HARD AGROUND

HARD AGROUND

A LEWIS COLE MYSTERY

BRENDAN DuBOIS

PEGASUS CRIME

NEW YORK LONDON

HARD AGROUND

Pegasus Books Ltd.
148 W 37th Street, 13th Floor
New York, NY 10018

Copyright © 2018 by Brendan DuBois

First Pegasus Books cloth edition April 2018

Interior design by Maria Fernandez

Library of Congress Cataloging-in-Publication Data is available.

ISBN: 978-1-68177-652-1

10 9 8 7 6 5 4 3 2 1

Printed in the United States of America
Distributed by W. W. Norton & Company
www.pegasusbooks.us

This novel is dedicated to my older brother

Neil DuBois

Raconteur, bon vivant, entrepreneur, and deep ocean sailor

May you always have fair winds and following seas.

CHAPTER ONE

From the vantage point of my bed, I looked out the near window to a cluster of rocks and boulders, which had been tossed and turned over the years by storms and long-ago glaciers. The view had been the same for nearly two centuries and for the past two hours. I gritted my teeth and rolled over, wincing from the pain of my recent surgeries.

From this side, the view was quite different, as I looked through a glass door that led to a small second-floor deck facing the Atlantic Ocean. Not a bad view—and one that's been with me since I moved some years ago into this house on Tyler Beach after being pensioned off from my short and not-so-brilliant career in the Department of Defense. The ocean was always just there in the background, something to look at while getting up in the morning or preparing to go to bed at night.

Since coming home from the hospital a few days ago pretty much bedridden, with another couple of dreary weeks of recovery waiting ahead for me, this view had become my new best friend. I had to lie mostly on my left side, trying to breathe easy, because my right shoulder and back were a mess, with scores of stitches and two drains coming out of my cut-up skin. Even lying on my back to stare up at the ceiling wasn't an option.

So what to do? I love to read, but the pain and discomfort of what was going on with my back and shoulder made it hard to focus on the printed page, and, what's more, it was hard even to hold a book or newspaper in my weak hands. I know there are e-book readers out there, but I'm terribly old-fashioned and can only read the real deal, with real paper and cardboard.

My friend Felix Tinios had brought in a television set that now dominated the corner of my bedroom, but there were only so many movies and History Channel programs one could watch before becoming bored to death. (And when did reality programs about lumberjacks and hunting Bigfoot equal history?) My taste in music was about twenty years off, and listening to what passes for talk radio made me wish we were still governed by the British Crown.

That left the ocean. In the two weeks since my surgeries, I had grown to like watching the way the light played upon the moving waters, seeing the boats working out there, the different types of birds that floated in and out of view. Most days, the view helped pass the time.

But not today. I was facing two problems—one immediate, and one not so immediate.

The immediate issue was the status of the two drains in my back, intended to drain out blood and fluid into little plastic bladders. They were held in place by an elastic bandage wrapped around my upper torso, and they needed to be emptied twice a day, with the output measured so my doctors would know to remove them when the output dropped far enough.

But there was something wrong. I could feel it. There was a cool moistness on my skin that didn't belong.

That meant I had to get off the bed and go to the bathroom. It was only about twenty feet away, but for the past few days that twenty feet had seemed as challenging as twenty miles.

I shifted some in the bed and, damn, now it felt as if I was sopping wet back there. If I didn't do something soon, I was going to soak the bedding, and at this rate it wouldn't be long before the leak soaked right through to the mattress.

If I had been at the hospital, I would have just needed to press the call button. If I had a health aide at home, I could have just called out. But the hospital, insurance company, and the home health aide company were currently feuding over who was supposed to pay what and for what services, so I was home alone. Nice name for a cute movie, but not so cute when I was the one alone, my back and shoulder wounds ready to burst with blood and fluid.

"Okay, partner," I whispered to myself. "Time to man up. Let's do this thing."

I scooted to the side of my bed, took a deep breath, and swung my legs out and—

I nearly screamed as pain rippled up and down my back. But at least my feet were on the wooden floor. I took a series of deep breaths, but it felt like a blowtorch set on low was sweeping along my back and right shoulder. Two weeks ago, Paula Quinn, assistant editor of the *Tyler Chronicle* and now an intimate friend, had been giving me a back rub when she found a lump near my right shoulder blade. The lump turned out to be the latest souvenir of my time in the Department of Defense, and when the surgeons at Mass General started cutting to take it out, they found two more tumors down closer to my spine. A number of years ago I was a research analyst for an obscure intelligence group within the DoD, and one day my little group was out in the Nevada high desert on a training mission. During the mission, we stumbled into a highly secret and highly illegal biowarfare experiment that killed everyone—including a woman I loved—save for me.

Many times over the years, as the biowarfare exposure caused an occasional tumor to appear, I was told how lucky I was that I was still alive.

Yeah. Lucky me.

I was still waiting to hear the report on whether or not the tumors were malignant. Several times in the past, after similar surgeries, I've lucked out and gotten the report that they were benign.

I guess that should have cheered me up, but I also remembered the hard and fast rule of gambling: at some point, the house always wins.

I stood up in bare feet, wobbled some, and then started making my way to the open door. On the second floor of my home, there's a bedroom, a large office, and a bathroom. When I got home two weeks ago, I had been tempted to sack out downstairs, with the comforts of the kitchen, living room, and fireplace, but my bathroom needs banished me upstairs.

One step, two steps . . . I was doing fine.

I finally reached the bedroom door. Beyond and to the left was my office, with boxes of books and pieces of unbuilt bookshelves. To the right was the bathroom; I wobbled my way in. I tried not to stare too hard at my face. I turned and glanced at my back.

Damn.

Two brown splotches about the size of a baby's hand had soaked through my extra-large white T-shirt. My drains were leaking somewhere.

Double damn.

I pulled up my T-shirt, grunted at the pain, and examined the yellow bandage wrapped around my upper back and chest. Two plastic tubes were running out of my upper back—kept in place with tiny black stitches—and went into plastic bladders tucked into little cloth pockets. Both bladders were full, with blood oozing out of their plastic tops.

On my new bathroom counter were a plastic measuring cup and a notebook, where I kept track of the output. If the daily output fell below a certain number of milliliters, then the drains could get removed. Based on what I was seeing back there, that wasn't going to happen anytime soon.

I bent some, then reached back with my left hand and grabbed ahold of the near bladder. I pulled it out and was able to lower it to my side. I slid the tube out, emptied the bladder into the measuring cup, and then wrote down "12 oz." in my little notebook. Replacing the empty bladder was a chore. Since it was now flaccid, it took some twisting and pushing to get it back into the cloth pocket.

All right.

One more to go.

I reached over again and—

Missed.

All right.

Tried again.

I grimaced and reached back further, and it was like a hot fire poker was being driven into my back and shoulder. I had tried a real heavy-duty painkiller the first day I got back home and the hallucinations and gastric distress made me give them up. I was regretting that decision now.

"All right," I whispered to the scary-looking man in the mirror. "Third time will be the charm."

I gritted my teeth and heaved my left arm across. My fingers grasped the top of the bladder, and I tugged and tugged and—

The damn thing popped out like some freak alien egg, and the top of the hose pulled free from the bladder. Within seconds, blood was spraying around the bathroom as if it were a scene in some deranged slasher flick. When I moved and tried to get ahold of the spurting bladder, my bare feet slipped on the bloody tile floor and I fell, striking my head against the wooden vanity.

I must have passed out because when I woke up, the blood had already started to cake on my hand. It was everywhere. I sat up against the vanity, looking at the mess I had made.

I tried to get up, but I was too tired and I hurt too much.

But I was also cold.

I reached up with my left hand and snagged a dark blue bath towel. I pulled it down and covered myself. And then I waited.

Eventually I made out the sound of a key rattling around in the downstairs door, followed by the sound of the door opening and closing. There was the thump of someone dropping her purse and coat on the floor.

I waited.

The sound of someone coming up the stairs was now audible, and when her fine blonde hair became visible, I saw that it was my Paula Quinn, who stopped with a hand on the railing and said, "For the love of—"

"How was your day, dear?" I asked.

"Shit," she said, as she came into the bathroom and got to work. Even in the midst of this, I took a moment to take her in. Paula's younger than I am, and over the past few years we've been friends, then lovers, then friends, and now lovers again. She was wearing tight blue jeans that hugged her bottom and a pink low-cut buttoned blouse with the sleeves rolled up. I admired her pert nose and the cute ears that poke through her hair, which she hates, and which I find adorable.

"What happened?" she asked, picking up a face cloth, running water over it, then scrubbing my hands and face.

"My drains were leaking," I said. "I got to the bathroom and tried to get them drained. I did fine with drain number one. Number two proved to be a hell of a challenge."

"I guess so," she said. "Your T-shirt and pajama bottoms are a mess. Let me get a clean set."

Paula went out to my bedroom, where there was the sound of a closet door opening and closing before she came back in. "Sorry I'm late. Some news broke and—"

"Please, no apologies," I said. "I'm grateful for everything you're doing and have done."

She put the new clothes—another oversize white T-shirt and a gray pair of pajama bottoms—on a clean part of the vanity and said, "Time to get you up on your feet."

"Got it."

She pulled on my left arm while I pushed myself off the floor with my right, and then I was standing, resting both hands on the bathroom vanity. Off came the soiled T-shirt and bottoms, and she helped wash my back, returned the second bladder to its proper place, and dressed me.

"Here, this is for you." She gave me a sweet kiss, which I received with thanks, and then she said, "Time for you to go to bed."

"Ma'am, I love the way you talk."

That earned me a swat on my tired bottom. "You're out of service for the foreseeable future, Mr. Cole, until I get a note from your doctor. So in the meantime, behave."

Back in the bedroom, she tidied up the sheets and pillows, and I slid back to my regular position on the bed. This time I patted her on the bottom as she went back to the bathroom, which got me a soft laugh, and soon enough, the clothes washer was running.

Paula came back and sat on the edge of the bed. "You eat today?"

I nodded to the tray on the nightstand. "I did. Thanks for leaving me lunch."

"Good. Now, I'm sorry to do this, but I'm going to have to leave you dinner. Something broke this afternoon, and I've got to get back to the story."

"What's the story?"

"Homicide."

I was stunned. "In Tyler?"

"Yep," she said. "Our little New Hampshire town. Maggie Tyler Branch, who ran Border Antiques on the Exonia Road. Got murdered sometime last night."

"Holy shit. I knew her. I even wrote a couple of columns about her for *Shoreline*."

"Of course you knew her," Paula said. "Practically everyone in town knew her. Hold on, let me go downstairs, get something together for dinner."

Paula went downstairs and I listened to her work in the kitchen, heard the refrigerator door open and close, the microwave start whirring. I blinked and looked out at the ocean again. Maggie Tyler Branch, whose middle name marked her as one of the descendants of the Reverend Bonus Tyler, who settled this strip of New Hampshire seacoast more than 350 years ago. Widowed, no kids, she owned a large farmhouse on the main road leading to Exonia. She sold antiques and gave out sharp opinions for a living. In my years here in Tyler, I had done two columns about her. The first was just a feel-good piece about her being descended from one of the first settlers, but the second was a newsier story. It was about how she had purchased a framed reproduction of the Declaration of Independence at a yard sale up in Porter, and later found out the reproduction was one of the very few printed in Philadelphia back in 1776, and worth a lot of money.

I still remembered talking to her in her cluttered and dusty barn. Smoking a Marlboro—and nearly a half-million dollars richer—she had shrugged and said, "You get old enough, and eventually instead of being shat upon, a unicorn will drop by and crap out gold coins in your lap. It was just my turn, that's all."

I heard Paula trot up the stairs, go into my bathroom, and put my clothes into the dryer. She went back down before I could ask her anything.

Maggie Tyler Branch.

Damn.

Some long minutes slid by until Paula brought up a covered plate on a tray, with a salad bowl nearby. "All right, favorite patient, best I can do. Hot steak and cheese melt, on French bread, with a side of salad and some healthy potato chips, if such a thing could exist."

7

She put the tray down on the empty nightstand, where she knew I could reach it with no difficulty. "Any questions?"

"A couple," I said. "How did she get murdered, and any word from the police on who did it? Or why?"

Paula stood up, brushed her hands together. "No suspect, so far as I know. As for a motive . . . you've got an elderly woman living alone with lots of pricey antiques and jewelry kicking around, plus whatever spare cash she might have gotten from that Declaration of Independence sale back in the day. Plus she's located about five minutes from I-95. In these troubled times . . . Lewis, our fair state is now number one in the country, per capita, for opioid deaths. For someone needing cash to score a good supply of heroin, Maggie's place would be a good place to start."

She checked her watch. "All right, time to go back to the cop shop," she said. "I'll see what I can pry from your best pal, Detective Sergeant Woods."

"Tell her I said hello."

"Will do."

Paula leaned down, giving me a nice look at her cleavage—I hoped it was a deliberate move on her part—and gave me a nice long kiss. She stood up and said, "Leave the laundry alone. I'll see you sometime tomorrow."

She had made it to the door leading out of my bedroom when I called out, "Hey! That other question. How did Maggie get murdered?"

Paula turned, grimaced. "Yeah. A bloody mess. Somebody blew off her head with a shotgun."

Later that night, after eating my dinner and pushing the tray back on the nightstand, I turned on the television, and I lucked out with HBO rerunning its *Band of Brothers* series. I watched for three hours, enjoying the great actors and well-written, realistic scenes of the invasion of Normandy, as well as the moral clarity of a time when enemies controlled a state and, most of the time, wore uniforms.

When episode three, "Carentan," wrapped up, I yawned and switched the television off. I swung from the bed again and made it to the bathroom to do my evening business. I checked the dryer and saw that my clothes were dry. I dragged them out, winced again at the pain, but managed to fold the T-shirt, underwear, and pajama bottoms, and leave them on top of the machine.

I knew Paula had told me to leave the clothes, but I wanted to prove to her—all right, to myself—that I wasn't totally helpless.

Back to the bedroom I walked, and then got into bed, switched off the lights, and looked out the window to the Atlantic. It was dark, with no lights out there, and I managed to fall asleep.

I woke up about an hour later, when my second problem of the day made itself known.

The house was quiet, with only the sound of the waves' endless march, until I heard the noise of the front door gently opening.

I cleared my throat. "Paula?"

No answer.

I shifted some in my bed, checked the time. It was 1:16 in the morning. "Hello?"

The door gently closed.

I shut my eyes.

My second problem of the day. It had happened several times in the weeks since I came back home from the hospital. At various points during the night, I would hear someone enter my house. Twice I had called my friend Felix Tinios, and once I had called the Tyler Police Department, but each time Felix or the police arrived, they didn't find anything. The door had still been locked, and there had been no sign that anybody had been in the house.

"Hello?" I called out.

No answer. But now I heard what seemed to be cabinet doors opening and closing.

I remembered the patient yet quizzical looks on Felix and the nice policewoman who had responded earlier, both no doubt thinking poor recovering Lewis Cole was hallucinating.

I reached under the mattress, wincing, and took out my 9mm Beretta.

So my night continued, and so did my second continuing problem.

CHAPTER TWO

woke with a man looking down at me, and, half-asleep, I reached for my Beretta—but it was missing.

"Looking for this?" he asked, holding it up by its butt.

"Yes, Felix, damn you."

He went "tsk-tsk" and put the pistol down on my nightstand. Felix Tinios, originally from Boston's North End and now an independent security consultant—he even had business cards, which I always found surprising—opened up a folding wooden table he had brought into my bedroom.

"You look like a college professor dressed for a class," I said, nodding at the tweed jacket he wore over a white button-down shirt and pressed blue jeans. "Preferably an all-female one."

"We all have our dreams, don't we," he replied.

Felix moved surely and swiftly through my room, taking out my breakfast from a dark green insulated bag. There was coffee, cold milk, and two covered plates. On the larger plate was a collection of freshly made crepes with a side of maple syrup—and, Felix being Felix, I had no doubt it was the real stuff, and not that horrid sugar cane syrup flavored maple. The smaller plate had five thick pork sausages.

I started eating and he wandered more about the room. "Why was your pistol out?" he asked.

"Guess."

"Your alleged visitor came back last night?"

"Nothing alleged about it, Felix. He was there."

"Sure," he said, coming back and sitting on the edge of the bed. "How are you feeling today?"

"Like I fell into a farmer's thresher," I said. "Cut up, banged up, and bruised."

"You'll get there."

"Right now I can't get out of my bedroom."

"Where did the ever-cheerful Lewis Cole disappear to?"

"Someplace warmer and safer," I said.

When breakfast was done, I checked the time and saw Paula was late. Damn. Felix saw me looking at the clock and said, "What's up?"

"My nurse is late."

"What, your insurance company and your doc figure out their dispute?"

"No, that looks like it's going to be another Thirty Years' War. The nurse is Paula."

Felix smiled. "Ah, the young and sweet Miss Quinn. Well, you can't wait, so let's get it done."

"What?"

"You heard me," he said, coming over to me. "I'll take care of those drains."

"But . . ."

He grabbed my hands, nearly yanked me out of bed. "What, you think I'm afraid of blood? Really?"

Felix worked quickly and efficiently, gently removing each plastic bulb, squirting it in the measuring cup, writing down the amounts, rinsing out the bulbs, and then securing them again.

"There you go," he said. "Uncle Felix's drain and repair company, at your service."

"Thanks."

"You're probably going to need a sponge bath by and by, but I'll leave that to your reporter friend. In the meantime, I've got some dishes to do."

"Bring me back to bed, you can do what you like."

"Um, not going to happen, grasshopper. You're coming downstairs with me and you're going to keep me company while I wash up."

"But Felix . . ."

"When was the last time you were downstairs?"

"The day I left to go to the hospital, and the day I came back. The end."

"Then it's time to go down and check it out, make sure your mysterious visitor hasn't stolen a book or a rug."

"But Felix . . ."

He gave me a look that, were I anyone else, would have caused me to lose control of certain bodily functions. "Trust me when I say this, you're not getting around enough."

"It hurts."

"Of course it hurts, moron. That's part of the healing process. Better a little hurt now than lots of hurt later on, trying to get your muscle tone back while lying in that comfortable bed and watching *Ellen*."

"I can't stand *Ellen*."

"Why?"

"Too much fake fun, fake dancing, fake smiles."

"Everybody's a critic. Let's go."

Felix took my arm and I moved slowly out of the bathroom, leaning on him as we went out to the landing and took our time going downstairs. "You poor fellow," Felix said. "You're walking like a sailor who hasn't touched land for six months. Later today I'll come by, drop off a cane that my Uncle Paulie used back in the day."

"Does it have a hidden bottle inside to carry around some illegal hooch?"

We got to the first floor and Felix laughed. "No, Uncle Paulie was around too late for Prohibition, but it does have a cute hidden secret."

"I look forward to it."

We walked through the living room, with the large stone and brick fireplace, and into the adjacent kitchen. The kitchen appliances were new, as was most of the furniture on this floor, since my house nearly burned down several months earlier. In the living room were a couch, three comfortable chairs, a coffee table, and the television. There were also scores of boxes of books, bought either at local used bookstores or from the megamall that is the Internet.

Felix helped me onto the couch, trotted back upstairs, and came down with my breakfast dishes. As he started washing them he called out, "Did Paula call to say she was going to be late?"

"No, but I figured she was busy. She's covering the story of Maggie Branch's murder."

Felix had taken off his tweed jacket and rolled up his sleeves. He turned to me, dishcloth in hand, and said, "What do you know?"

I shifted some on the couch. I didn't want to admit this to Felix, but I was glad to be down here. It was nice to be out of the bedroom, to have a different view and different light coming in.

"Not much," I said. "Homicide. Killed by a shotgun."

Felix nodded, the dishcloth clenched in his strong hands.

"What's up?" I said. "You know Maggie Branch?"

"I knew Maggie Branch," Felix said.

"How?"

"Occasionally she would help look over antiques, other items that I had that were of interest," he said. "A sassy, smart woman."

"Sounds . . . interesting."

He frowned. "Oh, come on. Nothing illegal. In fact, a week ago I brought in an old silver service that had belonged to a great-grandfather from the old country, back when it was the Kingdom of Sicily. It was just banging around in my house and I thought it would be good to get an estimate, either to sell it or to figure out whether I should stop using it as a place to drop off my keys when I came through the door."

"Oh."

He went back to drying the dishes. "Anything else you can tell me about her murder?"

"Paula said she hadn't heard if anything was stolen, but since her home and shop were so close to the Interstate, she thought robbery would be a good option."

"Hardly," he said, "unless whoever was doing the robbery had a specific target in mind."

Felix's eyes narrowed, and I said, "Like old silver from Sicily?"

He carefully folded up the towel. "I guess I'll just have to find out."

"Good luck with that."

"Luck has nothing to do with it, just reality," he said. "And speaking of reality—"

"Please don't start," I said. "I've had a rough month."

"So have a lot of people. But your mystery visitor . . . tell me more about last night's visit."

I tried the stubborn approach, but Felix stared at me until I gave up.

"I heard the door open," I said. "And then it closed. Then I heard footsteps."

He leaned over my clean kitchen counter. "Anything else?"

"I called out to him. Or her. Or it."

"No answer, then."

"Nope."

"Did you call the cops?"

"No, and as you can tell, I didn't call you either."

He drummed his fingers on the counter. "Do you ever hear the person leave?"

"No."

"They just come in and stay and . . ."

"That's right," I said.

"Maybe you just sleep through it."

"Maybe," I said.

"Want me to spend the night?" he asked.

"I may be a patient," I said. "But I'm not helpless. Maybe hapless, but I can manage on my own."

Later Felix said he was bored and he set up some of my bookshelves. I supervised him from my position on the couch, and seeing my old books emerge from the dusty cardboard boxes cheered me up, which I was sure was Felix's plan all along.

So the morning went by and the sun was coming in stronger, and Felix washed his hands in my clean kitchen and said, "You know there's new technology, don't you, where you can have a little handheld device and store hundreds of books?"

"I've heard the rumor," I admitted.

"Then why don't you make the technology leap? Enter the new century? Be one of the cool kids?"

"I like books," I said. "I love the feel of them, the scent of them, just the pleasure of holding them."

"But technology marches on."

"And when some idiots set off a nuclear EMP to fry all of our electronics, I'll still be here with my books, and you'll be stuck with a nice piece of plastic and glass."

"Boy, you've got one dark imagination."

"Can't help it."

Felix gathered up his tweed jacket and said, "You need a hand going upstairs?"

"No, I think I'll be fine," I said. "It'll be nice to stretch my legs later."

"All right, then."

"What are you up to for the rest of the day?"

"Some personal business," he said, putting on his jacket, and from the look in his eyes and face, he no longer seemed like a college professor.

"Relating to Maggie's murder and your silver?"

"Personal," he said. "By the way, you got plans for lunch?"

"My big plans are not to pass out while going upstairs."

"I'll arrange something from the Lafayette House."

"What's on the menu?"

"I think I know what you like," he said. "How does noon sound?"

"One o'clock sounds better," I said. "Had a generous breakfast from a generous chap."

"Glad to do it," he said. "In the meantime . . ." He came to the couch, briefly squeezed my good shoulder. "Get healed, get better. You aren't cut out to be a hermit."

"Thanks for everything," I said.

He smirked. "Wait until you get my bill."

When Felix left, I found the remote and switched on the television. I thought of the Springsteen song once again: fifty-seven channels and nothing on.

I flicked the television off, found a three-month-old issue of *Smithsonian* magazine, and stretched out on the couch, only shivering twice from the pain, and started reading a fascinating story about the status of Biblical-related archaeology in the Middle East.

Eventually the pages slid through my hands and the magazine dropped to the floor, and I took a midmorning nap.

A knock on the door got me up, and a few random and dark memories popped out as I rolled and sat up on the couch. I checked a new clock on the fireplace's mantelpiece. It was 11:45 A.M. I doubted very much that it was my lunch delivery from the Lafayette House, because Felix is quite specific in his instructions, and with Felix's look and attitude, they are never forgotten.

The knock repeated itself.

I closed my eyes. The memories . . . of when I was back at the Pentagon, working in a small and obscure intelligence agency, and that day when we went out to Nevada for a training drill, a drill that killed everyone but me.

Including the love of my life back then, Cissy Manning.

In my dream I had been with her, and it had been one of those dreams that dug deep into memories, so you could hear the person's voice, feel their touch, taste their skin . . . it wasn't a dream as much as it was a time machine visit, and then the knock woke me up. I had briefly spanned two worlds, wondering how in hell I was going to tell Cissy and Paula about each other.

Cissy.

Dead all these years.

I wiped at my face, surprised to find my eyes moist.

The knock came again, harder.

"Hold on!" I yelled, and then kicked myself for this mistake. I should have kept my mouth shut and the insistent visitor would have probably gone away. Because of where my home was located and the lack of a real driveway, I usually didn't get much in the way of visitors, just the usual poll workers every four years trying to save their candidate, or religious missionaries intent on saving my soul.

One more knock.

Damn it.

"Coming!" I yelled out, and later I realized too late that I should have never answered the door.

CHAPTER THREE

I opened the door and a man and woman were standing on my granite steps, both smiling widely at me. The man was in his fifties, with a closely trimmed white beard and bright blue eyes. He wore khaki slacks, a flannel shirt and open blue cloth jacket, and a tweed cap on his head, and there was a bulging manila file folder under his right arm. His companion seemed to be about the same age, though she looked colder, wearing a down jacket and a bright, multicolored knit cap even though it was probably in the low fifties. Her steel-gray hair fell across her right shoulder in a thick braid.

"So sorry to bother you," the man said, still smiling. "Do you have a minute?"

"Barely," I said, holding onto the doorknob, thankful for the support. "If you're on a religious mission, congratulations and no, I don't want to hear any more. If you're selling something, I can't think of anything you have that I might want to buy."

The woman frowned but her male friend wasn't giving up. "My name's Dave Hudson, and this is my wife, Marjorie. We're neither selling nor preaching. We've come all the way from Albany, doing some genealogical research . . . and my"—he raised his head to look up at my house—"I'm so thrilled to see this structure standing. You're Mr. . . . Cole, correct? The magazine writer?"

"That's right," I said. "And I'm sorry, I've just gotten home from the hospital. I'm not really up for a talk."

"Dear me, dear me, I'm sorry," he said. "It'll just take a minute. You see, my grandfather was once stationed here, at this very same house. Though it does look different from back then."

"He was with the Coast Artillery?"

"Nope, later than that."

"I'm sorry, there was nothing after the Coast Artillery shut down, except for a radar station looking for Russian bombers, back in the fifties. And this place had been abandoned by then. Before the Coast Artillery used it for officers' quarters, it had been a lifeboat station, back in the mid-1800s."

Marjorie rubbed her hands together and looked like she wished she were back home, among the charms of New York's capital city, rather than here on this particular stretch of the chilly New Hampshire seacoast.

"Well . . . hate to correct you," Dave said, "since you're the current owner, but there was a time right around when the artillery station was being shut down that this was a facility for Navy corpsmen, during the Korean War. They did training at the old hospital in Exonia, and this was where they were put up. My grandfather was stationed here."

My hand was starting to lose its grip on the doorknob, and my bladder was sending alarm bells that a bathroom visit was urgently required.

"I'm sorry," I said. "Maybe I'm being dense, but I don't see how your grandfather being stationed here has anything to do with genealogical research."

Marjorie said, "David . . ."

"Just a sec, just a sec," he said. "The thing is, there's always been a rumor in the family that granddad was a bit of a tomcat, and that he met up with my grandmom here, and well, you know. This was the place where my dad was probably conceived. Isn't that funny?"

"Hilarious," I said, and my bladder was now sending emergency signals to my brain. "Look, I don't mean to be rude but—"

"I know, I know, and I appreciate your time, but all I'm asking is for a quick tour of your house, take a few photos, a few measurements, and—"

I shook my head. "Not today, please. Maybe in a couple of weeks."

Dave stepped forward as I started to close the door, and the folder under his arm slipped out and fell to the rocky soil. Papers and long sheets with scribbled notes flew around. Marjorie swore and his face went red as they both scrambled to retrieve the papers.

Dave squatted down, grabbing them before they could fly, and Marjorie bent over and grimaced—it looked like her back hurt or something—and I felt guilty, but more than that, I really, really had to go to the bathroom.

"Please," I said, shutting the door. "Two weeks, all right?"

And through a lot of hard work and some swearing, I made it upstairs just in time.

At one P.M. I was back on the couch, rereading the section of *Smithsonian* that I had read earlier, when there was once again a knock at the door. It didn't sound as harsh as before, so I didn't bother looking through the peephole before opening it up.

A young, tired-looking woman was there, dressed in black shoes, black slacks, and light blue down jacket with frayed sleeves, carrying two bulging plastic bags. Her face was red from the blowing wind and her blonde hair was cut short, like some sort of rich aristocrat from the 1920s.

But there was nothing about her demeanor or clothing that said rich.

"You Mr. Cole?"

"I am."

"I got a dinner for you, all prepaid. I was told you just got out of the hospital and if you'd like, I can come in and set it up."

I stepped aside.

"That would be great, thanks."

She came in and announced her name was Mia as she took off her jacket. From her white blouse and short black apron, I could see that she had probably just come over from the dining room at the Lafayette House. Mia went through my cabinets, looking for plates and such, and then expertly doled out the food. And there was a lot of it: sautéed sea scallops, hand-cut French fries, a large bowl of salad. Holy God, it looked like Felix had sent over enough food to feed a squad of hungry soldiers.

Mia washed her hands and said, "Is this okay, then?"

"It's great," I said. There was something about her look that just . . . got to me.

Couldn't explain it.

"Do you need to go back to work?"

She shook her head. "Nope. My shift is done, thank God."

I sat down on the near stool. Mia stood on the other side of the kitchen counter next to the three extra stools.

"This is going to sound odd, but please listen. Look at all this food." I waved my hand around the full plates. "There's no way I can eat all this. I won't even be able to finish the leftovers. Please join me."

Her eyes were warm but suspicious. "I don't think so."

I put a blue cloth napkin on my lap. "Mia, I'm a few days out of the hospital. Lots of people know me here in Tyler. I'm a magazine writer, and I have nothing untoward in mind. In fact, I'm so weak, I can't even think of anything untoward. It'd be a shame to let all this food go to waste."

I could sense her hesitation, and added, "And your time here, well, it'll be reflected in a tip. Does that sound fair?"

A quick nod. "Yeah, it does sound fair. And Christ . . ."

She picked up a knife and fork and I asked, "What's that?"

Mia started working on a scallop. "This'll be the first time I get to eat one of the meals I serve to all those rich people that stay across the street."

After a few awkward moments, my meal and my guest both settled down. I was hungry, but not compared to Mia, who looked absolutely starved. As she ate I learned she was an only child, came from a very small town up north called Wentworth, and had graduated from the University of New Hampshire in Durham more than three years ago with a B.A. in Journalism. Her parents had moved south outside of Porter, looking for work: Dad was a construction contractor, and Mom kept the books and did some hairdressing on the side. Still, even with her college degree, Mia couldn't afford to work full time as a journalist.

"Don't get me wrong," Mia said. "The professors—all former reporters themselves—did great, and I learned a lot working on the student newspaper. I managed to get a summer internship at the paper up in Dover, but . . . look at me. I'm no reporter. I'm a waitress here and at another place, barely making enough not to starve, all the while my student loan debt keeps on climbing up and up."

"Sounds rough."

"Yeah, good word, rough. You see, as much as I learned about being a newspaper reporter, what I really should have learned is that I was getting trained for a dying industry. It's like being an apprentice at a buggy whip factory back when Ford was setting up his first assembly line. My aunt, she used to be a reporter here thirty, forty years ago, and back then, there were lots of papers competing in this part of the state, weeklies, semiweeklies, dailies. Lots of pressure to get the news. Now? One Texas-based outfit owns all the local newspapers, so there's no real competition."

Mia paused, shook her head. "I do what I can. I've done freelance, I've done some web stuff, but most of them want stories for free. Ugh. Like it's gonna give me exposure and I should be grateful for that."

"And the waitressing?"

Another pause. "Up at the Lafayette House it's okay. Make good tips because of the rich folks who stay there. But the other job, up in Porter. A fish shack that, for some reason, a bunch of grumpy retired cops hang out at, and the three commissioners that supposedly oversee the Porter cops. Bigger bunch of clueless jerks you've never seen, and they tip like shit."

We ate some more and she said, "What's your story?"

"Magazine columnist. Used to work for the Department of Defense. Had some surgery recently. Trying to bounce back."

Mia nodded, looked around my house. "Cool place. Up in the dining room at the Lafayette House, you can see the top of your place. Nice and remote. And old. Am I right?"

"Built in the mid-1800s. Almost as old as I am."

She laughed. "You're not that old—but maybe old enough."

A flash then, of déjà vu, and in that moment, this young lady reminded me of my Cissy Manning. Not that they looked alike: Cissy was taller, skin more pale, and she had thick red hair. No, it was her attitude, the way of carrying herself and her lack of shyness when talking to someone she had just met. That had been my Cissy, back at the Pentagon, a strong woman who could talk to anyone without any fear.

21

"Hey, I'm curious about something," Mia said. "Where did you go to college?"

"Indiana University, in Bloomington."

"How long after graduation did you wait before getting a full-time job, you know, a real job with the start of a career and benefits."

"About a month."

Mia's eyes widened with amazement. "Lucky you."

I took a sip of water, thinking of that short career, and the dead bodies of friends and a loved one left behind and forgotten. "Yeah, lucky me."

She wouldn't let me help her with the dishes, and when she was finished with them she packed up enough leftovers for me to have a second meal. I walked her back to my door and she checked her watch. "Good. Enough time to get up to Porter and start another shift, and then try to write something freelance for the *Porter Herald*."

Mia put her coat on, smiled. "Hey, at least I'm having a better day than some other people around here."

"Like who?" I asked.

"When I walked over there was this couple in a car, talking to each other—okay, maybe yelling. They didn't look very happy. At least the woman didn't."

"Did she have gray hair in a thick braid, a knit cap on her head?"

Mia and I were at the door. "She sure did."

"And the man in the car with her . . . short white beard, tweed cap?"

Mia nodded. "That's them. What are they, friends of yours?"

"No," I said, opening the door for her. "Not friends."

CHAPTER FOUR

After the generous meal supplied by Felix and the Lafayette House, I felt full and almost content as I slowly took my time going back upstairs. Each step hurt, of course, but not as much as before, which I took as a good sign. In my bedroom, the disheveled bed seemed to mock me. I was brought up to always make your bed in the morning, and there was just something creepy about crawling into a sloppy bed.

I sat on the edge of the bed, careful to avoid resting on my drainage tubes, and picked up the remote to navigate the television's complicated on-demand menu and find the fourth episode of *Band of Brothers*. I managed to stay awake to the very end.

Late afternoon I was up again, but definitely not about, staring out the window at the cruel sea. But it didn't look too cruel at this moment, just a dark gray swelling movement, with lobster pots visible and the sharp rocks of the Isles of Shoals.

A knock at the door caused me to say a few naughty words in the direction of the islands, and then a woman's voice called out: "You decent up there?"

To which I yelled back, "Not hardly!"

I was rewarded with a laugh and there were footsteps on the stairs, and into my bedroom came Detective Sergeant Diane Woods of the Tyler Police Department. She was wearing black sneakers, black slacks, a waist-length brown leather jacket, and a red blouse. Her brown hair was cut in a bobbed style that went out of fashion years ago—which I've never had the heart to tell her—and she looked pretty good, with the recent scars and bruises on her face finally fading away.

"This is a treat," I said.

"You bet it is," she said.

"No, I mean it. I know you're up to your ears in the Maggie Branch killing."

"Yeah," Diane nodded. "A real freaking mess. But I got some free time and Paula rang me up, asked if I'd come over and give you a hand with your drains."

"You're kidding me."

"Nope," she said.

She walked over, held out two rough and strong hands. "Come along, tiger. Let's get this job done."

I worked with Diane, getting up on the floor, and she walked me to the bathroom. I said, "It might be bloody."

"What, you don't think I've seen blood before?"

As with Felix, Diane got the job done with little fuss or muss, and she said, "Looks like your output is decreasing. A good sign?"

"Very good sign," I said. "Means in a couple of days I'll get these drains removed, and I won't feel like Dr. Frankenstein's practice creation before he figured everything out."

I eased back into my bed and Diane brought in the chair from my office. She kicked off her sneakers and stretched out her legs, putting her feet on my bed.

"What's the latest?" I said.

She ran her hands through her thick brown hair. "What we got is that somebody met up with Maggie Tyler Branch sometime after five P.M. two days ago. We know the time because a half hour earlier, she had left Hannaford's with some groceries. She was due to have a late dinner with a neighbor at eight P.M., and when she didn't show up, the neighbor drove over and found her."

"Where?"

"In the barn where she kept her antiques. She has a little office in the back with a rolltop desk, some wooden filing cabinets, and one of those old-fashioned swivel chairs. That's where she was found."

"Paula said she was killed with a shotgun."

Diane sighed. "Very messy, very bloody, and . . . very unnecessary. What's the point? She was an old woman, no threat to anyone. And if you're going to rob the place, why not just bop her on the back of her head, or tie her up? What's the point of blowing off her head?"

"Maybe the thief or thieves didn't want to be recognized."

"Maybe . . ."

"And no one heard anything?"

"You've been there before, right? I recall you did a column for *Shoreline* about her."

"Two," I said.

"Must have missed one, then," she said. "Her place was probably the most remote piece of property left in Tyler, with brush and trees around it. One shotgun blast . . . we can see why nobody heard anything. Or saw anything."

"Anything of value stolen?"

"What, you planning on writing a magazine column about this?"

"Not anytime soon," I said. "But humor me, Diane. I'm stuck in this house, I'm tired of reading, tired of watching television."

"Looking for stimulation, then?"

"Looking for adult conversation."

She laughed, folded her hands in her lap. "Nice to be called an adult. Well, the place was tossed, like they were looking for something. But there were small vaults that had gold jewelry in them, and those weren't touched. And some cash."

"Any valuable, antique silver?" I said, remembering Felix.

"Not that I'm aware of," she said. "You have any particular interest, Lewis? You have anything that you were having Maggie check out?"

"No," I said, being honest. "I didn't have anything there for her to check out."

"Uh-huh."

"Paula thinks maybe it was a robbery," I said, changing the subject. "Maybe something to get money for heroin, since her place was so close to the Interstate."

"Mmm, maybe," she said, her voice skeptical. "I can tell you that the surveillance tapes from the tollbooths leading off the Interstate are being reviewed, but people who steal to get a fix, they're in a hurry, they're trembling, they don't have time to check out an antiques shop and fumble around. No, they like quick and easy hits. Convenience stores, liquor outlets, places like that."

"So what's the theory?"

She smiled. "You know our methods, Watson. Collect the evidence, see where it takes us, and leave the theorizing for later. And I'm afraid later has just arrived."

Diane got up and came over and gave me a kiss to the cheek. I said, "How goes the wedding plans?"

"Oh, it's on all right. This June. The social event of the year. Kara and I can hardly wait." Diane pulled away and said, "How are you?"

"You know what I look like, Holmes. Any other questions?"

"Your nighttime visitor?"

I paused, thinking of what I could say to her.

"Lewis. The truth."

"Came by last night."

"How do you know?"

"Heard the door open and close. Heard footsteps."

"Why don't you have Felix sleep on your couch?"

"He's already done that a couple of times, to no effect. Hey, I have an idea. Why don't you sleep on my couch?"

Diane smiled one more time as she walked out of my bedroom.

"Don't tempt me."

Paula called at about five o'clock. She was desperately trying to finish a piece before she had to go to a selectman's meeting at six. I told her to do her job and do her best to get the Pulitzer Prize committee's attention. She laughed and said she might try sending the committee a photo of her in a new bikini, and would I be interested in helping her? I said yes.

Felix stopped by an hour later, as promised, carrying dinner and an on old cane. "Dinner is fettuccine Alfredo with lobster, and a salad," he said, passing over a plastic bag. "Pretty warm so you should go right for it."

"Thanks," I said, putting it on the kitchen counter. "That I will."

"And here's Uncle Paulie's cane," he said, handing that over as well. The cane was dark brown, with a metal tip and a knobbed end that was carved in the shape of a wolf's head.

I held it with both hands. It felt heavy, solid. "Nice to see Uncle Paulie was discreet in making a fashion statement."

"Uncle Paulie's statements were usually more direct and didn't involve fashion sense."

"Thanks," I said, trying the cane out for size as I went down one length of the living room and then back.

Felix gave a slow-motion clap and said, "Work it, boy, work it. Show us what you got."

"Thanks, old bean," I said.

Felix nodded. "There's a cool secret with the cane. You want me to show you?"

I hefted its weight again. "Nah," I said. "Let me figure it out. Gives me something to look forward to."

He checked his watch. "Sorry, friend, have to leave."

"And where are you off to in such a hurry?"

"Lowell," he said.

"Massachusetts?" I asked, surprised. Poor Lowell, a former mill town that had been struggling to recover for decades, had the unfortunate distinction of being a hub in this part of the world for cheap drugs and other nefarious dealings.

"No, silly boy," he said. "Lowell, Alaska. What do you think?"

"What the hell are you going to be doing in Lowell?"

He smiled, but it wasn't one of those cheery smiles that makes one think of sunshine and lemonade and listening to the Red Sox on my rear deck. It was a smile of a man going to a place where he's well prepared and well armed, and has no qualms in doing what has to be done.

"Research," he said.

"Okay, you got me there. What kind of research?"

"Finding out why a Toyota Corolla with Massachusetts license plates was seen departing the residence of Maggie Tyler Branch on the night of her murder."

"Felix . . ."

"Yep, that's my name, don't wear it out."

"The police have been chasing down leads, and last I heard there were no witnesses at the time of the murder, and definitely no sign of anyone leaving Maggie's place that night. Not to mention a Toyota Corolla."

"Did I mention a Toyota Corolla? Funny, I thought I didn't."

"You don't have to worry," I said. "Your dastardly secrets are mostly safe with me. Just be careful, and . . ."

"Yes?"

"Let me know what you find out. With all of this healing, I'm getting bored out of my mind."

"Will do."

One of my many faults is that I get impatient whenever friends or strangers come to me and are desperate to tell me about their dreams. "You see, it was my house, but it wasn't really my house, it had a secret basement, and the property went down to the river, but in my dream, the river was an ocean and we never got down there as we should, and there was buffalo grazing on the front lawn and then the dump trucks arrived . . ."

And that's when I usually nod politely and make an excuse to leave the room.

But tonight the dreams came back, and I woke up, trembling. It was like before. I was with Cissy, pretty fuzzy but . . . it wasn't a dream. Like before, it was as if deep in my memory cells, a bit of videotape was replayed, and I was there. I swear to God, I was there, not only experiencing what I was experiencing with Cissy—and God, it was so good just to taste her, just to be with her—but also becoming the man I had been back then, young and cocky and full of confidence, sure that I was the person I was meant to be, in confidential service to my country, with the woman I was meant to love and be with for the rest of my life.

"Cissy," I whispered when I woke up, sheets tangled around me, heart racing, wondering why in God's name I was dreaming about those long ago days. Why? Was it the surgery that brought my past into rough view? Was my body—now cut free of tumors once again—conspiring with my mind to bring up a mirror to the past, forcing me to look, forcing me to flinch at the good and bad, forcing me to account for what I had become? Or delayed aftereffects from the strong painkiller I had taken days earlier?

And what had I become? For a number of years I had thought about being in government service, working quietly and behind the scenes, against what I thought was an implacable foe . . . and I was fortunate enough to find a woman to join me in that life, and the dreams we had . . .

Now I was alone. A magazine writer with too many scars and bad memories, with a woman now, Paula, but for how long? For how long about anything?

I had that strange mixture of dread, sadness, and melancholy, for having briefly revisited who I had once been in the past, and facing who I really was now.

I didn't like it.

I kept on not liking it up until I heard the door open downstairs.

I was going to call out but I kept my mouth shut. Enough was enough.

I kept the lights off, kept everything off.

I just listened.

The sound of footsteps down there, once more.

The phone was nearby but it was going to stay right there.

It was time for me to take care of things.

I slowly got off the bed, gritting my teeth from the pain, and I reached under the mattress and pulled out my Beretta. I forced myself up and reached for the flashlight on the nightstand. I was now standing, flashlight in my left hand, pistol in my right.

Okay, then.

I slowly walked across the bedroom floor, hoping the creaking wasn't warning whoever was down there.

At the upstairs landing, office just ahead and to the left, bathroom to the right.

I took a step and then lost my balance for a moment, and I almost dropped everything as I grabbed the railing to the right.

Damn.

That was close.

Movement downstairs for sure.

My legs started trembling.

Maybe there was enough time to go back to the bedroom and make that phone call . . .

And face the impassive faces of either Felix or whatever Tyler patrolman was on duty at this hour?

No.

I managed to keep myself upright by using my right hand—still holding the pistol—to guide myself down the stairs. Now all I heard was the ocean. Ambient light from the outside and from the few electronic devices gave me some visibility.

Two more steps.

I paused.

My legs were really trembling now.

From fear or from still being a recently discharged patient?

I took two more steps and reached the kitchen, with the living room visible to my left. My foot slipped again, making a very loud thump, and with all surprise being lost, I switched on the flashlight, yelled, "Freeze, whoever you are!" and swept the wide room with my light.

Nobody was there.

My heart was thumping loud enough to make a nice counterpoint to my shaking legs, and I stepped forward, breathing hard, swinging the light back and forth, back and forth. "Just so you know," I called out, "I've got a pistol here."

Nobody jumped up and surrendered.

I moved slowly through the living room, past the boxes and the shelves, flashing the light behind the couch and the two chairs. I slowly made my way back to the kitchen. Nothing seemed amiss.

What the hell?

I retraced my steps. Flashed the light again, even pointed it up at the ceiling, just in case my visitor was pretending to be Spiderman.

No joy.

The sliding glass door leading out to my first-floor deck was locked, and the length of wood I put in the runners to jam it from any potential burglar was still in place.

All right.

I moved back through the living room, my back screaming at me that it was time to wrap up this nonsense, go back to bed, and when it comes time to ask the good doctor to remove the drains, perhaps she could also recommend a nice head doc to find out why I was hallucinating.

I checked the front door.

Locked.

I shrugged, felt desperately tired all of a sudden, and turned and looked at the two other doors tucked away near the stairs going up.

One door belonged to my closet.

The other led downstairs, to my oil furnace and a dirt crawl space that marked my cellar.

That door was ajar.

I took another deep breath, leaning back as best as I could against the locked front door.

Hold on, hold on, just hold on, I thought.

Four days ago, a technician had come in to give my oil furnace its annual spring cleaning. She had spent a couple of hours down there, cheerfully banging away and swearing and making the whole house smell of #2 fuel oil for the rest of the day.

But had she closed the door behind her when she was done?

Or had I closed the door at some point?

Or, it being an old house, still settling, still getting used to the repair work after the arson last year, maybe the door just popped open by itself?

I could close the door and jam something up against it, I thought, and then call Felix. Or the cops.

Sure. And wouldn't they really be in a mood when the door was opened and the cellar was empty.

"Man up, buttercup," I whispered to myself.

I switched off the flashlight.

Just inside the door to the cellar was a light switch, right above the fuse box that controlled the power for the house. I could open the door, take a step down, flip on the switch, and surprise the hell out of whoever was down there. And with Beretta in hand, I'd make sure he stayed there, while I closed the door, blocked it, and called the cops.

Not Felix. Based on the times I had called Felix and had woken him up, he would probably shoot my intruder, yawn, announce he was going back to bed, and leave me to clean up the mess.

I got to the cellar door, opened it wider with my right foot. Stepping down into the darkness, I was ready to pause, switch on the light, and see what was what down there in the dark cellar.

Instead, my foot slipped, and I fell down the stairs in one long, loud, magnificent, and painful tumble.

CHAPTER FIVE

When I gathered my scattered senses and rolled over on my side, the funny thing was that the pain wasn't bothering me as much as the mouthful of dirt I had picked up while plowing into the cellar floor. Like a lot of the old houses in this part of the state, this home had never taken up with that newfangled trend of cement floors. In my case, that turned out to be a blessing.

I moved about, got up on my hands and knees, spit and spit, and then wiped my hand across my mouth. Blech. Besides the taste of centuries-old dirt, there was also just the faintest taste of Saudi Arabia's most famous refined export.

I swiveled, sat down.

It was dark as hell. I blinked, waiting for my eyes to adjust to the darkness, but after a couple of minutes, I figured my eyes had adjusted as much as they could.

Sure was dark.

I moved my hands through the dirt, feeling dirt and nothing else. Somewhere around here was a 9mm Beretta pistol, along with my flashlight. I was hoping to find either one, no rush to find one before the other.

Then I changed my mind.

The floorboards above me were creaking. My intruder was on the move.

Time to find the pistol first, especially if he heard me go ass over teakettle down the stairs, and knew I'd be in rotten shape to put up any resistance if he decided to come down and check me out.

I groaned and got back on my hands and knees, started spreading my hands through the dirt, looking for the pistol.

No joy.

This was nuts, I thought. My cellar was just a crawl space. You couldn't even stand up without hitting your head. How come it felt as large as a ballroom down here?

No lights, that's why. My active mind was expanding the little space.

Okay, maybe finding the flashlight first would be something. The only light switch for the cellar was at the top of the stairs, which I knew was a lousy design—I always said that one of these days I would have to get someone to come in and install another switch here. Yeah. Funny how "one of these days" always manages to arrive at the wrong time and bite you in the ass.

My hand felt something metallic.

About time.

I grasped it, picked it up, put it down.

A wrench.

I caught my breath, tried to ease the trembling in my arms and legs, and the creaking noise continued over my head. I moved my hand again and this time, I had found my prize.

My Beretta.

I slowly got up, hunched over, pistol in hand. Now it was time to find the stairs.

Okay. Where are the stairs?

I rotated slowly and then a little bit of light caught my eye. Some of the ambient light up on the first floor was seeping through the gap between the door and the cellar stair landing, or as it should really be called, the cellar stair falling.

I moved up one step, then another, staying to the side, pistol out, breathing hard, my incisions back there screaming at me to stop climbing

34

the stairs, stop bumping into the railing, stop moving, damn it. But I gritted my teeth, got to the top.

There you go.

I grasped the doorknob, turned, and tugged.

The door didn't move.

One more time.

Wouldn't move.

Was it blocked? Did my intruder jam something on the doorknob on the other side, trapping me?

One more tug.

Then I felt like taking the Beretta and rapping it on the side of my very thick skull.

I turned the doorknob and pushed, and the door moved easily enough.

"Nice going, dopey," I whispered. "Forgetting which way the door opened."

I got out and flicked on some lights, then turned on some more lights, and went to the kitchen and washed my face, took a glass of water and got a healthy swig, and spat it into the sink.

The water was gray.

Ugh.

I checked everything out, went to the front door that was—surprise!—still locked, and then I came back to the cellar, opened the door, turned on the light. The cellar from my mind's eye shrunk dramatically, and I spotted the flashlight up against the first step. Good. It was going to stay there. I switched off the light, closed the door, then looked to the stairs going up to the second floor. They looked steep, and they also looked like they stretched about a hundred feet above me.

Not going to happen.

I went back to the living room and kitchen, switched off most of the lights, then went to the couch, stretched out, and pulled a blanket over me. I only yelped twice as my wounds and drains rubbed up against the couch, and then I closed my eyes. I drifted off to sleep, occasionally reassuring myself by touching the nearby metal of my Beretta.

The morning sunlight was blasting right in when my front door was unlocked and Paula Quinn stepped in. She had a black knapsack over one shoulder, along with her purse, and she was also carrying yet another black bag that held her laptop.

She stopped. "What are you doing on the couch?"

"I was sleeping."

"And why aren't you in bed?"

"My secret lover Greta kicked me out, that's why."

My little joke went unnoticed. She said, "Did I wake you?"

My first lie of the morning. "No, not really."

She closed the door, dropped her stuff. Her face was red and her eyes were swollen.

"What's going on?" I asked.

"Had a rough night."

"Come over here and tell me about it."

I shifted on the couch. She sat down and then started weeping. I moved some more and put my arm around her and said, "When you're ready . . . go ahead."

She wiped at her eyes. "Oh, I'll be okay. And when it's over, you think, maybe you were overreacting."

"Knowing you, I doubt it. What happened last night?"

Paula took a deep breath. "Busy day, getting the latest out about Maggie Branch's murder. Not much more was released at the press conference the Tyler cops held, and then I had a quick take-out sub for dinner, and then went to the regular scheduled Tyler selectmen's meeting."

I squeezed her and she patted my other arm. "Meeting went on, blah blah blah, and then I heard the Tyler cops and Diane Woods are going to have another press conference later today. Okay? So I had a bind of getting my copy in today to make deadline, and making sure I could have the time to get to the press conference."

"Let me guess," I said. "You went back to the *Tyler Chronicle* offices to write your selectmen's story."

"Yeah," she said. "It was past midnight when I got the story wrapped up and done. Then I slipped to the front office to grab a drink of water, and then I heard the rear door bang open."

"Oh."

"You bet," she said. "There were voices, and some guy swore, and . . . I panicked. There are two conference rooms by there, and I ducked into the smallest one, locked the door behind me. Then—my cell phone was back at my desk, and there was no phone in the conference room."

"Paula . . ."

She snuggled into me, took another breath. "I stayed there, under the conference room table, for hours. I could hear them moving around."

"How many?"

"I don't know. Two at least. Maybe three."

"Could you hear what they were doing?"

"They went through the office upstairs, and then I heard someone shout that he had found it, and they went downstairs to the cellar. Spent at least an hour down there, I could hear them tossing things around."

"The cellar?"

"Yeah, pretty weird, right? You'd think they'd go through the desks on the ground floor, break them open, looking for laptops or some petty cash, but no, they stayed mostly in the cellar."

"When did they leave?"

I could feel her head shake. "I don't know. I . . . was under the conference room table, curled up, and I know it sounds strange, but I actually dozed off for a bit—until I heard a door slam."

"Them leaving."

"That's right. But I was so scared that, oh, I don't know, that one of them had stayed behind. So I waited, and waited, and when it started lightening up from the sunrise, well, I felt brave enough to get out. I ran out the front door and went over to the Common Grill & Grill to make a call. The cops got there in about five minutes, thank God."

"What was taken?"

She turned, smiled, which was nice to see. "Hard to tell, because they left the basement a mess. Filing cabinets with old clips, bound back issues, that was all tossed around. But I told the cops I was sure I knew what might have been taken. The sludge."

"The what?"

Paula smiled and I could feel her tension easing. "For decades, the *Chronicle* has had a darkroom down there in the cellar, processing film, before digital cameras came on the scene. Don't ask me the ins and outs of everything, but the chemicals and papers used in photography back in the day had silver in them. A year or two . . . big deal. But years after years, if certain sludge was collected, well, I told the cops the silver there could be worth a bit."

"How much?"

"No idea," she said. "But the containers with the sludge were gone. What else could it be?"

"Must have scared you something awful," I said.

"It did." Paula moved and looked up at me. "All right if I crash here for a day or two?"

"Stay as long as you want," I said, which earned me a kiss, and then a wrinkle of her nose.

"What's wrong?" I asked.

"No offense," she said. "But you taste like dirt."

Despite her offering to do so, I made us both a quick breakfast as she set up her laptop on the kitchen counter, and when we were finished with our instant coffee, scrambled eggs, and English muffins, she said, "Good. Two more hours before I have to head to the cop shop."

Paula yawned and I said, "I need to go upstairs for a second. Don't go anywhere."

"I won't."

So I took my time going upstairs, did some morning business, and when I came back downstairs, Paula was stretched on the couch, fast asleep.

Well.

This now posed a problem, because I was counting on Paula to help me with my two drains, but she was sleeping and I wasn't going to wake her up, not after the night she'd had at the *Chronicle*. So what to do?

Adapt and overcome.

I walked away from the couch, made my way to the stairs.

In the bathroom I got my oversize T-shirt off, looked at the situation in the mirror. Situation approaching extreme. Both bladders were full, and needed to get emptied. Okay, then.

The near bladder looked like it was reachable, as before. I moved my arm, my fingers brushed against it. Close.

I forced myself again. Almost.

"One more time," I whispered. I used my other arm to push my right arm and—

Snagged the little bastard. I pulled it out of the pouch, the bladder warm and obscene-looking in my hand. I gently tugged it away from the tube, emptied it in the measuring cup. Eight ounces. I washed out the bladder, popped the tube back in, and then grunted one more time and . . .

Success. The empty bladder was back in the pouch.

Okay. I took a few more breaths. Leaned over the bathroom counter. My head was light. That was some effort.

I calmed myself down and turned back once more.

The second bladder . . .

It could have been in Concord for all the good it was doing me.

All right.

As someone I greatly admired once said, work the problem.

I slowly walked out of the bathroom, went into my office, still in disarray. Desk, shelves, computer, printer, and monitor, plus cartons of books and shelves and other clutter.

Including a toolbox, overflowing with tools. I got down on my knees and went through, seeing what was there. Hammer, screwdrivers, hex tools, nuts, bolts, and a plier set.

Yes. A nice set of 11-inch-long needle-nose pliers.

I went back to the bathroom, struggled, swore, dropped the pliers four times, but by the time I was breathing hard and sweating, I had gotten the bladder out, drained, washed, and put back in place.

Then I blundered my way out of the bathroom and fell on the bed.

The smell of coffee and a woman's voice woke me up, and I got out of bed, made my way downstairs with Uncle Paulie's cane in hand to see a pretty sight indeed: Paula Quinn sitting at my kitchen counter, working on her laptop, cup of coffee at her elbow. I poured myself a cup and sat across from her, as she typed furiously along, her blonde hair cascading, her cute ears sticking out. I just sipped and watched her work and admired the way . . . well, the way everything was just working for her.

Paula looked up, smiled. "Have a good nap?"

"I did. And you?"

"Very much so," she said. "Nice cane you got there. What horror movie set did you get that from?"

"From Felix Tinios's long-departed uncle." I held it up. "See the wolf head? I'm told it can scare off vampires, or zombies, or bookies."

"I'm sure."

"According to Felix, it also has a secret inside."

"Probably a vial of brandy."

"Probably," I said. "How goes your work?"

"Oh, it goes well," she said. "I'm getting ready for the 11:00 A.M. press conference, and I'm trying to get a follow-up piece for the *Chronicle*'s website done before then." She picked up her coffee and gave a slow glance around the place. "You're making progress."

"Not enough."

"Enough for me to have a good sleep, refresh myself," she said. A little sip and she said, "Thanks."

"No thanks necessary."

"I came in, pretty wired up, scared . . . and I woke up feeling a hundred percent better. I'd feel a hundred and ten percent if I had time to slip into the shower."

"We could save time if I volunteered to wash your back."

A sly smile. "Knowing you, you'd feel compelled to wash my front as well."

"Never leave a job half-done," I said.

"Hah."

She went back to her keyboard and I said, "Hey, if you're up and running, can you do me a favor? What's the number for the Tyler Historical Society?"

"Hold on," and her fingers went tap-tap-tap and she gave me the number. "Who do you want to call over there?"

"Whoever answers the phone, or whoever runs the joint."

"I thought you knew who—"

Her cell phone rang, and she picked it up. "What?" she said. "For real? Thanks for the heads-up."

She clicked off, shut down her laptop, got up, and said, "Sorry, Lewis. For some reason the assistant attorney general has taken over the press conference, and he's moved it up fifteen minutes."

"Why would he do that?"

Paula gathered up her knapsack, coat, and put her laptop into a carry-on bag. "Because by starting the press conference earlier, he's pointing out that he's running the show, that's why."

A knock on the door caught our attention. Paula said, "Is your secret lover Greta returning from shopping or something?"

"Let's find out," I said, thinking it better not be the genealogical couple from the other day. I didn't have the patience. I went to the door, opened it up, and there was Felix Tinios, standing on my granite doorstep. He nodded in our direction, stood there rather stiff and formally, with his jacket over his left arm, although it didn't seem that warm.

"Lewis . . . and the ever-charming Paula Quinn," he said, brown eyes twinkling. "Have I interrupted anything?"

"Just me leaving, Felix," Paula said. "Hey, you do anything illegal lately?"

Felix just smiled a bit. "Depends on your definition of illegal, I guess, and since you're a journalist, and not a lawyer, why don't we just leave it at that."

"I guess so," she said, and she turned for a kiss goodbye before starting up my rough dirt driveway. I watched her slim form go up to the parking lot that belonged to the Lafayette House from across the street, and Felix said, "Paula . . . reasonably attractive, reasonably smart . . . but you're a man of the world, Lewis. What more do you see in her?"

"More than you can imagine, Felix. Come on in. Up for a cup of coffee?"

He grimaced as he came in. "What you call coffee . . . not at the moment, thanks. But I was hoping you could do me a favor."

I closed the door and followed him into my cluttered living room. Felix was moving slow, hesitant.

"What do you need?" I said.

He turned and dropped his jacket from his left arm. A bloody bandage made of paper napkins and kept in place by gray duct tape covered his forearm.

"I've been shot," he said.

CHAPTER SIX

On the couch, now," I said.

He went to the couch. "Turn around. Lay down. Legs up," I instructed.

Felix settled in and rested his wounded arm on his chest, then he raised his legs over the far armrest. I had lots of questions to ask and no time to ask them. I went upstairs as fast as I could—not fast enough, not fast enough, my mind was screaming at me—and from the bedroom closet, I tugged out a thick black zippered bag. Back downstairs I pulled a chair and the coffee table close to the couch, and opened the bag.

"Is the bullet still in you?"

"No," he said. "Looked like a clean hit before I bandaged it up . . . with what I had on hand."

"Why didn't you go to any ER in the area?"

He shifted his arm, frowned. "You know the rules, son. Anything that appears to be a gunshot is reported to the authorities. Need I say more?"

"Nope," I said. "Hold still."

I went to the kitchen and took out a plastic bottle of hydrogen peroxide from the refrigerator. I gave my hands a good wash, dried them off with a paper towel, went back to Felix. From the interior of the first aid kit, I tugged out a pair of latex gloves, slipped them on, and took out some sterile bandages, still in their paper packages.

Felix eyed me and said, "You look pretty prepped for a magazine writer."

"You know the rules, papa," I said, taking out a pair of stainless-steel shears. "In these troubled times, it's nice to have things in reserve, just in case. Hold tight. You need a stick to bite on?"

"Just do it."

I slipped the shears underneath the gray tape and started clipping. Felix's face tightened but he didn't say a word. I got the tape cut in half and then tugged away the tape and the paper napkins. Blood oozed and bubbled up from a wound at the side of Felix's wrist.

I tore open the gauze bandages and gently wiped away the blood so I could see the open wound. About two inches in length, a half-inch in width, and bleeding like hell. I dabbed and dabbed, and then soaked another bandage with the hydrogen peroxide.

"Going to hurt," I said.

"Gee, you think so?"

I gave the wound as gentle a wipe as I could, and Felix's arm jerked a bit, but he stayed still. One more wipe and I said, "It's going to need stitches."

"I know."

"I really don't want to stitch you up," I said. "The wound's pretty jagged. Somebody with a hell of a lot more skills than me would have to give it a good cleaning and trimming to make sure the stitches work."

"That's all right," Felix said. "I have somebody . . . on call. Just my bad luck he's out of town today. But he'll be back tomorrow. Just wrap it up, the best you can. I'll get it fixed and stitched tomorrow."

"All right, then."

In my kit was a small bottle of distilled water, which I cracked open and used to irrigate the wound. Then I patted everything dry, folded over a piece of gauze, placed it into the jagged opening. I did my best to pull the wound together with butterfly bandages, and then put another gauze bandage over that, taped it up, wrapped the area with a length of gauze, and taped the whole thing in place.

"Sloppy and amateur," I said, "but it'll keep you in one piece until you see your doc."

He nodded, gently put his wounded forearm on his chest. "Thanks."

"No thanks necessary," I said. "But how about a pain pill? I've got some Percocet upstairs from my surgery that I'd be happy to share."

A violent shake of Felix's head. "No, not at all, I wouldn't dare use that stuff. I like to think I'm tough, but I'm not taking something that'll end up with me injecting street stuff between my toes. Nope, Extra-Strength Tylenol or something like that."

I found the pills and a tall glass of water for him; he swallowed the first and sipped the second as I cleaned up the joint. I sat across from him and said, "I thought I told you to play nice."

"Yeah, you always say that, and the other people decide not to play nice. So what's a boy to do?"

"Tell me the story," I said.

"From where?"

"The beginning."

"Once upon a time there was the Big Bang, and—"

I gently kicked the side of the couch. "Bad jokes about cosmology belong to me. Cut it out, or I'll tell everyone you were crying when I was bandaging you up."

"Hah, like anyone would believe you." He took another sip of water and said, "I got a lead on a car that was in the area of Maggie's place the night she got murdered."

"How?"

"Because . . ."

"Because you haven't told me that part of the story yet," I said. "You said that a Toyota Corolla with Massachusetts license plates was seen leaving Maggie's place during the time frame when she was murdered."

"I did."

"Was it you or someone in your employ?"

"My employ."

"Doing what?"

"Working a surveillance for me. Another house up the road. Nice family with a college-age daughter, commuting to UNH. One of her professors is harassing her—not enough to get the university's attention, but enough to get Mom and Dad's attention. Sometimes he stops by unannounced, leaves gifts in the mailbox. She's afraid that if she makes too much of a stink, it'll impact her grades."

"And your contractor?"

"Was working surveillance on the house in question, which was quiet. No love-struck professor with receding hairline and glasses approaching. But one house over, where Maggie lived, he did see a Toyota race out, nearly clip a tree, and head off toward the interstate, about the time when the police said Maggie was murdered."

"I see. And you traced the license plate and what did you find?"

"A not-so-nice man named Pepe, who leads a gang of not-so-merry men in and around Lowell and Lawrence. We met up in one of those three-story tenements that used to be called Irish battleships before the latest round of immigration."

"Okay, then, what next?"

Felix shrugged. "Had a chilly conversation that eventually went full Arctic."

"Did they take your silver?"

"Not sure."

"Did they kill Maggie?"

"Well, see, that's where it got interesting, right from the start. I asked them about that and I half-expected some brave talk, tough talk, crap like that. You know, 'Yo bro, the bitch gave us grief, so we capped her.' But no go. In fact, they used an excuse I've used on occasion, when I was much younger and much faster."

"And what excuse was that?"

"The one that goes, 'Sorry, officer, he was dead when I got there.'"

"Really?"

"That's right. Pepe and friends said that Maggie was already dead when they went into her place. They were looking for a quick score, thinking antique places like that must have a lot of cash and jewelry lying around. So they parked halfway up her driveway, went into the barn, and . . . found dead Maggie in her chair, bone, blood, hair, and brain splattered on the wall behind her, papers and books all over the floor. Pepe claimed his guys saw the scene and got the hell out."

"Do you believe him?"

"Well . . ."

"Felix, do you think he was telling the truth?"

He thought for a moment. "I think he was leaning more toward the truth. He said something like, 'What, we gonna smoke a grandma and for what?' Plus, the way my guy saw that Toyota drive out of Maggie's place, it was like they were spooked and needed to get the hell out."

I refilled his water glass and made my way back, and he saw the cane and said, "How's Uncle Paulie's cane treating you?"

"Just fine. I'm waiting to scare little kids off with the wolf's head."

"Do you want me to show you what—"

"I can figure it out," I said. "Now, tell me the interesting part of the story, the one that ends with you getting shot in your forearm."

Felix took a long swallow, put the glass down on the coffee table. "No, wasn't that interesting. I kept on asking about my great-grandfather's silver, coming at them from different approaches, and then Pepe's buddies got angry. Then they got really angry, and it deteriorated from there."

"Why so angry?"

"Kids nowadays . . ."

A pause. I said, "Go on."

"Are you sure?"

"Felix . . ."

"Kids nowadays, not only don't they respect their elders, they also don't respect much of anything. Institutions, ways of doing business, past agreements and such. What I saw was one of Pepe's gang start raising a fuss, and I knew what was going on. The guy was making a play, wanting to show Pepe that he was tougher than tough, that he wouldn't allow anybody to 'dis his *jefe*,' or something like that."

"Spun out of control then?"

"Well, after I shot the guy making the play." Another pause. "I had to make an example, to all of them."

"I guess they didn't appreciate the lesson."

"Not hardly. No more talking but some more gunplay . . . and here I am."

I just nodded. "What next, then?"

"Short term, I'd like relax here for a bit until the Tylenol kicks in. Long term, I'm going back to Pepe and company to get a final and clear answer on my great-grandfather's silver."

"You know, the Tyler cops might be interested in talking to Pepe's boys."

"They didn't have anything to do with her murder."

"Still . . ."

"Good lord," Felix said. "I can't believe you didn't make Eagle Scout back in the day, Lewis. Okay, once I'm satisfied with the status of my antique silver, then I'll make sure Pepe's boys make an appearance at the Tyler police station."

"Sometimes you're so civic-minded, it helps restore just a bit of my faith in humanity."

"Just a bit?" Felix asked.

"No need to get ahead of ourselves."

Felix napped for an hour and I offered him lunch before he left, but he declined. "I just want to get to my home turf and collapse. See if I can convince a nurse or two to come over and ooh and aah over my latest wound."

"Based on past experience, I doubt that'll be a problem."

"You never know," he said. "How are you set for dinner?"

"Fine."

I walked him to my door and he stepped out, took a look at my house and the scraggly yard and rocks. "I know this joint has a lot of historical significance for you and all that, but don't you get tired of these old boards?"

"Not for a moment."

"Damn thing almost burned down around your ears some months ago."

"True, but the rebuilding's almost finished."

"Yeah, that it is," he said. "Just keep on watching out for arsonists and tourists."

And just then, there was a shout up at the top of my driveway, as a man and a woman began to come my way.

"So who are they?" Felix said. "Arsonists or tourists?"

"Worse," I said. "Amateur historians."

Felix took his time walking up the driveway past the couple from Albany, Dave and Marjorie Hudson, and I really hoped that seeing an injured Felix Tinios come their way might turn the couple around so they would decide to beat a retreat back up to the Lafayette House's parking lot, but maybe that fresh bullet wound had weakened Felix's superpowers, such that they kept on coming.

Having been spotted in my open door, I also thought that going back in, locking the door, and ignoring any knocks would be in bad form, so I tried to paste on a reasonably blank face as they approached.

The husband-and-wife team had on the same clothes as before, including the tweed cap for him and the brightly colored knit cap for her, and Dave Hudson still had a bulging file folder under his arm.

"Mr. Cole, so glad to see you again!" he called out, and I just nodded politely and waited in my doorway. His wife, Marjorie, kept quiet as they both approached.

"Please, I'm really not up for a visit today," I said.

Hudson nodded politely. "I know, I know, but I assure you, we won't take too much of your time."

"I appreciate that, Mr. Hudson, but I'm not in a mood or a position to host visitors, so . . ." I started going back into my house, and he came up the steps, surprising me.

"Look, Mr. Cole, my wife and I have driven a long way here from Albany, to do genealogical research, and I don't think you appreciate the time and effort we've spent on this."

"I do appreciate that, Mr. Hudson, and I hate to be rude and flippant, but that's not my problem. You didn't write, call, or email me ahead of time to tell me that you were coming. If you had done that, I could have explained my situation, and we could have set up a mutually agreeable time for you and your wife to visit."

His wife came up behind him and I said, "As it is, and I hate to repeat myself, but I've just come out of the hospital. I find it exhausting just to stand up for a while. I also get exhausted just being awake. In fact, I get exhausted from talking about being exhausted. I'm not in the mood nor condition to receive visitors. Please. Give me some time and space, and I'd be happy to let you in and have you look around."

He said, "Mr. Cole . . . if I may, all you have to do is go into your house, have a seat on your couch, and we'll be as quick and as quiet as we can. You'll hardly notice we're there."

"While you're doing what?"

"Taking photos. Measurements. Recording what this place was like back when my grandfather was stationed here during the Korean War."

I took a breath, trying to keep my temper in place. "Really, I'm trying not to be rude here, but this place—my home!—is not the same place as it was when your grandfather was here. It's changed, it's been built, expanded, some parts torn down, and just last year, a good chunk was burned down in an arson. I did my best rebuilding it with old lumber and timber from the nineteenth century, so I don't see what you'd gain."

His voice got sharp. "What I gain is none of your business, Mr. Cole." And then, like he knew he had gone too far, he added, "Sorry, I didn't mean it that way. Mr. Cole, your home doesn't just belong to you. It belongs to history. It belongs to future generations. Certainly it has changed over the years—I do realize that—but the basics of your house, the foundation of your house, it's remained the same. And all I ask is some time and courtesy to let me record a part of it."

"History and future generations don't pay the utility bills or the property taxes," I said. "I do. Is that clear enough?"

"I—"

His wife, Marjorie, got up on the granite steps, tugged at her husband's jacket. "David please, that's enough."

His face was red and he stepped down hard from the steps, like he was making a statement. Marjorie rubbed her hands—she looked pretty cold, even with the April sun up high and warm—and she said to me, "I'm sorry. David . . . he's a bit of a compulsive, you know? The kind of guy who eats M&Ms by putting them on a plate and organizing them by color, or who makes sure his shirts are hung by sleeve length and fabric. When he gets a notion in his head . . ."

Her husband stepped back a few more steps. Marjorie glanced back at him and then turned back to me, lowering her voice. "I know he's being a pain." She gave me a wide smile. "You should try being married to him."

"No thanks."

A pleasant nod. "I understand, and I'm sorry for disturbing you again."

"I appreciate that, Mrs. Hudson. And honest, just give me two more weeks, all right? I'm sure I'll be in a better position then."

She nodded. "I get it. Again, sorry."

Marjorie stepped back and went to her husband, and there was a brief yet spirited discussion that I couldn't quite make out, and then she took his arm—not the one with the folder—and started walking back up my dirt driveway. Marjorie turned and gave me one more sympathetic look, and then she turned back to her husband.

I watched for another minute or so as the couple walked away, heading up to the parking lot of the Lafayette House, and then Hudson shook off his wife's grasp, stood, and then looked back at me.

His gaze wasn't friendly or open or forgiving.

It was pure hate.

CHAPTER SEVEN

After that dreary event, I had a lunch of defrosted frozen soup and some cheese and rolls, the soup having come from Diane Woods's fiancée, Kara Miles. And as chance would have it, Diane called me and we made a date for an early dinner. So I napped and poked around and, thanks to Paula's help, I called the Tyler Historical Society three times. Each time, the call went to voice mail, except the voice mail box was full and couldn't accept any more messages.

At five P.M., Diane came through the front door without looking at me and flopped down on my couch, barely missing my feet.

She looked very tired, wearing jeans, a black turtleneck, and short leather jacket. I said, "Thanks for coming by."

"Glad to do it."

"I thought you'd be busy at work."

She rubbed her face with her right hand. "Ah, yes, I would be, if there was any work for me to do."

"What's going on?"

"You're aware that this state is in the middle of an opioid crisis?"

"I know, but I'm sure I don't know enough."

A sigh. "Get this. Our little Granite State, our little slice of heaven, it's ground zero in the current heroin epidemic. Per capita, we're number one—not as newsworthy as having the first-in-the-nation primary, but it's right up there. Each day we lose a couple of men and women, boys and girls, to ODs. Over in Manchester we had a mom and dad who OD'd and died in a restaurant bathroom while their kiddos were having the early-bird special."

"I don't remember hearing that or seeing that in the papers."

Diane stretched her legs, rubbed her hands along her jeans. "That's because it didn't really officially happen. Sometimes, if there's no real crime involved, like an underage victim or someone forcing the drug into a person, the families like to keep it quiet. You'll see it in the obits if you read it the right way. 'Died unexpectedly.' 'Died at home.' 'Died with friends at his bedside.' Saves the family a bit of grief, though that's changing now. Lots of families want to get the word out, even if they're embarrassed, so they can help save another family."

She took a breath and I interrupted. "Then what does this have to do with Maggie Branch's murder?"

"Yesterday morning, it had nothing to do with Maggie's murder. Then after we did another sweep of her barn office, it had everything to do with Maggie's murder. We found a little plastic envelope of high-grade heroin. Goddamn stuff even had a stamp on it, that's how brazen the goddamn dealers are getting."

"What kind of stamp?"

"Oh, just a stamp with a bird on it. A bluebird. Your stamp of approval that you'll be getting one honking good high, accept no substitutes."

"And who's doing the stamping?"

"Some outfit out of Lowell. Not to pick on Lowell and Lawrence, our distressed neighbors to the south, but they're currently the Axis of Evil when it comes to distribution up here."

Lowell, I thought. Where Felix went last night, talked to a gang that had its members at Maggie's place the night of her murder, and where they apparently had left a souvenir behind . . .

"Lewis?"

"Sorry, I was daydreaming. What did you say?"

She shook her head. "What I said was that when that little envelope of heroin was found, it was 'Katie, bar the door.' The Feds are pouring money and resources to help us local yokels do something, when the real temporary solution right now is to stop arresting people and getting them into rehab. But allocating money for rehab centers isn't sexy enough for our elected betters, so most of the money is going to law enforcement."

"They took the Maggie Branch case away from you."

"The state most certainly did," she said. "Including one handsome, young, and energetic assistant attorney general named Camden Martin, who's hell-bent on making a name for himself. He has a special task force set up with the authority and ability to go anywhere and take over any case that has a connection to heroin."

"One little packet doesn't seem like much of a connection."

"Ah, but what's more fun for our handsome young Attorney General Martin: meeting with local police chiefs to try to track down the midlevel dealers, most of whom live in distressed housing and are addicts themselves, or diving into a case that will tug at the state's heartstrings?"

"A lonely elderly antiques dealer, murdered by a shotgun blast to her head, connected to the opioid crisis."

"Yep. So they have it, and are being polite, but the Tyler Police Department has officially been shoved out. Even though it's my case, damn it."

A right foot snapped out, kicking my coffee table a few feet. "My case, damn it!"

I paid special attention to a pile of history books near me, all written by the famed British historian John Keegan, and Diane reached over and patted my arm, shaking her head in dismay.

"Sorry. Not enough sleep and I lost it there. You and your furniture and books don't deserve it."

"Don't worry about it. Forgiven and forgotten."

"Thanks." She moved on the couch to get a better look at me. "How are you doing?"

"Doing all right."

"And how are you when it comes to painkillers?"

"I took one prescription pill. Made me constipated for three days, gave me crappy dreams. That was it."

"Good for you," she said. "You know, if there was a blame game on this situation, I'd blame big pharma and the doctors. Big pharma for making these powerful painkillers and making it seem like your Constitutional right never to experience a twinge, and the doctors who go along for the ride, writing scripts for their patients because they're tired of hearing them whine about how it hurts so much. And when the scripts run out, and they can't get them refilled by any doctor, then the patients go another route. Just to satisfy the craving that hadn't been there in the first place."

I wanted to change the dreary subject so I asked, "How's Kara?"

That brought a smile to Diane's scarred face. "My honey is doing fine, thanks for asking. The Internet is a wonderful and dangerous thing, but Kara knows to keep on top of things. When a company or a person has a problem with their websites, Kara can dive right into the mess and make it right. I have no idea what the hell she's doing, but it makes her happy, so that's great with me."

Diane said, "Oh, crap, here I am, talking about my woes and worries. How are you doing? Any more mysterious visitors?"

"If there are, they're not making themselves visible."

"We've got an Explorer unit at the police department. I could arrange to have a husky lad or two spend the night, just in case."

"Any husky lasses?"

Diane smiled. "Not at the moment."

"Thanks, but I'll be all right."

"Good. Hungry?"

I made a point of looking past her. "I am, but I don't see anything with you."

Diane got off the couch. "I got a cooler I dumped on your steps before coming in. I was getting tired of the damn thing and I didn't want to trip and dump it all over your nice clean floor. Hold on and I'll got get it."

She took three steps and then glanced down at my floor, and stopped. "Your floor's not that clean, Lewis. Everything okay?"

"What is it?"

"This," she said, squatting down and picking something up, and then holding it out to me; I tried very, very hard to keep a friendly, bland expression on my face.

For "this" was a wad of bloody gauze, from when I had fixed up Felix earlier.

Long seconds dragged on for a long time. I held out my hand. "Thanks," I said. "Guess I missed that one."

"An accident?" she asked, giving me the dry and brown-looking piece of gauze.

"You could say that," I said. "Sometimes . . . well, sometimes you just don't know what's going to happen."

"Turn around."

"What?"

"Turn around."

I did as I was told, before she went from using her friendly-but-concerned voice and slid into hard-ass police-detective-sergeant voice, lifting up my T-shirt. I felt her strong fingers poke around back there.

"Mmm," she said. "Your two bladders are definitely filling up. You want me to empty them before I leave?"

"Paula might be by . . . but if not, that would be nice."

"Ah, Paula Quinn. Glad to see the two of you making a go of it."

"Trying," I said. "Did you run into her this morning?"

"About the burglary at the *Chronicle*? Nope, letting a patrol sergeant do that. Give him some experience if and when we ever get another detective hired."

Her fingers still gently traced my skin. "When do you hear about the pathology results?"

"Any day now," I said.

"Meaning what?"

"Any day now," I repeated.

"Huh," she said, fingers still softly back there. "Doctors."

"I'm hopeful," I said. "The other times I've had growths like this removed, they've all turned out to be benign."

"Yeah, benign, but still forcing you to get gutted like a goddamn chicken. And I hope you like chicken, 'cause that's what we're having."

And then, in a quiet moment, and before she lowered my T-shirt, Diane gave a gentle kiss to my back.

I tried to help in the kitchen but she shooed me away, although she did notice my walking implement.

"Good God, where in hell did you get that cane from? The estate of H. P. Lovecraft?"

"No," I said, at least laying out silverware and dishes. "It's a gift from Felix Tinios. It belonged to an uncle of his."

She peered at the wolf's head at the top of the cane. "The uncle the mob shooter, or the uncle the exorcist?"

"The uncle with the bum leg or hip."

As promised, dinner was a roasted chicken, with carrots, mashed potatoes, stuffing, and homemade gravy, and it tasted damn fine. We had glasses of ice water, and since Diane belongs to the same wine club I do—red goes with everything—we made do with a nice pinot noir from New Zealand.

When there was a pause in the meal, I asked, "Wedding plans still on for June?"

"They are, and you better be one healthy bastard to walk me down the aisle. So get going on that healing process."

"Doing the best I can," I said. "Funny . . . last year I thought you'd be going down the aisle in a wheelchair, and this year I thought it was my turn. Make sure Kara doesn't piss off any gods or goddesses related to medicine."

Diane smiled. "I'll pass that along to her. I'm sure she'll appreciate it."

We ate some more and I sensed something was troubling Diane—besides having the homicide investigation taken away from her and given to the state police—and since I've known her for quite some time, as she scooped up the last of the stuffing, I said, "All right, give."

"What? More gravy?"

"No, what's bugging you. Besides the state police and the charming and too-cool Camden Martin, assistant AG, complicating your life?"

Her chin scar whitened just a bit, meaning that emotions were now coursing through her, and a part of me thought, *Dummy, you should have just asked her if she wanted chocolate or strawberry ice cream for dessert.*

Then the scar went back to its normal color, and she said, "The deputy chief has announced his retirement."

"Okay."

"I'm thinking about applying for the job."

"Why not?" I said. "I think you'd be good at it."

Her eyes narrowed. "Why?"

I quickly didn't like where this was going. "Um, because you're good at everything you do."

"Hah," she said. "What do you think the deputy chief does?"

"Fill in for the chief when he's absent?"

"No," she said, "and I hope this doesn't burn your tender ears, but the deputy chief is the chief's bitch."

I struggled to keep my face expressionless.

It didn't work.

"Lucky for you we're having this discussion now, and not before dinner," Diane said. "Otherwise, I would have taken your meal away."

"What do you expect?" I asked. "I don't know much about softball, but I think you just tossed a big fat slow one right over the plate."

"Hah."

"All right," I said. "The chief's bitch. Details, please."

She shrugged. "Lots of scrut work. Doing financial research on budgets, wages, health-care costs. Being the bad-ass disciplinarian when the need arises. Representing the chief at certain civic functions. Pretty much any task that the chief doesn't want to do."

I took that in and said, "Doesn't sound much like police work."

"God, no," she said. "And I'd have to wear a uniform every day. Have you seen that thing? Ugly color not seen in nature, makes my ass look huge—no, I wouldn't like that. Plus, yeah, no more real police work. Investigations, helping people out, tracking down the scum that need to be put away. It can be a grind, it can be a pain in the ass, but it also gives me a real sense of satisfaction at the end of the day."

"I see what you mean. I can't see you feeling so satisfied by balancing a budget or disciplining a cop for using naughty language in front of grandma."

"Yep."

I wiped my fingers on my napkin. "Lots of negatives you're putting out there. But you are still considering applying for it?"

"Yep."

"Okay, help me out, then."

Diane leaned back on her stool. "Because . . . because I've been in the department long enough, and it's considered bad form not to seek advancement. Like you're not taking your job or the department seriously enough. If I don't apply, then some folks will see that as a weakness, and I don't like being thought of as weak."

"Especially with what just happened with the Maggie Branch homicide."

"Exactly," she said. "So I'll probably apply for the job and hope I don't get it, and if I don't get it, I'll manage to soldier on."

"But suppose you do get the job?"

"Bite your tongue, son," she said. "I don't want you jinxing anything. But at least I'm not up in Porter."

"What's going on up in Porter?"

Diane frowned. "The police chief up there is a good man, a fine man, and there's a witch hunt after him for something that happened in his department long before he became chief. Fools. They'll end up running him out of town and God knows how long it'll take for them to get a permanent chief to replace him."

I did my best to help clean up, Diane did her best not to bump into me, and as we were wrapping up, the door opened and Paula Quinn came in. Diane and Paula nodded at each other and I said cheerfully, "Dear me, my favorite fantasy comes true. Diane and Paula, under the same roof, at the same time."

Paula stuck her tongue out at me and Diane tossed a napkin at my head. Diane picked up her cooler and as she went out the door, she had a brief conversation with Paula, which Paula nodded at while closing the door.

"Hey, it looks like you've got enough leftovers for one hungry journalist."

"Sure does," I said. "Come on over."

"Don't have to invite me twice," she said. "And you can tell me about your interesting day, and I'll do the same."

It only took a few minutes to warm up what was left of the dinner Diane and I had shared, and Paula dug in enthusiastically as I watched in awe as she ate. Paula always had the capability of putting away big meals without it showing up anywhere. "A long day but not much to show for it," she said.

"Besides the story about Maggie Branch, I also had to do a story on a proposal to expand the town hall, which is getting all the poor overwhelmed taxpayers in a snit."

"What's going on with the homicide?"

"The state police and its opioid task force are taking the lead in poor Maggie's murder, and the Tyler police are grinning and trying to bear it. There'd be a time when the chief would have everyone's back and put his booted foot down, but not with heroin everywhere. The Tyler selectmen are just as happy to have the state police come in."

"Any more news on the case?"

"Depends. The news is the news, and they're tracking down whatever leads they might have. And that latest lead is the odd one, finding that little packet of heroin in her shop. I mean, hey, just because heroin was found there, doesn't mean it was left by the killer. It could have fallen out of someone's pocket, a week ago or a month ago."

"But budgets and resources have to be used where appropriated."

She dabbed at a little drop of gravy on her chin. "My, aren't we being the cynical one."

"You started it," I said.

The cleanup went faster this time, and we cuddled as best as we could on the couch, with me trying to avoid putting pressure on my bladders—such hot talk—and Paula tapping away on her laptop.

We watched a British comedy, one of those quirky little films that take place in a small English village, and it made us laugh so much that my sides ached, but not my back and shoulder, which was nice for a change.

As it got later we went upstairs and she pointed to the bathroom; I walked in without raising a fuss.

She got my bladders out, measured them, and shook her head as she emptied the measuring cup and washed it. "Sorry. Still on the high end. You're still going to be tubed up like a Borg or something."

"Without the skin condition, I hope."

"That's our next step."

I got my clothes off and Paula ran some water into the tub. I stepped in and she did a good wash of me with a hand cloth, and then using a small plastic container, rinsed off the soapy water on my skin. It felt good to be washed, and it felt good to be touched by Paula.

When she dried me off she gave me a teasing look as she patted the towel in a sensitive place. "Nice to see part of you is still working."

"Glad to see you noticed."

She helped me into fresh clothes, and feeling pretty refreshed, even with the throbbing aches back there, she helped me into bed and said, "Feel like company?"

"Always," I said. "But a lot of the time I get restless. You know that."

Paula kissed me. "What, you're warning me already that you're going to toss me out of bed?"

"I just don't want any surprises."

"Lighten up," she said. "I want some company, too, and if you get too restless, I'll kick you out and you can go to the couch downstairs."

"Deal."

Paula turned on the television, lowered the volume, and switched it to one of those reality televisions shows featuring rich housewives who tend to travel in groups, eat at fine restaurants, and yell at each other a lot. It was one of Paula's guilty pleasures, and who was I to tell her otherwise?

From the bathroom, water was used and flushed, and then she came back in, wearing an oversize Red Sox T-shirt. When she climbed in next to me, I saw she wasn't wearing much else.

"Put your eyes back where they belong," she said.

"I'm an invalid. Don't you have any mercy?"

"Maybe, maybe not."

She slid under the blankets and picked up the remote, toggled it so that it would switch off in a half hour, and we kissed some. Then she sighed, stretched out behind me, and said, "Nice to be here with you."

"It'll be nicer when I'm in better shape."

She patted my hip. "Slow down, cowboy. One day and then another."

"Got it."

So we settled in, and on the television screen one housewife was screaming at another for losing a historical piece of jewelry, and that triggered something. "Paula?" I said.

"You expecting Diane?"

"Just wanted to make sure you were awake."

"For the next several minutes, so make it worth it."

I said, "I called the Tyler Historical Society a couple of times today."

"Uh-huh."

"And nobody answered."

"Uh-huh."

"And the voice-mail box was full, not accepting any messages."

Paula yawned. "Well, what did you expect?"

"Sorry?"

"The Tyler Historical Society," she said. "Maggie Branch was its president."

CHAPTER EIGHT

ots of questions just popped up in my head, like a herd of prairie dogs, but they could wait. Paula was drifting off and I didn't want to wake her up. A few more minutes passed.

"Oh, Lewis?"

"Still here."

"I think I left the lights on downstairs. You want me to go back down there and switch them off?"

I reached around and took her hand. "No. Don't leave."

"Okay. Thanks. Because if you had told me to go downstairs, I would have said no."

"That's my girl."

She moved some and soon was slumbering behind me. Up on the television more overdressed and undereducated women were throwing drinks at each other.

I closed my eyes.

Tried to block out the sounds and memories.

Failed.

It had been a few years ago. The local news media was agog when news broke about Maggie Tyler Branch having discovered a printed copy of the

Declaration of the Independence at a yard sale in Porter. The copy was later certified as one of the original broadsheets printed in Philadelphia in 1776, and was worth several hundred thousand dollars.

I let the initial media buzz lighten up and then I made an appointment to see Maggie, on a pleasant early July day that was unexpectedly cool for the season. I parked my Ford Explorer in a dirt patch in front of her large barn, next to a wooden sign painted white and black that read, BORDER ANTIQUES, and swung gently in the breeze.

As I got out of the car, three black-and-white cats came trotting out. I stood still as they sniffed my feet and lower legs, and then flopped over for a belly rub. I bent down, let them sniff my hands, and I scratched their heads and rubbed their bellies.

"Hey!"

I looked up and Maggie Branch was there, smoking a cigarette, a glass of amber-colored fluid in her other hand. She was wearing shapeless blue dungaree pants and a gray sweatshirt. Her hair was white, short and styled, and her hazel eyes had a sweet tingle about them, like she couldn't believe the life she was now leading.

I introduced myself and she led me into her barn. The cats followed us in. The floor was made up of wide wooden planks, uneven and gapped, with lots of knotholes. There was a short wide area near the entrance, and around us were shelves upon shelves upon shelves. Up overhead there were rafters and a second floor, also jammed with shelves upon shelves.

The shelves were crowded with a mass of chaos, and you had to stare at just one at a time to bring everything into focus. That shelf with leather-bound books, that shelf with radio parts and speakers, and another shelf with shoes, and glassware, and Hummel figurines, and so forth and so on into the gloom.

Maggie stopped when she couldn't walk anymore. We stood in the middle of four wooden chairs in various stages of repair, an old-fashioned rolltop desk, and a collection of wooden filing cabinets. Another desk was covered with papers, file folders, bowls of cat food, and dishes of water.

She sat down in a wooden swivel chair, turned around to me, and flicked some ash on the floor. "You're probably the seventh or eighth reporter I've talked to," she said. "I imagine me finding that damn Declaration will be the first line in my obit, though for Christ's sake, I hope it's not for a while."

"Absolutely," I said. "But I hope you're not offended, your obit won't run in *Shoreline*."

Maggie cackled. "I like *Shoreline*. I got it for my two grandkids. One lives in Oklahoma, another in Idaho. I don't want them or their young'uns to forget where we all came from, about their history and such."

"Thanks for being so supportive."

"What, you think those three subscriptions make a difference?"

"It all makes a difference," I said, taking out my notebook and pen.

"You gonna do a story about me?"

"That's why I'm here."

She took another drag off her cigarette, flicked some more ash. A cat jumped up on the desk and started eating from its food bowl. Maggie leaned forward, grinned, and said, "I like *Shoreline*, so I'll tell you a story. You can use it if you want. But I think it's funnier than hell."

I opened the notebook's cover. "I'm always open for a funny story. Hit me."

I had confused her. "What?"

"Sorry, tell me your funny story."

Maggie nodded with satisfaction. "Okay, then," she said. "I like to drive around and scour yard sales, or garage sales, or tag sales, or whatever it is that they're calling them nowadays. Lots of time you get junk, and over-priced junk at that. Shit on a shingle, I'll see some old G.I. Joe dolls from—"

"Action figures," I interrupted.

"Huh?"

"The G.I. Joes, they weren't dolls. They were action figures. Trust me, I know from personal experience."

That made her laugh, and her laugh was so loud it made the three black-and-white cats hide for cover. When she was done she said, "Whatever you want to call 'em, I don't mind, but you'd see these G.I. Joes from the 1960s for sale, and sure, they're valuable, but they gotta be in good shape. And what can you say to someone who wants to sell a G.I. Joe with a missing arm for a hundred bucks?"

"But you must find some good things here and there. The Declaration, for example."

"Yeah, and that's the fun of it, though not as much anymore," she said. "I used to be able to go on these long road trips, just me, a road map, and some Dunkin' Donuts, and go out to Maine or to upstate New York, but after a while, it just got too hard. My ass and my back couldn't handle it. That's why I try to stick around here and there, not too far from Tyler."

"What happened in Porter?"

"Funny thing, purely by accident. I was just puttering around, Saturday morning, just enjoying the sunshine after a nice heavy breakfast. Was feeling drowsy so I thought I'd go home, but in one of the older neighborhoods up in Porter, somebody was having a yard sale. So I stopped right away."

"What made you stop?"

She smiled. "Didn't you hear me the first time? It was a house in an old neighborhood. You get out to some of the newer homes, when they have yard sales, it's mostly crap. Stuff from the 1970s—God, what a ghastly decade for fashion and collectables and politics. Anyway, at these older houses, you got nitwits who live there who either moved in, or who took the place over after grandma died. And when they try to clean out, they don't know what they have."

"Did you know it was the Declaration of Independence when you saw it?"

"Hard not to, with all those big letters at the top."

I smiled back at her. "Okay, how did you know it was one of the original prints, that it was rare?"

"Keep a secret?"

A quick flashback to my time at the Department of Defense. "Always."

She moved the chair from side to side with a sharp squeak. "I didn't give a shit about the Declaration. I just liked the frame. It was old and ornate. So I picked it up and the sweet young man told me it was for sale at five dollars, and I said I'd give him two, and we settled on four dollars."

"You bargained him down like that?"

"I'm an old Yankee trader, one of the oldest around," she said with satisfaction. "Then, a couple of months later, I needed the frame, and I took it apart and then, well, I held the damn thing in my hand. Hard to explain, but the texture of the parchment, the scent, looking at the printing . . . it just . . . it just whispered to me. That it was much more than a later reproduction. After a couple of appraisals and a visit to a rare bookstore owner in Boston, I knew what I had."

"And you didn't want to keep it?"

"Hell, no," she said.

She moved her chair over and gave a healthy kick to the wooden filing cabinets. "See that? Chock-full of papers from the Tyler family, going way back to some of the original documents from the Reverend Bonus Tyler hisself, one of the founders of our fair community. There's also lots of other historical papers in here about almost everything to do with Tyler. Do you think it's fun having the responsibility for holding onto something valuable like that? Christ, no. The same with the Declaration. If I had held on to it, I'd have tourists and noisy bastards—not like you, no offense—lined up all the way to the road to take a look at it."

Maggie took a deep drag of her cigarette, dropped the butt on the wooden floor, ground it out with her heel. "This way, I could sell it, use the money for good—like local animal rescue agencies—and people could go away."

"But what about those papers?" I asked, pointing to the filing cabinets. "Are you looking to sell those?"

"Nope," she said. "I wanna donate them to a place that makes sense, like the historical society or the Tyler library. But those folks, they can't promise me that they'll be taken care of. They say they don't have the space or resources to accept such a gift right now. Maybe one of these days."

"Maybe."

One of the cats suddenly jumped up on my lap and scared the wits out of me. Maggie laughed again and I stroked his back as he rotated three times before plopping himself down. I scratched his ears and cheeks and he rubbed up against me and purred and purred.

Maggie looked around her place with a mix of satisfaction and exasperation. "All this . . . stuff."

I lifted my head as well. "Lots of it."

"Yeah," she said. "Funny . . . I know the attraction that comes from stuff like this. You can read history books and old newspapers, and get a feel of what might have happened in the past. But when you pick up an object, like a hat pin, or a pair of lace gloves, or an inkwell, you can hold it in your hands, you can touch it and smell it, and you realize that it's the things that have changed. The people . . . not so much. Except for the loonies you get in every society, most people want to live, love, eat, and be happy."

"Good point."

"Even twenty years ago, or a hundred years ago, or—" She laughed again.

"What's so funny?"

"Oh, people. Let's say you could go back in time, say, the 1930s, and talk to a kid. Could you convince him or her that their Little Orphan Annie doll or book, that they shouldn't open it, they should put it away for decades, because at some point it would be worth a lot of money? The kids would laugh at you. It would sound crazy. And even now, we can't predict what will be worth something, what will be of value. For a while baseball cards were the rage, until that market collapsed. Then Beanie Babies. And metal lunchboxes. Who the hell knows what's next."

I looked again to the wooden filing cabinets. "But the papers in there, they must be worth something, to someone."

"Hah," Maggie said, reaching out to kick the cabinets again. "Sure. In there are old documents, papers, invoices, receipts, and such, concerning the history of the Tyler family, the history of the town and its historic and famous buildings, and a lot of other horseshit. You ever see horseshit?"

"Not lately," I admitted.

"Well, when they put down those mounds of turds, sometimes you see these little birds diving in, picking out little seeds of grain. That's what I got in these cabinets. A humongous pile of turds, and I don't have the time or inclination to go through and pick out the seeds of information that might be useful. Shit, I have eighty years' worth of invoices from the Tyler General Store, back when it existed and was run by my great-granddad. Who the hell wants to go through those? But buried in those invoices might be receipts for back when the place got expanded, and some historian somewhere might want to know that."

"And they don't?"

"The historical society has no room, the town of Tyler has no room. I've tried donating all this crap to various colleges and universities, and there's no interest."

Maybe it was the history geek in me, or my past life as an intelligence research analyst, but part of me wanted to slide by Maggie and just dive right into the files.

But I resisted the urge. "What's it like, being a Tyler, living in a town named after your famous ancestor?"

Maggie patted her jeans pockets and whispered to herself, "Damn it, must've left them in the basement." She looked up at me. "Huh? My famous relatives? Well, when they landed here in 1638, at least they pretended to buy the land from the surviving Native Americans who were wandering around, still dazed after what had happened to them. About a hundred years before the first settlement, this whole coastline of New England had been a series of prosperous settlements and villages. Then the Basque fishermen arrived on-site, and other Europeans, and in those brief meetings, the Indians probably passed on beaver pelts and such, and the Europeans passed on the measles and mumps. That's why the Pilgrims down south survived that first year. They raided abandoned villages to get at their seed corn."

The cat on my lap decided to make a leap for it, digging its untrimmed claws in my thighs. I grimaced, but Maggie kept talking. "The Reverend Bonus Tyler and his congregation, they were supposed to end up in Massachusetts but landed here, and decided enough was enough." Then she laughed at some memory. "Back during some anniversary event, I was asked by the historical society to write a commemoration about my ancestor, the Reverend Bonus Tyler. The story that had been passed on from generation to generation was that he left England with his congregation to get away from the oppressive government and godless society and discover a new land and life in the New World. Well, that was partially true."

"What was the other part?"

"One of my cousins, from the Maine branch of the Tylers, she was a funny sort and really got a kick out of doing some serious genealogical research. She even flew over to England, to the village where those first settlers came from, and after some digging around in the archives and old court papers, she found out the good Reverend Bonus Tyler had abandoned his pregnant wife before setting out across the Atlantic."

"That doesn't sound very saintly," I said.

"Yeah, especially since the Reverend Tyler came across the Atlantic with a new, younger wife. I wrote up that particular tale and wouldn't you know it, the historical society suddenly found out that it didn't have room for my article."

That garnered another laugh from Maggie and she kicked the wooden filing cabinets one more time. "History. Here in this part of the world, it's all around us. But beware of what you look for, or what you dig up. You might just be goddamned surprised."

In the darkness of my bedroom—the television having switched off automatically, just as one housewife tossed a glass of white wine into the heavily made-up and Botoxed face of another—I thought about Maggie, and who she was, and what she sold, and what she had . . .

History. It often had a violent past, but did Maggie ever dream or even consider that hers might end with a shotgun blast to the face, in the safety and comfort of her own antique shop?

A hand gently caressed my shoulder. Paula.

"Hey," I whispered.

No reply.

I turned around some, expecting to see her awake, or perhaps dreaming, but when I rolled over, there was the smiling and aware face of my long-dead and long-missing Cissy Manning.

CHAPTER NINE

I froze, just staring, all the memories and thoughts and sensations coming down at me, like I was standing in the middle of the old Boston and Maine railroad tracks, as a train came barreling right at me, unable to move or even lift a hand.

"I . . . I . . ."

Cissy smiled. "You're doing well."

I think I found my voice. "I've done better."

She kept on smiling, her full red hair on the pillow, lacy straps of something black on her shoulders, freckles prominent, and old sweet melancholy memories of rainy Sunday afternoons spent at her condo in Maryland, playing "freckle hunt" . . .

"Let it go," she said.

I tried to speak again but couldn't. So much to say. I shook my head.

Her smile got wider.

"Let me go," she said. "Please, my old love."

I couldn't say anything.

I woke up. I shivered and shivered and shivered.

The house was here, it was all the same.

I shivered some more.

I wrenched around, a sharp pain driving into me, and Paula was there, sleeping away, her face peaceful and soft.

A pang of guilt joined the earlier pain, making me wince. Paula was here, Paula was loving, Paula was taking care of me.

So why was I dreaming about a past love, a dead love?

Guilt? A memory? A sense of loss of what had once been, what could have been . . . if not for that training accident in Nevada that had killed her and the others.

I rolled back, shivered again, and stared out into the darkness of the room until I saw the sun rise out over the Atlantic.

Paula breathed easy behind me. The pain in my back lessened a great deal, but the guilt stayed.

Restless, I got up and went to the bathroom, twisted around, and saw it was time once again to empty the bladders. "Work, work, work," I whispered.

I swung around and got the first one out with a minimum of strain and effort. Well done, although the amount of blood and fluid coming out was the same. At least I got the bladder back into the cloth pocket without any problems.

Then it was number two's turn, and with the long pliers, I did get it out, sweating some and gritting my teeth. Once it was emptied, measured, and put back in place, I was bone-tired again.

I avoided looking at myself in the mirror when I got back into bed, careful not to wake up Paula.

But about an hour later, she didn't return the favor when she jostled my feet and pulled away my blankets to wake me up. Still dressed in her sleepwear, she yawned and said, "Up and at 'em, patient Lewis. Time to get your blood sucked away."

"It's already been sucked, drained, and measured, you meanie, you."

Paula yawned again, her ears sticking through her hair. "How? You got a secret nurse stashed away in the attic?"

"Ain't no attic here, sweetie, and I got them out myself about an hour ago." I checked the time. "You were in deep sleep and I did it myself."

That got her more awake. "With what?"

"With blood, toil, tears, sweat, and a pair of very long needle-nosed pliers."

She sat down on my bed, held my hand. "You could have woken me up."

"I didn't want to."

"Wait . . . I didn't take care of you yesterday morning. Right? Is that when you figured it out?"

"I did."

"Then why didn't you do it yourself last night."

"Because I like your touch."

She leaned over and kissed me. "You keep on doing things for yourself, I'm going to think you don't want me anymore."

I kissed her right back.

"Don't ever think that."

Paula saw that I was still droopy so she told me to stay in bed, which didn't take much convincing, and she came up a while later holding a bowl of oatmeal with cut strawberries and brown sugar sprinkled in, along with toast and a mug of tea.

I gave the tray a severe look. "What, no meat products?"

"I know you're typical Irish and think the major food groups are beer, meat, chips, and sugar, but this is healthier for you, and that's what counts."

"If you say so."

"I do. And eat it up, and don't let me catch you tossing it out the nearest window."

I ate while she showered and got dressed, then she took the tray down. She came back up later, purse over one shoulder, her computer bag in her hand.

"Have a good day at work, hon," I said. "Do you need a dollar for the lunch lady?"

"Not today," she said, and we engaged in a bit more kissing and cuddling.

"That'll make me feel better than a meatless day," I said, and Paula surprised me and made my face turn red with a comment about her suffering through a number of meatless days herself.

Something came to me as she headed out of the bedroom. "Hey," I said. "Got a moment?"

She checked her watch. "For you, two moments."

"When Diane Woods left yesterday—"

"And interrupted your *Penthouse* fantasy," she pointed out.

"Yeah, that," I said. "Just before she went out the door, it looked like she said something to you. Anything important?"

Paula smiled. "I guess it was, since it involved you."

"Me? How?"

Smile still in place, Paula said, "Diane said that she was very happy to see the two of us together, but if I did anything to hurt you, she'd kill me and make it look like an accident."

When she was gone I flopped back in bed, struggling to fight the onset of an early-morning nap. Too much sleep, too much lying around like a lump of flesh, not being active—it wasn't part of the road to recovery. Heck, I wasn't even on the on-ramp to recovery. But when your belly is full and your eyes get heavy, that sweet, sweet surrender of sleep is tempting indeed.

It was approaching noon when I got up for good. I made a phone call to the Lafayette House across the street, and as one o'clock approached, a knock on my door announced—I hoped—that lunch had arrived.

I opened the door, leaning on my borrowed cane, and Mia, the waitress and would-be journalist, was there on my steps, yawning.

"You should think about getting a doorbell," she said. "My knuckles get scraped from knocking on the door."

"I'll think about it," I said, and I gimped my way back into the kitchen. Mia followed, ditching her coat along the way. Again she went through my cabinets and we sat down to lunch, a roast beef sandwich and broth for me, and a lobster roll the size of my forearm for her.

Mia noted my look and said, "Hey, you said I could order anything I wanted from the menu, so I did."

"And I'm glad you did."

As we ate, we talked some about the high cost of living on the seacoast and she yawned throughout her meal—"Sorry, didn't get a wink of sleep last night"—and said that the *Porter Herald* had accepted a freelance piece about Revolutionary War–era forts for the upcoming Sunday edition.

"I'm pretty happy with the article," she said. "The problem will be what it looks like once it hits print. Clowns up there delight in inserting typos and spelling errors that weren't in the original copy."

"Happens to the best of us," I said.

"Yeah, I guess so. Hey, the last time I was here, you said you were a magazine writer. Which magazine?"

"*Shoreline*," I said.

"Oh," she said. "I don't know it. Is it like *Yankee* magazine?"

"Fewer recipes and B&B ads, more articles about the history and future of the New England seacoast."

Mia chewed, swallowed. "Cool. Do you know the editor?"

"I do," I said. "If you have an article query, let me know, and I'll pass it on to him. Get past the usual crew of gatekeepers who've just graduated from Brown or Northeastern and think they know everything."

"Yeah, lucky bastards," she said.

After we were finished she helped me clean up and put away the dishes, and I said, "Can I ask you a question?"

"Sure," she said. "But only if you answer one of mine."

"Go for it."

She pointed at the cane. "What horror movie set did you get that from?"

"The one called real life," I said.

After I paid Mia for the meal and for her time, we went into the living room; she took a chair and I took the couch. "Your aunt," I said. "The former newspaper lady. Is she still around?"

"Yep," she said. "Lives up in Rochester, at a so-called retirement community, though I never mention that phrase out loud to her."

"What's her name?"

"Gwen Aubrey."

"And you said she worked around here in newspapers, back thirty or forty years ago."

Mia laughed. "Oh, God, don't get her going. She says she's writing a book about what it was like, being a journalist in the Seacoast years back, and I don't have the heart to tell her that nobody cares."

"Wrong," I said. "I care."

"What's that?"

"Your Aunt Gwen. If possible, I'd love to meet her, talk about the old days, about what it was like here back then."

"You're not kidding, are you?"

"Not at all," I said. "But if she can, I'd like to have her visit me. I'm still stuck here."

Mia reached over to her purse, poked in, and came out with an iPhone or an Android or a Yoda for all I know; she scrolled through and said, "Yep, got her number. I'll give her a call later."

"Tell her I'll compensate her for her time as well."

Mia eyed me and looked around my cluttered living room and at my baggy clothes and cane, and said, "What, are you rich or something?"

"Or something."

Her eyes narrowed. "Magazine writers make shit. I know for a fact. So what's the deal? How did you get this cool place on the beach?"

"Retirement package from the government."

"Some package."

"Back then, some government."

I made a cup of coffee and resolved to stay awake for the afternoon, but that resolution lasted about as long as those made every December 31. When I woke up on the couch, I puttered around and tried to shelve some books.

I reached nine volumes before I was too tired to continue. I looked out the sliding glass doors to my deck. I hadn't been out on my deck in weeks. I limped forward, balanced the cane against the wall, unlocked the sliding glass door, and pushed.

Oomph.

Pushed again.

Nothing again. Had I really become that weak?

I glanced down at the runners and saw the length of wood I had dropped in a long time ago, to prevent burglars easy access through these sliding glass doors.

I hadn't become that weak, but maybe I had become that stupid.

I grabbed on to the door's handle to keep my balance, slowly knelt down, and got in a good position to pull the wood piece out. I grabbed one end and tugged.

And tugged.

And tugged.

Nothing budged.

By now my breathing was labored, and I saw what had happened. Wet weather had dripped in and caused the wood to swell just a bit, enough so it was stuck.

The old Lewis could have popped it out in seconds.

The new and not-so-improved Lewis let it be.

I got back up on my feet without falling, grabbed the cane, and went back to the couch.

Later that afternoon I managed to get hold of Diane Woods, and after an exchange of pleasantries and a promise by her to come for dinner tomorrow, I got right to it.

"Can I see the crime scene photos from Maggie's barn?"

"What?" she said. "I just thought I heard you ask to see the crime scene photos from Maggie's place."

"You did."

"You know I can't do that."

"I know you can't do that for a normal person during normal times. These are neither."

"Lewis . . ."

"You know my methods, you know I can be trusted. And it just might help you out."

"Might, or will?"

"Might," I said. "I had a thought I wanted to share with you, but only after I see the photos."

She waited a few seconds, and I wondered why it was taking her so long. We had done many a favor for each other over the years, so this one more shouldn't have been causing her pause.

Yet it was.

I didn't like it.

"Okay," she said. "Just this once. And I'll only show you after we eat. These aren't photos to look at and then keep your appetite."

"Great," I said. "See you tomorrow."

One more power nap to break up the afternoon, and I had a brief flash of excitement: this was the first time since I had come home from the hospital that I spent most of the day on the first floor, and not upstairs in my bed. To celebrate, I grabbed the phone and called to find out when I could expect the pathology results from my surgery, because they were at least two days overdue.

After some navigating of prompts, press one for this, two for that, and saying "agent" a few times in an increasingly loud voice, I finally caught up with a sweet young lady named Rachel.

"All right, sir," she said. "We just need to verify who you are. Could you give your name and date of birth?"

"I already did that, when I made my first call."

"I'm sorry, I need to ask you again."

So I complied.

"Very good, sir," she said. "And could you verify your membership number?"

"But the fact that I'm in your system, doesn't that mean I'm a customer of yours?"

"Sir . . . in order for me to proceed further for you, I need your membership identification number."

"But that was one of the first things I put into the system."

"Yes, but now I need to reconfirm it, please."

"Hold on," I said, and I got up and went over to that section of kitchen countertop where I toss car keys, various bits of mail that need immediate attention, and I got my wallet.

Which I promptly dropped on the floor.

Some swearing and sweating minutes later, I retrieved it from the floor, dug out my membership card, and made it back to the couch. It now felt like two little embers of fire were at play on my back and shoulder.

"All right," I said. "Here you go."

After rattling off the numbers, she said, "Very well, Mr. Cole. And could you verify your address for me?"

I rubbed my free hand across my forehead. "Rachel . . . with no disrespect, please, why do I need to do that? It should be right there in front of you."

"That's how our system is set up, Mr. Cole."

"Why? Because you're concerned some random criminal folks out there will try to go through all these prompts, armed with some of my personal information, so they can find out the status of my pathology report?"

She didn't say anything. "Mr. Cole," she said. "Could you verify your address for me?"

I gritted my teeth. "Physical or mailing?"

"Oh," she said in a chirpy voice. "Either one will work."

I gave her my post office box number, there was some more *tappity-tap* of the keyboard, and she said, "All right, Mr. Cole, how can I help you today?"

I took a breath. "I had major surgery recently. Two tumors were removed from my shoulder and lower back. They were sent out for biopsies, and I've not heard back yet."

"Uh-huh," she said. "Well you should have heard back by now. Let's check this out."

More *tappity-tap* and she said, "Um, Mr. Cole, can I put you on hold for a moment?"

It felt like ice was gathering around my heart. "Go right ahead."

So I was put on hold, some elevator music started swooning in my right ear, and I took a breath, looked out at the wide and cold and endless Atlantic. A good place to be, no matter what.

Click.

"Uh, Mr. Cole."

"Still here."

"It seems we have a situation concerning your biopsies."

"Go on."

"The reports haven't come back yet."

"I already know that."

"It seems that . . . there was an error."

"Go on."

"Uh, the samples were supposed to go to one of our associated testing laboratories in Massachusetts."

"All right."

"But they were sent to California. It appears that one of the attending physicians checked off the wrong box on the pathology request, and the samples were sent to our facility in San Diego."

"In California? The Golden State? The one on the West Coast? The Pacific Ocean?"

"Uh . . ."

I tried to take a moment to calm down. I failed. "Let me get this straight. My tumor samples, the ones that are going to tell me if I have cancer or not, they could have been hand-delivered to your testing lab a few streets down—and now they're in California?"

"Er, not really."

"What do you mean, not really? Isn't that what you just told me?"

"Not exactly, Mr. Cole. They were sent to California. The tracking number indicates that they haven't yet arrived. It looks like . . . they were misplaced."

I hung up the phone.

I was still on the couch when Felix came into my house, one arm in a sling, his good arm carrying a large grocery bag with twine handles. He caught my eye and said, "I'll remind you that I'm the one that's supposed to be blue, the one with a bullet wound in his arm."

"And I'll remind you that I've also been shot."

He snorted in disdain, put the shopping bag on the counter. "Yeah. In the lower leg, by a professor from UNH using a .22 pistol. When it comes to shooting and other complex tasks, most UNH professors couldn't pour the proverbial piss out of a boot with the instructions printed on the heel. I got hit by a pro."

"How's your arm?"

He pulled it free from the sling. "Doing great, and thanks for bandaging me up. I was able to locate my freelance physician late that night. Got everything cleaned up and stitched."

He started pulling packages from the bag. "Barbecue sound okay?"

I looked outside. "Might start raining."

"It's all right."

"Could you get the sliding glass door opened? I tried . . . well, the stick I use to block the runners was stuck."

"Sure," Felix said. He walked around the kitchen counter, bent down, and flipped it out with one motion.

Using his wounded arm.

He spotted my look and said, "I'm sure you loosened it."

"Yeah."

I got off the couch, limped my way to the sliding glass door, unlocked it, then slid it and the screen door open. I stepped out on the deck, breathed in the cold salt air. It felt good. There were wooden chairs and a square wooden table out on the deck, as well as my gas barbecue grill. Felix went to the grill and took the cover off, lifted up the lid, and lit it off.

There was sand all across the deck. Any other day I would take a push broom and clean the sand off, but yeah, this wasn't any other day. To the south was the bulk of Weymouth's Point, and the houses scattered on top, as well as the seawall leading up to it. Not much traffic on Atlantic Avenue. Out on the waters the sharp forms of the Isles of Shoals were as clear as ever, and up to the north, the woods and grassy mounds of the Samson State Wildlife Preserve. Decades before it had been a Coast Artillery Station, and this little house of mine had been converted from a lifeboat station to officers' quarters, and now, according to an amateur historian and genealogist from New York, it had been something else for a year or two, during the Korean War.

Felix came to me and said, "You look cold."

"I'll be all right." I leaned over the far railing, noted the large rocks and boulders, the dark waves rolling in and splashing up and roaring, moving to and fro, the waters out there sliding to Hampton Shoals, the Gulf of Maine, and the Atlantic . . . all those constant waves, all the endless motion, year after year.

"This will be a good place," I said.

Felix stood next to me. "What kind of place?"

"When the time comes, to spread my ashes. Be part of the ocean. Forever."

"Pretty grim talk," Felix said.

"Sometimes it's necessary. Have you thought about what's going to happen to your remains?"

"Sure," he said. "I have it all figured out. I'm going to die in bed at a hundred and ten years old, after a fine meal and sponge bath by two sweet nurses, and then I'll be buried in a large lot with a headstone so years afterwards, sobbing women will throw themselves down upon the ground and mourn me."

"Mine sounds simpler."

"Mine sounds more fun, more fulfilling," Felix said. He looked up to the darkening and thickening clouds. "Going to rain soon."

"Yeah."

"You get the pathology report back on your tumors yet?"

"Nope."

"What's the holdup?"

"One of my attending physicians checked off the wrong box on a form. Instead of going a few blocks down in Boston to be tested, my tumor samples are in San Diego."

Felix went over to check the grill's temperature, came back. "In California?"

"No, Vermont," I said. "And even with the tracking number, they've lost them. Still some waiting ahead."

"So there's a part of you getting a free trip to California."

"Some guys get all the luck."

He stood quietly and said, "You should go back in. It's cold."

"My first time out on the deck in a while. I'll stay."

Felix said nothing, went into the house, and came back with one of my winter coats. He draped it over my shoulders, gave my good shoulder a squeeze, and went to work.

The rain started coming down.

I didn't move.

CHAPTER TEN

Dinner was barbecue steak tips, some sort of potato logs—fresh-made, not frozen—and asparagus spears. I'm usually not fond of green items at dinner, except for a salad, but Felix had expertly grilled them and sauced them so that even I would eat most of what he served me.

We ate at the kitchen counter, just as the heavy rains rolled in and started their drumming on my roof and deck. Remembering what I had experienced that morning, I said, "You get lots of dreams?"

"All the time."

"Weird ones? Scary ones?"

"Yes, yes, and more than that."

"Like what?"

He shrugged his strong shoulders. "You know the kind. Little snippets of memory, running like video clips."

"Yeah. Those disturb you?"

"Well . . . I've done things in the past I'm not proud of. You try to move on, try to forget, try to atone if necessary. And I do hate those little night reminders. Especially if they involve gunfire or blood. Funny how those types of dreams don't bring back happier times."

We ate some more and he asked, "What brought that up? You have an odd dream?"

"Pretty damn odd. I . . . somebody from my past was there, in my bedroom, talking to me."

"Male or female?"

"Female."

"Where is she now?"

"She's been dead—for a while."

"Oh. Chrissy, the one you were with, back at the Pentagon."

"Cissy," I said, saying her name aloud, so she would not be forgotten. "Cissy Manning."

"You dream of her often?"

"No, which is odd. She came to me and told me—"

"What?" Felix asked, eyes steady on me.

I went back to eating. "Never mind."

When we were through and the dishes were done, I made some coffee and we retired to the living room. "What's up with the arm?" I said.

He twisted it to and fro. "A little weak, but I'm working on it. The stitches should come out in a few days. In the meantime, I'm on the hunt for Pepe and his gang of merry men."

"They scatter?"

"Oh yeah," he said. "And I think once they found out I was still mobile, still looking for them, they scattered even further, like the proverbial herd of cockroaches scattering when the light hits them."

"You still believe their story? About going to Maggie's place to do a quick robbery, and that they found her there dead?"

"Maybe, maybe not," he said. "What I'm looking for now is the whereabouts of my great-granddad's silver, and making an . . . arrangement concerning the young man who shot me."

"That should be interesting for all involved, but it'll be a crowded hunt. The Tyler police and the state police know about Pepe and his friends being there."

There was the slightest tightening around Felix's eyes. "Go on. Do you know how this amazing bit of information got to them?"

"Maybe I gave you up."

The eyes tightened more and then his face broke out in a wide grin, showing me once again why he does so fine with the ladies.

"Yeah. Right. What was the real deal then?"

"The forensics folks found a glassine envelope with heroin in it, marked with a bluebird, which signified it came from an outfit in Lowell and Lawrence."

"Okay."

"So how did it get there? Dropped during the panic?"

"Maybe."

"Because I don't see Maggie Branch dealing."

"Maybe she was a customer," Felix said quietly.

"Felix," and then I shut up. I had read the news stories, seen the news reports. The heroin epidemic was cutting a wide swath through my home state, and it wasn't picky about age or condition.

"Maybe she was," I said.

"I'm sure the police will be looking into it," he said.

"Have you gone to them about your granddad's silver?"

"Have you taken leave of your senses? Never talk to cops unless otherwise necessary, and always have a couple of alibis and stories ready to come out when needed. Besides, they're busy with Maggie and other crimes, right?"

"Not sure about other crimes, but—"

Hold on, I thought. *Just hold on.*

"Felix."

"Yeah."

"I'm not keeping track of such things, but how's the market for silver nowadays?"

"Up," he said. "Like all precious metals. Gold, silver, platinum. Usually goes up when news is bad."

"You collect?"

"Nope," he said. "I collect other valuables. Freeze-dried food, water, ammunition. I figure if and when the collapse comes, the essentials will come first. What are you driving at?"

"You mentioned other crimes," I said. "There was a break-in at the *Tyler Chronicle* the night before last."

"What did they take? Old lead letters?"

"Close. Darkroom sludge. From chemicals that have been used in developing film at the *Chronicle* for decades. Supposedly sludge like that can contain a fair amount of silver, especially when market demand is up."

Felix nodded slowly. "Interesting. Great-granddad's silver goes missing, and silver sludge is stolen from the *Chronicle*. Could be a coincidence, but you know me. There's no such thing." He glanced at his watch. "In the meantime, I need to go hunting."

"Wish I could go along with you."

Felix stood up. "Are you nuts? Long hours driving around, asking questions, visiting grungy places, meeting people out in the shadows. Doesn't sound much like fun."

"I didn't say it would be fun," I said. I took a long view around my living room. "I'm going a bit stir crazy. I need to get out and about."

Felix smiled, gave my good shoulder a squeeze. "What are you complaining about? Part of you is already in California."

That night I watched three more episodes of *Band of Brothers*. Once again I envied the clarity of what was going on back then, though I'm sure if I had been a paratrooper in the famed Easy Company of the 506th, I'd be more concerned with food, sleep, my buddies, and not getting my ass shot off instead of the great moral issues of that war.

It was getting late and I was wondering if I would be able to fall asleep— the caffeine consumption and the news was keeping me awake. Heroin found at Maggie's place. A gang from Lowell and Lawrence claiming they came across her when she was already dead. Felix's silver missing. Silver stolen from the *Chronicle*. And my own condition, and my own home misadventures. I couldn't get that dream of Cissy out of my head. It had been so real, so alive, so . . . true.

But it couldn't have happened.

So what had occurred? A leftover from my first and last experience with a heavy-duty painkiller? Or something else that might be connected to my surgery, when my body was so violently opened up and closed by the skilled surgeons?

And another thought came to me, about my invisible and late-night visitor.

Maybe that needed to be filed along with my Cissy Manning sighting.

Maybe.

Then the lights went out.

All right. I had no fire going in the fireplace, which meant the living room was plunged into darkness. Eventually my eyes would adjust and the ambient light from outside would at least outline where the furniture was, so I could walk around without tripping over anything.

Flashlights. Since I'm right next to the ocean and my house is on the end of the power circuit for this part of the beach, I've been a madman about keeping flashlights in every room of the house, but that had been pre-fire. Now? Well, the only place where I was certain there was a flashlight was upstairs in my bedroom.

I got up. Couldn't locate my borrowed cane.

All right, we'll just go upstairs without it.

I started shuffling my feet, and stifled a chuckle, knowing that the way I was slowly shuffling with arms held out was akin to what poor Mr. Karloff had to endure in filming some of his classic horror movies. I got through the living room without tripping, and then I made it to the stairway without encountering an angry, torch-bearing mob, so that was good.

With hand on a banister, I got upstairs in a fair amount of time, and feeling pretty cocky, made a right and—

Promptly ran into the open door. Edgewise.

Crap, that hurt.

I moved around, arms still waving some, and then I got into my bedroom.

Fantastic.

My eyes must have adjusted somewhat and the bedroom looked pretty well lit-up. I could even make out the tumbled pile of blankets and sheets.

I stopped just as I got to the bed.

Something was wrong.

Something wasn't right.

Okay.

I looked around and with the ambient light coming in—

Wait a sec.

I made my way to the near window, which overlooked my tiny yard and a pile of large boulders and stones that rose up to Atlantic Avenue, and right above that was the steady glow of lights coming from the Lafayette House and the streetlights. I moved around, peered south.

More lights.

Only my home was suffering a blackout.

I moved around and got to the nightstand, picked up the phone.

No dial tone.

All right. No power, no phone.

I went to the door leading out to the small deck facing south. Through the glass I saw all the lights of Tyler Beach at nighttime.

And I saw something else.

What looked to be a bobbing light, up by the edge of the Lafayette House parking lot. Someone holding a flashlight.

I watched for another minute. The bobbing light kept bobbing.

But now it was coming down my dirt driveway.

Back to the nightstand, I picked up my own flashlight, and reaching between the mattress and box spring, retrieved my Beretta. I wasted some important seconds, wondering how I would carry the pistol with no holster. In my saggy pajama bottoms, I couldn't shove it between my waist and waistband.

To hell with it.

I switched on the flashlight, cupped my hand around the beam so it wouldn't light up the nearby world, and got out of the bedroom without smashing my nose and face again.

Down the stairs, and then I switched off the light, and waited.

Waited.

Lots of dark thoughts dancing around back there, thinking about locked doors, windows, setting up a line of defense, and then a line of retreat.

But I didn't feel like retreating tonight. I unlocked the door and stepped out.

Outside, the cool spring air was refreshing, especially since I was sweating like the proverbial swine. A quick look to the left, up to my driveway, showed not one but two bobbing lights coming toward me.

I moved to the right, across my tiny, scraggly lawn, where there was a line of boulders and rocks. I banged my shins twice—one for each leg, of course—and settled down.

Outside was better than being inside. Offense is better than a good defense. Patton said something about any fortification built by man can be surpassed by man. Or something like that.

The two lights paused where my driveway flattened out and approached my new one-car garage. A dark stream quickly plowed though my mind: if I saw anyone light a match, flare, or Molotov cocktail, I was going to start shooting without asking any questions at all.

The two lights were close now, as though their handlers were conferring. About the best way to approach my house? To break in? To do what?

Over the sound of the waves, I could make out the soft murmur of voices. The lights split up and started to the front door. The lead light went up to the front door, knocked hard, three times.

Another quick confer.

Two more hard knocks.

No response from inside the house.

What a surprise.

The two lights backed off, and then it looked like there was another chitchat session. I was cold and worried and uncomfortable, and there was a heaviness at my back and shoulder that told me it was way beyond time to empty the bladders, but still, I was enjoying myself.

Why?

Because I was in control, I was in charge, and I was no longer going to be a victim.

The conference seemed to have ended; the lights started going up the driveway, then stopped, and there were some harsh voices. One light came back, the other one following, and back to the door.

More harsh whispers.

Then a shape bent over, and the other light backed away, illuminating my doorknob.

Enough.

I stood up, keeping the rocks in front of me as a barrier, and switched on my own flashlight. "Freeze right there!" I yelled.

My flashlight was a good one, not one of those five-buck jobs you pick up at a gas station or hardware store. It lit up half of the front of the house, the door, and the man and woman attempting to break in.

Dave Hudson and his wife, Marjorie, amateur genealogists from Albany, and now attempted burglars.

CHAPTER ELEVEN

They were shocked, both standing up, mouths open, and I took advantage of that by yelling, "I'm armed! So point your flashlights on the ground and stay put!"

Their arms moved as ordered; I switched my light off and moved a few feet, just in case one of them was armed as well. We were all struggling to see after my flashlight went out, but as our night vision recovered, being able to see their own lights would give me an advantage.

"Hey, Mr. Cole," Dave started, and I said, "Shut it, right now."

I settled myself in another position among the jumble of rocks and boulders, and as my vision improved, it was easy to make out the shapes of Dave and Marjorie. "Just for the benefit of you two folks from away, you're trespassing on private property. Police departments and juries in this state tend to take a very dim look at that, so whatever happens, I've got the locals and the law on my side. Clear?"

Dave didn't answer, but his discouraged wife did. "We understand," she said, her voice sullen.

"Outstanding," I said. "So what the hell are the two of you doing on my property?"

"We were concerned about you," Dave said.

"Say again?"

"We were worried about you," he said. "We've been staying up at the Lafayette House while we've been doing our research, and we were going to take a drive into Porter to see a movie, and then we saw the lights go out at your house."

"Just a couple of good Samaritans, right?"

"Absolutely," he said. "We saw the lights go off, and then we went back to the Lafayette House, found out what utility provides power for you, and then we put in a call. Then I told Marjorie we should just come down and check on you, to make sure you were all right."

"Did you pass any unicorns along the way?"

"What?"

"You really think I'll believe that nonsense?"

Marjorie said something sharp and nasty, and her husband sounded hurt. "Mr. Cole . . . I know we've been pressuring you, and I'm sorry. I tend to let these things control me. But we know you've been in the hospital. We know you've had some serious surgeries, and when we saw you lost all your power, we wanted to make sure you were okay. Honest. That's all we were doing."

I was beginning to feel less comfortable. "And when nobody answered the door, you decided to break in?"

"No, nothing like that," he protested. "There were no lights on at your house. No lanterns. No candles. After we knocked a few times, Marjorie was worried that maybe you had fallen, that you had hurt yourself."

"And how were you going to get in?"

He kept silent for a moment and said, "Not proud . . . but when I was a juvie, back in New York, I did some time for breaking and entering. My uncle . . . a locksmith. He taught me some things."

I was going to ask him if he was so concerned about my safety, why didn't he just call the police? But I was getting cold, tired, and I wasn't having fun anymore, and this interrogation wasn't going where I expected.

"Go away, then, all right?"

"Why are you over there in the rocks?"

"They looked lonely," I said. "Now, please. Go away."

He whispered to his wife, she whispered something louder back to him, and he turned back to me. "You know, it would only take a few minutes and—"

"Dave, don't push it," I said. "Don't."

His wife grabbed him by the arm and hauled him off my steps; they started back up the driveway, and he called out, "We were just trying to help! That's all! Just trying to help!"

Back in my house, I didn't feel like doing much of anything, but the drains demanded release. I got upstairs and into the bathroom, and managed to spray around only a little blood before I got things squared away. The blood was cleaned up pretty easily from all the practice I'd had. I worked with the flashlight on the counter, pointed at the mirror, and when I was done, I said to the odd man looking back at me, "I'm so sick and tired of being sick and tired."

Then I went to bed, but not before putting my pistol down on the nightstand.

Two hours and one minute later according to my watch, the power in my house came back on. I turned the little clock around so I wouldn't see the flashing red numerals, and I knew that lights were on downstairs, but I didn't care. I rolled over and went back to sleep, and kept on sleeping until a beautiful woman appeared in my bedroom.

And this one was real.

Paula looked down at me and said, "Rough night?"

"You know it," I said, sitting up. She sat at the foot of the bed and passed over a plate with a Dunkin' Donuts breakfast sandwich on it.

"Me, too," she said. "Damn selectmen went on yapping until past midnight. Then I got to work this morning and found out that one of my freelancers who's supposed to cover a criminal trial over at the county courthouse in Bretton called in sick. So that's why we're feasting on takeout this morning."

"I don't mind, not at all," I said, and we went through our sandwiches, Paula beating me with her impressive appetite. Then she helped me get up and get washed, and emptied my morning output, which was still too high.

"Where now, sport?" she asked.

"Back to bed for a while," I said. "And why did you stay until the bitter end for the selectmen? Usually you bail out at around eleven or so, make a follow-up phone call the next day to see what you've missed."

"Yeah, well, this particular board is getting sneaky," she said, helping me into bed, pulling the blankets up. "They like to sneak in things at the last minute, or adjourn the meeting and sit around and have a coffee break, where, oops, some town business gets discussed with nobody else in the room."

"Tricky."

"Yeah, well I'm one trickster who won't let that nonsense get by." Paula smoothed out the blankets and sheet and said, "I may be getting older, and the First Amendment's getting creaky and well-worn, but at least in Tyler, I won't let journalism die."

She stroked my face, sat down next to me on the bed. "What kept you up last night?"

"Power outage. Lasted a few hours. And then when the lights popped back on, well, that woke me up and kept me up for a bit."

"I see," she said. "And what else?"

I didn't want Paula to worry but I also didn't want to dance around what had been going on. For all she had been doing for me, she deserved at least that.

"Had two visitors with flashlights stop by," I said. "Knocking at the door."

That caused her concern. "Mormons are usually too polite to pull off stunts like that, and Jehovah's Witnesses don't go out at night. And I don't think it's Girl Scout cookie time, though I may be wrong."

"They were amateur genealogists."

She made a face. "Ugh. The worst. What the heck were they doing at your house?"

So I spent a few minutes explaining who Dave Hudson was, and his apparently supportive yet embarrassed wife. When I was finished, Paula said, "Good for you. This place has history, but it's still your place. I'd tell them to go to hell and not come back."

"Well, I told them that when I felt better, I'd let them in."

Paula got off the bed, kissed me. "Not so fast, buddy o' mine."

"What do you mean?"

"I mean that when you feel better, I intend to take a day or two off, and make meals for you, and give you a nice bath in your tub, and wash every inch of you, and when you're nice and dry, I intend to give you a nice, close, thorough examination by visiting nurse Paula Quinn."

A grumpy part of me wanted to say that the last time that had happened, she had found a lump on my back, but by God I wasn't going to say that. "Will you wear one of those sexy nurse costumes you see at Halloween?"

She kissed me again. "Who says I'll be wearing anything?"

I slept some more and then found my way downstairs to get the lights off. After I spent an exhausting ten minutes or so restocking books, Diane Woods came by, with lunch in one hand and her large soft leather briefcase in the other. She looked tired but she also looked good. There were still scars on her face, but I had seen her for weeks in a bed at a rehab center, when she had looked much worse.

Seeing her like this, mobile and in better health, was always good.

We set up at the kitchen counter, and soon enough we were dining on lobster stew, Caesar salad, and warm French rolls.

As we ate and talked, I kept looking at her innocent-looking briefcase, which I knew contained her laptop, whose chips and circuitry held a series of ones and zeros, the crime scene photos of a dead woman who didn't deserve to die from a violent crime in her home.

"What have you been up to?" she said.

"Oh, you know, jogging and weight lifting, trying to get back my girlish figure."

Diane made a serious point of leaning over to look at my baggy T-shirt, sweats, and overall flabby appearance. "Hate to tell you, Lewis, but you've got a hell of a ways to go."

"Gee, ya think?"

Diane buttered another roll. "No dancing, then. Have you gotten your biopsy work back yet?"

"Not really."

"Lewis, it's an either/or. What the hell does 'not really' mean?"

"It means my tissue samples were removed and sent to a testing facility."

"All right."

"But the testing facility is in California."

"How the . . ."

"Human error. And to make it more fun, it's been lost in transit, even with a tracking number attached to it."

She stopped buttering her roll. "You seem to be holding up pretty well."

I took a spoon of the lobster stew. It was hot, sweet, and filling. "Not much else I can do. Panicking and swearing and all that—what would it get me?"

"I'd tell you what it'd get me. I'd be down at the doctor's office and I'd raise some hell."

"For what purpose?"

"To make them upset and make me happy." She took a healthy bite of her roll. "Some days, that's a good combination. Even if you can't get an answer to what you're looking for, making people miserable for making you miserable is a reasonable payoff."

After another spoonful of stew, I asked, "What's up with Maggie's investigation?"

"The state police's investigation, overseen by Assistant Attorney General Martin and assisted by the Tyler police, don't forget that."

"With you bitching about it all the time, how can I?"

She laughed and said, "It's going. The net is widening. The state police have gotten surveillance camera footage from the tollbooths on I-95, to run the license plates, see if anybody suspicious came off and on the exits during that night. We've also done another canvass of the neighborhood, and the only bit of info is one of the neighbors saw a car parked deep into some woods off the road . . . no license plate, no make or model."

"Meaning what?"

"Meaning how the hell do we know? It was parked near a neighboring house of Maggie's. First thought was maybe the car was keeping an eye on the road, the house, who knows what . . ."

I kept my face as bland as possible, knowing the car belonged to the man hired by Felix to keep surveillance on the house.

"Yeah," I said. "And the AG?"

"The honorable Camden Martin? He's still up front, still running the show. The guy will probably be governor one of these days, you know? Lots of excess energy and smarts that have to go somewhere."

"He still thinks it was something to do with heroin?"

Diane rubbed at her chin. "Well . . . the autopsy shows nothing in Maggie's system except for some THC."

"THC? Maggie was smoking dope?"

"Her personal doc said she had bad arthritis. But there was no sign of any opioid in her system, no track marks on her arms, thighs, or between her toes. Pretty clean. But still . . . there was that packet of heroin on the floor."

"The bluebird," I said. "Your sign of drug quality. Anything from the Massachusetts end?"

"Nope," she said. "Massachusetts State Police—in a shocking development—is cooperating with us and the staties. Heroin doesn't know state borders. And the local cops in Lowell and Lawrence, they've been helpful, too. But there's something funny going on with that gang . . ."

Her voice dribbled off.

I had a queasy thought of where this was going, but I decided to take it there anyway. "What's the funny thing?"

"The gang members, they've scattered, gone to the wind. Two days ago, there was a firefight and two of them were wounded at a tenement building in Lawrence. They've been keeping their mouths shut about what happened, who did the shooting, or why it happened in the first place. But whatever happened, it scared the shit out of them. It's hard tracking them down."

"Maybe Maggie's pain was getting too much. Maybe—"

Diane shook her head. "Doesn't make sense. If her pain was getting too much, why go the illegal route? Her doc would have prescribed something to take the edge off."

We changed the subject and spent some time talking about Diane's upcoming wedding. I remembered that she was considering applying for the deputy chief's job, but I didn't want to bring it up, and it seemed like neither did she. When trash was disposed of and dishes were washed and put away—and I actually had the energy to do the bulk of the dishes this time—Diane wiped her hands dry and said, "I guess it's time."

"I guess so, too."

"Where do you want to do it?"

I thought about the kitchen counter but no, I'd be cursing this area for the rest of the time I'd be here, seeing those death photos over and over again. "Let's go to the couch," I said.

"Fine."

We sat down on the couch. Diane dragged the coffee table over, pushed over a pile of magazines—*Smithsonian* and *Astronomy*—then took out her laptop, put it down, and switched it on. The computer made its usual *bloops* and *bleeps*, and as Diane worked the buttons, she said, "Just a reminder that I'm going out on a limb here."

"I appreciate the reminder," I said. "I promise not to come along with a saw."

"That's nice," she said. "Okay, here we go. What are you looking for?"

"Where she was found."

A little grunt—of acceptance, concern?—and then she double-clicked an icon, and up came a photo. I grimaced and forced myself to keep looking.

"From the entrance to her office area," Diane said. "Wide shot."

"Okay."

I took my time, just looking around the edges, trying to get used to what was there in front of me on the screen, in all its bloody and colorful horror. The shelves of books and antiques and other knickknacks were crowded on either side of the area that had been cleared for use as Maggie's office.

There was a shape at the center of the photo. I glanced, looked away, glanced again.

It was the shape of a human, sitting in a chair I also recognized, wearing baggy jeans and what was once a light blue sweatshirt. I could only tell it was once light blue because of the end of the sleeves. The rest of it was smeared and stained with blood and other fluids.

The only tiny saving grace was that Maggie's body had been thrust backward by the force of the shotgun blast. There was just a mound of bone, blood, tissue, and brain barely visible between her shoulders. Her legs were splayed and a portion of the jeans were stained from where the body's internal fluids had let loose.

I could sense Diane sitting next to me, smell a fresh soap scent, hear her breathing.

I looked away from the body. Papers and file folders were strewn across the wide planks on the floor.

"Well?" Diane asked.

"Give me a minute more."

"As long as you want," she said.

To the left were the rows of wooden filing cabinets, and I could make out that at least two drawers were open.

"Okay," I said. "Do you have a photo that focuses on the left here, where the filing cabinets are?"

"Hold on."

She reached forward, picked up the laptop, and went to work. I saw one close-up photo pop up on her screen of Maggie's shattered head, and I looked away and stared at my dark and quiet fireplace. More boxes of books around the side of the fireplace. One of these days, these books would be removed, lovingly examined, and put up on shelves. And one of these days, my dear friend would leave my house with these horrible photos.

"Okay," she said. "How about this?"

"This" seemed to fit the bill. It was a photo of the wooden filing cabinets that were to the left, and three drawers in one cabinet were pulled open. I looked closer and there was splintered wood in the upper right corner. A lock there had been smashed open.

"Any others in this area?"

"Thought you'd ask," Diane said. "Give it back."

We flipped back and forth and yes, this new photo was aimed toward the floor, where again, papers and file folders had been strewn around. Blood was splattered over the paper and cardboard, and there were pink and gray pieces of tissue that I recognized came from Maggie's brain matter.

I swallowed.

"Interesting," I said.

"How's that?"

"The papers and folders here on the floor, they have blood spatter and tissue on them. Meaning that Maggie was shot after the papers were pulled out."

"Good point," Diane said.

"Maybe she was shot because they had found what they had been looking for, or she had been shot because they didn't find what they were looking for."

"Why 'they'? What makes you think there was more than one?"

I knew why, from what Felix had told me, but I wasn't going there quite yet. I said, "I don't know. Just made some sense to me. Intruder number one with a shotgun, intruder number two talking to Maggie, going through the filing cabinets."

"Not bad," she said.

"Speaking of shotgun, any forensic evidence from that?"

Diane shook her head. "Always a pisser, trying to do that where there's a scene involving a shotgun. We've got a number of shotgun pellets recovered from Maggie and the rear wall and a painting that was hanging up there, but you know the rule. It's not like recovering a bullet with the barrel marks and scrapes so you can match it to another bullet or a pistol barrel. With shotguns, no joy."

I focused on the filing cabinet. "The intruders were in a hurry," I said. "They wanted what was in that cabinet. Maggie either didn't have the key or couldn't get to it in time. So they took a hammer or something, pounded on the cabinet, broke the lock, dug out the files."

"It was a crowbar," Diane said. "No prints, of course."

"Of course," I said. "Did you determine if anything was taken from the cabinet?"

"Who could tell," she said.

"What was in there?"

"A lot of nothing," she said.

"Diane . . ."

She sat back against the couch. "A mess. One file folder had planning board minutes from twenty years ago. Another had a collection of blue-prints for old homes and town buildings from a hundred years ago. Then a collection of letters to the water precinct commissioner from businesses on Fourth Street at the beach from 1952. Stuff like that."

"Any chance there was another copy of the Declaration of Independence stuffed back there?"

"That's what we first thought, a robbery gone bad, but you've been there, seen the mess the place is. She could have Martha Washington's recipe for apple pie in her own handwriting, and how would we know it was missing?"

"Then you have the packet of heroin left on the floor."

"Yeah, funny thing, that. Another theory is that robbers came in, looking for a quick score—gold coins, jewelry, stuff like that—and when it went bad on them, with Maggie telling them to go to hell, she was shot."

"But that doesn't explain one opened filing cabinet, filled with old papers. Or . . ."

I glanced back at the crime scene photo, at Maggie's bloody and stiff remains, and I looked away.

"Give it up. Or what?"

"Maggie was in her chair. Why was she in her chair? If she was being robbed, and maybe executed, would you shoot a woman in the face while she's looking right at you? Or would you shoot her from behind? It's like . . . she was placed there. Like the robber or robbers were having a conversation with her, one that ended badly."

We sat there in silence for a few seconds, and Diane said, "We done here?"

"Huh? Sure. I don't need to see the photos anymore."

"Good." Diane closed out the photo viewing program, and her laptop went back to a screensaver shot of Tyler Harbor. "I know you and others have a vision of me, Diane the ice princess who can go anywhere, investigate anything, and do so without feelings . . ."

I reached over, gave her hand a squeeze. "Thanks for coming over. And you're no ice princess."

"Thanks."

"Maybe a frost queen, but definitely not an ice princess."

And that got me a kick in the shin.

A few minutes later I walked her to my door and I said, "Had a little power outage here last night, gave me a few sleepless moments."

"Why's that?"

I sensed she was running behind so I didn't want to get into a lengthy discussion of my late-night visitors. "It's okay when the lights go off," I said. "But if you're sleeping when the lights come back on, well, the smoke detectors here are hardwired so they set off an unholy screech when they come back on, as well as all the lights you forgot to switch off."

"Yeah, I saw something about that in this morning's police log. Looked like vandalism."

"Somebody cut the power line to my house?" I asked.

"Nothing as simple as that," Diane said. "I don't know what you know about power lines, but up on the street, there's something called a step-down transformer, which leads to a cable heading to your house. Somebody took a pot shot at the transformer, blew it out of service, and then cast you back into the nineteenth century."

I took that in and she said, "Hey, you got any enemies out there?"

"More than I can recall."

"Yeah, well, be careful."

"Always," I said.

Just as she got through the open door, I said, "Hey, when you ran into Paula the other day, did you really say that if she did anything to hurt me, that you'd kill her and make it look like an accident?"

Diane kissed me on the cheek. "Silly girl, she must have misheard what I said. I told her that I was thrilled for her, and that seeing you with a woman like her was a happy accident. That's all."

CHAPTER TWELVE

The rest of my afternoon just dribbled away, with another long time spent in phone purgatory, pressing numbers here and there, only to find out that my biopsies were still lost somewhere in California. I removed eight books from a cardboard box, which I declared a major victory before celebrating with a late-afternoon nap.

The ringing phone got me up twice. The first call was from Mia Harrison, who told me she'd gotten hold of her aunt, the ex-newspaper reporter.

"Oh, thanks," I said, reclining on my couch, looking at the late-afternoon light play against some of the clouds out there above the Atlantic. "How is she?"

"Nutso and full of opinions as always," Mia said. I could hear the sound of a busy kitchen in the background, plates and pots and pans rattling around, voices raised. "She said you're lucky, that she's bored as crap, and she'd welcome a chance to come back and check out her old stomping grounds."

"Thanks, I appreciate it."

"Would eleven A.M. tomorrow work for you?"

"Lucky for us both, my schedule is wide open," I said.

"She just had one question."

"What's that?"

Mia laughed. "Like I said, she's a bit nutso. She wants to know if you're single or not."

Funny question. "Legally, yes. Technically, no."

"Fair warning, she'll take that as a challenge," Mia said.

"Did you tell her I just got out of the hospital?"

"Yeah, and she said that was just fine by her. She said most men she's seeing nowadays are either going in or coming out of a medical facility. Good luck."

"Thanks," I said. "I think."

Later in the day Paula Quinn checked in, and we made a dinner date—surprise, at my house. I asked her to pick up some groceries on the way over. She said yes but I detected a lack of enthusiasm, and I couldn't blame her. Being the assistant editor of a struggling daily newspaper, being short-handed and covering a homicide, that was enough to fill anyone's plate, but asking her to also be a home health-care aide was like filling up the buffet table.

When she arrived and came in, I helped her with one of the plastic grocery bags, and I said, "All right, go settle down."

"What?"

"Have a seat on the couch, put up your feet, and relax," I said. "My turn to make dinner."

"Lewis . . ."

"Go on, young lady, mind your manners, and your elders."

She gave me a quick kiss, sat on the couch, kicked off her shoes, and put her feet up on the coffee table. Then she laughed as she picked up the remote.

"What's so funny?" I asked.

"I should have known something was up," Paula said, turning the television on and going to the local ABC affiliate, Channel 9 out of Manchester. "You had me pick up some veggies. You and veggies? As if."

I went through the plastic grocery bags, found a bottle of Bass Phillip pinot noir from Australia, struggled some to get it open, and then I poured a glass for Paula and limped over. She took a satisfying sip and asked, "What's for dinner, then?"

"Ham and cheese omelet for me," I said. "Stir-fried veggie omelet for you."

"With ham and cheese," she asked.

"Got it."

I went back to the kitchen, dug out two frying pans, and got to work. Pretty soon my kitchen was filled with satisfying cooking aromas and I got dinner up and served in less than thirty minutes.

Paula came back to the kitchen and we started eating. "Tastes good," she said.

"It should," I said. "Every meal tastes better when you don't have to make it, am I right?"

She giggled at that and we kept on eating.

After dinner and the dishes, we cuddled up on the couch, and blundered our way through *Jeopardy!* She put her head on my shoulder. "How was your day, dear?" I asked.

Paula sighed. "Oh, the usual. Board meetings, police logs, trying to get the latest on Maggie Branch's murder."

"What do you have?"

"What, and give you a scoop before reading tomorrow's paper? How in heck do you think the *Chronicle* will survive if you don't pay for it?"

"I do pay for it," I said. "I have an online subscription, and when I've been on my feet, I've bought the print edition as well."

"Okay, then," she said. "The Tyler cops are still shoved aside, and the state police and the task force are trying to squeeze her murder into the opioid crisis, but I don't think it's going to fit."

"Why's that?"

"Because there was just one packet of heroin found in her place of business, there were no opioids found in her system, and come on, can we believe that Maggie had anything to do with the heroin trade?"

"But there's a chance she was murdered by somebody looking for cash or gold to buy heroin, right?"

"Right," she said. "But that means a robbery that turned into a homicide. Not anything to do with heroin."

"Okay," I said. "Thanks for that criminal update. How about the break-in at the paper? Anything new on that?"

Paula snuggled in closer. "One of Tyler's finest is working on it, helping out Detective Sergeant Woods while she plays with the state police. So far, nothing untoward has been found. No fingerprints on the door, no apparent break-in. And it still looks like the silver sludge was taken."

"But didn't you say that some filing cabinets and bound back issues were disturbed?"

"Yeah, disturbed like tossed all over the place. Who knows. Maybe they got in the mood of wrecking things while hauling out the sludge."

"And how's the assistant editor's job coming along?"

She laughed. "Well, not much more of a bump in pay, and a hell of a lot more responsibilities, but it's a step forward. I'm beginning to like the editing process, especially with the freelancers we have working for us. Lots of dedication, lots of enthusiasm, not much in the way of grammar and style."

We sat there for a while longer, then she said, "All right, fess up. Have you heard anything about your biopsies?"

I told her about my traveling tissues. She groaned and swore in all the right places, then asked, "Feel like being the subject of a story?"

"About that?"

"Why not? Our health-care system is one big screw-up from one end to the other. Why not publicize it?"

"Well . . . tell you what. When I get my results back, if it's benign, you got it. If it's not, I'll have more important things to worry about."

"I can see. You get any writing done lately?"

"Um—no."

"I thought *Shoreline* gave you your job back."

"In a manner of speaking, they did."

She squirmed around so she was looking up at me. "That's some kind of speaking. Do tell me more."

"The guy who runs the magazine told me, quote, 'We'll run something under your name for now, in the meantime, get your ass better.' Unquote."

"But it's not your ass that's a problem."

"Thanks for noticing."

On the television there was now a network program airing, something ridiculous going on about some single guy with bright teeth—said number of teeth approaching his IQ level—and a group of tanned, taut, and trimmed women who were competing for his attention. I didn't have the mood or energy to change the channel. At this point, ridiculous was just fine.

"You miss the writing?" she asked.

"At the moment, no."

"Really?"

"I know there's probably a bolt of lightning up there coming down from the spirits of Morrow and Halberstam, but I'm not that much of a writer. I'm more of a snoop. I like finding things out, historical things, events and people from the past."

"Once a spook, always a spook?"

"Probably."

On the television screen a group of women and the dopey single guy were in a hot tub. The old phrase came to me: Youth is wasted on the young.

"Tell me more about what you did at the Pentagon."

"I thought I already did that."

She squirmed around some more, so one arm was loosely draped over my lap. "Bits. Here and there. Give me a typical day."

"No such thing."

"Then make it up."

I wondered what it would be like to be in a hot tub with five drop-dead gorgeous women, all of whom were pretending to be interested in me. It would be a challenge, but I think at some point I'd be up to it.

"You get in early," I said. "No reason for it, because the world and the DoD operates on a 24/7 basis. And this was pre-Internet, so stuff was sent around as reports or memos. We'd read what was called the O-S-R, the Overnight Status Report, one-paragraph summaries of what happened during the previous twelve hours in all the world hot spots. A quiet week would mean those reports would be one page, two pages maximum. A busy week meant eight, nine, ten pages."

"Wow, all those secrets."

"Not so much," I said. "They just glossed over what was really going on. If you needed more information, you had to dig deeper past the synopsis."

"Mmm, what then?"

"Then we'd do our jobs," I said. "Our unofficial title was the Marginal Issues Section, meaning that all the quirky requests or questions that the big boys and girls didn't want to handle came to us. Then we'd be asked to research them and get back to the requestor. More often than not, by the time our reports went up the food chain, the issue had been resolved or forgotten."

"Sounds incredibly dull."

I said it before I could catch myself. "Before the end, it was the best job I've ever had."

Paula squeezed me. "Oh, do go on. Why's that?"

I hesitated. Oh, the secrets I was revealing . . . but so what. It was all history, now.

"It was a different time, different place. The world wasn't as fragmented, or filled with pure anarchy and hate. There were fuzzy boundaries and rules, but they existed. And all of us felt that we were in a fight . . . not both sides tossing ICBMs at each other, but a fight between one sloppy but relatively free way of life and another system that was sending poets and writers to the gulag. No doubt too basic and too clichéd for some. We were in a fight, and we were dedicated to it. Now . . . I'm dedicated to getting better so I can woo you better."

"Woo you? What, you learned fifties-speak back there at the Pentagon?"

"Learned lots of things."

Paula squeezed me, laughed, and said, "There was a woman back there, wasn't there."

"Yes."

"You told me she was dead."

"I told you right."

"You miss her?" Paula asked.

I tried not to hesitate as I slipped an untruth past her. "Sometimes."

It was warm and fine and the meal was settling in. "You know, I could spend the rest of the night here on this couch," Paula said. As I was about to answer that it sounded like a good idea, her phone rang.

Paula said something so vile and obscene for someone so pretty and slender, and grabbed her cell phone out of her leather bag. She answered it with, "Quinn," and I bit my lip not to add "medicine woman" to her sentence.

"Uh-huh," she said. "Uh-huh. Hold on."

One more rummage trip through the bag, coming out with a Bic pen she uncapped with her teeth, and looking for something on my coffee table; she found a subscription card to *The New York Times* and started scribbling.

"Okay, okay," she said. "Got it."

She got off the phone, muttered yet another fantastic expletive, and said, "Two-car crash over in Bretton. Tractor-trailer truck and SUV, tractor-trailer on its side, SUV flipped over three or four times, ended up in some birch trees. Route 101 from here to the middle of the state blocked off. Med flight coming in. One hell of a mess. I gotta go."

I got up and saw her to the door, got a brief kiss, and she said, "Look, not sure when I'm coming back."

"I understand."

"And when I'm done, I'll probably end up back at my condo. Quicker to get to bed."

"Understand that, too."

Then she was out the door, and I was there by my lonesome, like it had been planned or something.

Karma, maybe, or the spirits Up There who were having fun sending parts of me around the West Coast were responsible.

Back to my couch I went.

The sloggy routine continued, with a bit more of television downstairs, and then my usual routine of emptying out the blood and fluid upstairs. Measuring the blood—a slight improvement, but still not enough to get the drains taken out—and then, filled with a burst of optimism and energy, I decided to take a shower.

It took some doing, but I got my top and bottoms off, and turned on the water, letting it run nice and hot. I did the best I could, ducking my head in, washing my hair, trying not to get my midsection bandages wet, the ones next to my drains. The angry-looking stitchwork wasn't as angry-looking anymore, more disgruntled-looking. I flipped around and washed my other leg and arm; it took a long time and I got water splashed all around the place and on the tile floor, but damn, it felt good.

Drying off took some time and a couple of grunts, and by the time I was done, I was exhausted. There was great temptation not to get dressed, but I plowed ahead. Then I resisted another temptation to put some dry towels on the floor and stretch out and sleep there.

I got ahold of my borrowed cane, went out to the bedroom, took a gander at my sloppily made bed, and knew at some point I'd have to strip it and put fresh sheets down—but not tonight, maybe tomorrow.

Maybe tomorrow.

The slogan of all recovering patients everywhere, I guessed.

I slipped into bed and switched off the lights and rested.

And rested.

Okay, why aren't we sleeping?

I thought about the oddest things, bouncing from one to another. Maggie's murder. Paula and her sweetness and her being by my side. Diane Woods, being shoved aside by the state police, and also considering applying for the deputy chief's job. My memories of my dear Cissy, bustling in at the oddest time . . . and that dream. Oh, that dream. Heroin, here, there, and everywhere. The little planned power outage. Dave Hudson and his poor wife, Marge, trying to gain entry to my house for genealogical purposes, and me . . . well, maybe me being a jerk about it.

Then there was the whole writing business. Unlike for some, to whom it came easily, writing had always been a struggle for me, especially when it came to nonfiction, for—unless you worked for some websites or newspapers of notoriety—you had to write the truth, and keep the facts straight.

I positioned myself in bed, and winced, just as there was a creak or a groan as the new wood continued to settle, still getting used to being part of the landscape.

My old house, still not there yet.

My somewhat old body, still not there yet either.

Let the healing resume, and eventually, sleep did come.

To be disturbed about two hours later.

I woke from a dream I couldn't remember, but I was hearing rain coming down, rattling on my new roof and my small, second-floor deck, and there was another noise as well, of someone closing the door downstairs.

I called out. "Paula? Is that you?"

No answer.

Had I been dreaming?

I switched on a small bedroom lamp, checked the time: 1:05 A.M.

Maybe I had been dreaming.

Then came the sound of a floorboard creaking.

"Paula, if that's you, I'd really appreciate you letting me know."

Still nothing.

I thought of something else, and called out, "Dave Hudson, if that's you or your wife, Marjorie, you better leave now. Right now. Or I'm calling the Tyler police."

More rain falling. A gust of wind rattled the door leading out to the deck on this floor.

"Last chance."

Another creak of a floorboard.

I reached for my phone, thought better of it. One more call to the Tyler cops, finally arriving once more to an empty house? Nothing like helping along the growing story of the nutty magazine writer living alone on Tyler Beach.

Felix?

No. At this hour, he would come, no matter where he was, but I wasn't going to put him through that. Besides, he was still recovering from a gunshot wound, and he didn't need to come out here for one more empty reason.

Nope.

I called out one more time. "I don't know who you are or what you're up to, but if you come up the stairs, I'll blow off your goddamn head."

Then I thought some more and said, "And whatever you do, don't steal my books. Anything else down there is fair game. But not my books."

A pause, and I said, "Good night."

Still no reply, but it didn't take long for me to get back asleep.

CHAPTER THIRTEEN

My unplanned and unanticipated wake-up call came at just past eight A.M., and it was Paula, checking in.

"You sleep okay last night?" she asked.

I wasn't about to get into my mystery visitor, so I said, "Pretty fair. How about you?"

An intake of breath. "Hardly got a wink. Last night . . . a bloody mess it was. Two dead, both from the SUV. Neither one was wearing a seat belt, and when their car got hit by the tractor-trailer truck, they were both ejected between roll number two and roll number three."

"Damn," I said.

"Oh, yeah, it gets better. So you have the SUV in one tangle of birch trees, and what's left of the driver and passenger in another. Plus a big-ass tractor-trailer hauling fuel oil on its side, leaking, with the local fire guys freaking out that it was gonna blow."

"Rough night."

"Oh, it was long . . . but you know what? I owned that story. Nobody else did. I even caught some video and sold it to the nice TV folks in Manchester, and today, it's going to be follow-up city."

"Which means no sensuous back rub with scented candles later on?"

She didn't laugh. Maybe she hadn't heard me or didn't like what she had heard, but she pressed on. "I'll drop by if I can," she said. "Rollie Grandmaison is out sick again. Poor guy's been editor since I've been there and I think he'd rather die in his editor's chair than a hospital room."

"Who wouldn't?"

"Not me," she said. "I want to die when I'm over a hundred, looking out a window and seeing the Eiffel Tower. But that's for another day. You take care."

"You, too."

I hung up the phone and wondered if I had enough energy to get up and check my drainage tubes and have breakfast.

I fell back asleep while in the middle of contemplating just that.

Breakfast was breakfast and I got the usual tube-drainage task done without spraying blood everywhere or falling on my increasingly flabby ass. At about eleven in the morning, a force of nature called Gwen Aubrey blew into my house, raising my hair and nearly lifting up the rafters in the process. She had been dropped off by her niece, Mia Harrison, who was up at the Lafayette House for a bit, trying to straighten out a time sheet.

Mia's aunt was in that odd age range that could be late sixties, early seventies, but she dressed and carried herself like she still had fond memories of being a head cheerleader back in high school. She had a thick mane of styled blonde hair, a tanned face with enough makeup to think she wasn't wearing makeup, and gold jewelry around her neck, on her ears, wrists, and practically every finger. Gwen was wearing a tight white turtleneck with tight acid-washed jeans, said jeans decorated with glitter and stones along the pockets and rear.

She was an inch shorter than I am, and her shape was what could be politely called full, or bosomy, or zaftig. She barreled into my house and gave me a big kiss on my cheek. "Christ on a crutch, Mia didn't tell me you were such a good-looking boy. Wow!" she said in a booming voice.

I managed to step back and avoid any other further kisses. "Come on in, and thanks for coming by."

She waved a hand dismissively and took the near couch; I dragged over a chair and sat down across from her. She brought in a scent of lilac that was strong enough to linger in my house for another week or two after she left.

"Shit, it's good to get out and about," Gwen said. "I'm living in one of those active senior places up in Porter. Expensive as crap but at least you don't have to make your own meals, beds, or laundry. I've gone through three husbands and twice as many boyfriends, and I figure I sure as hell have done my share. Life's too short when you get to be my age to waste time on deciding what kind of laundry detergent to use."

"Well, I can see—"

"Plus, it's stuffier than hell up there, you know what I mean? You got the older guys who spend all day on the computer, keeping track of their investments. You got the older ladies who sit around and gossip and stick invisible knives in each other's backs, and you got the old couples who are in a new place and still fight over grudges from three decades ago. Jesus Christ on a crutch, it's nice to be out and around."

"Why are you there then?"

Gwen laughed. "Good goddamn question. Thing is, I'm on my own, I like it most times, and I got a nice nest egg. Thing with the place I'm at, once you're in, you're in . . ." She slapped a thigh for emphasis. "That means once this old broad's body starts falling apart, I'll have a place that will have to take care of me, per the contract, and they have to provide the care until I shuffle off to the great beyond. Can't kick me out or put me in a wheelchair and abandon me at the mall. Pricey as shit but it's worth it."

She shifted on my couch, looked around the inside of my house. "You know, I've driven past this place for decades, and this is the first goddamn time I've ever been in. Not bad . . . but what the hell happened here a few months ago?"

"There was a fire."

"What? Electrical? Hot ashes from the fireplace?"

"No," I said. "It was arson."

"Holy shit," Gwen said. "Did they catch the guy who did it?"

"Sort of."

"Sort of?"

"Well, he's dead."

"Did he die in the fire?" Gwen asked.

"No," I said, remembering a very dark and unpleasant time from last fall. "He died up in a town called Osgood."

"Jesus . . . did he die in a fire that he set? That would be freaking karma, wouldn't it."

"No," I said. "Somebody cut his head off."

Gwen's roaming eyes froze and came right to me. "You kidding?"

"No."

"You're a fine-looking guy, even though you look like you've been battered around some. A man gets his head cut off . . . bet you have lots of interesting stories. Am I right?"

I felt like I was being sprayed from a fire hose with a torrent of words and interest, and that I couldn't move.

"Funny you should mention stories," I said, trying to change the subject. "Because I'm looking for—"

"Yeah, well, before we get there," she said, grinning, teeth too white and perfect. "I want to ask you one."

"That sounds fair," I said. "Go ahead."

Gwen nodded. "Okay. For as long as I can remember, this place has always belonged to the government. It used to be a lifeboat station, then officers' quarters when the artillery station got set up, and then for a while when the artillery station was replaced by radar to see if Russian bombers were coming this way."

"That's what I've heard, too."

"Yeah, well, the question is, how in hell did you get this house? It's always belonged to the Feds, it's on a nice isolated part of the seacoast, and the value. I mean, Christ, I know the place is old but if it got torn down and replaced by a condo with four or six units, a paved driveway instead of that goat path you've got—could be worth millions, you know?"

"I do know," I said. "And the reason I got this house . . . a favor was owed to me."

"Last I knew, this place was under the . . . whaddya call it . . . stewardship of the Department of the Interior. The secretary of the interior steal your car or something?"

"No," I said. "The secretary of defense stole my health . . . among other things."

"Hell of a story," she said slowly. "Mind telling it to me?"

"Not today, I'm sorry," I said. "Look, can I get you something to drink? Water? Tea? Coffee?"

Gwen glanced at the chunky jeweled watch on her wrist and said, "Damn, not afternoon yet, I really shouldn't have anything strong. Coffee will be fine. Black."

"Be right back."

A few minutes later we were both having late-morning coffee. "Before we start, mind telling me what the hell put you in the hospital?" she asked.

"Some surgery on my back and shoulder."

"What the hell did they do?"

I don't know why she got me in a talkative mood—maybe it was her age or her presence—but I said, "Had two nasty tumors taken out."

She swore like a sailor on dry land for the first time in two years. "You okay now?"

"Think so."

"They malignant?"

"Don't know yet," I said. "They're out for testing."

Another impressive string of expletives, and she said, "Okay, if it comes back malignant, you let me know. My age, I got lots of doctor and nurse contacts, get you first in line. If it's benign, you have a party of a lifetime, okay?"

"Deal," I said.

She took a slurpy sip and said, "Okay, what can I do for you? My sweet little Mia told me that you wanted to know what was happening in this little slice of paradise back in the 1950s."

"That's right."

"Hoo-boy," she said. "I was just beginning to write for the newspapers back then, doing church raffle reports, collating school lunch menus, crap like that, when I got wind of a big story happening right under this roof, back in 1954, a year after the Korean War ended."

"I heard this place was being used as barracks for Navy corpsmen while they received training over at the old Exonia Hospital."

She laughed. "Sure. Barracks. Training. Story back then was that with the war over, lots of training was winding down. Them's the rules of war, right? They can end on a certain date but lots of things are in the pipeline, like planes and ships being built, bullets being made, and training going on. With the war over, the corpsmen were getting their training, but they didn't give a shit. Nobody gave a shit. The training was ignored or postponed, stuff was getting stolen, the barracks here was on a beach in the summer, and you had guys in their teens or early twenties who stayed here and partied because they knew they weren't going to be sent to some bombed-out frozen landscape where you had thousands of Chinese boiling over the hills coming at you."

"And what was the story?"

"Story was that some young girls from Tyler Beach and other locales came up here and got a hell of an education in sex, drinking, drugs, and other nefarious activities."

I didn't say anything for a moment, and Gwen leaned over the couch and slapped me on the knee. "Sweet Jesus, every generation thinks they invented sex or drinking or drugs. Everything you have now, from pot to whatever, was easily available back then. Guys and girls were humping to and fro in the backseats of cars or in the dunes. Nothing new."

"A scandal, then?"

"Hell yes, a scandal. Somehow a North Tyler cop found out his niece was sampling the Navy wares, and he came down to get her. A fight broke out, then the shore patrol came down from the Porter Naval Shipyard and raided the place. Cleaned it out tight. And found out that one of the girls was a cousin to a U.S. senator from Maine—and that was that. Within twenty-four hours the place was cleaned out and locked."

"What paper did your story get in?"

Another laugh. "I was working for the *Wentworth County Dispatch*—God rest its inky soul—and that story was spiked."

"Got killed."

"Like a zombie on TV getting its head blown off. That's when I learned one of the unwritten rules of small-town journalism, that you don't embarrass the locals or put them in a bad light. There was enough bad light with this one to light up a football stadium. So I ended up writing a story about how the brave trainees at this barracks were sent home, thanked everyone for their service, and that was that."

"Do you remember any of the names from back then?"

"Whose names?"

"The corpsmen who were here."

"Oh, Lewis, c'mon, I'm about ninety percent ahead of my neighbors in keeping my noggin straight, but I don't remember that. I don't even know if my notes still exist."

"Okay, thanks."

She shook her head. "Boy, you give up easy."

"What?"

"You heard me, youngster. Just because I don't know doesn't mean I can't find out. In fact, I can guarantee it."

"Why?"

"Because I ended up dating one of the corpsman before he got out, and he's still alive, and he's living just over the line in Massachusetts. Bobby Turcotte, bless his soul."

That got my attention. "You always keep track of your former . . . acquaintances?" I asked.

"Aren't we being the gentleman," she said. "Yeah, you know why? Because it gives me great joy to outlive them or outdo them. They say revenge is a dish best served cold. Honey, growing old and being in good shape while your rivals and old friends are shitting in diapers and eating Jell-O is the coldest dish you can think of."

I limped back into the kitchen to wash our few dishes, and Gwen insisted that she come along to help; I was being polite and tired and decided to let her do so.

When the washing was done and Gwen wiped the dishes and put them away, she said, "Ask you a favor?"

"Ask away."

"I spotted your deck over there. I'd love to take a look outside."

"Sure," I said. "As long as you give me a hand getting it open."

Gwen got the length of wood out and got the door open with no difficulty. I followed her out. "Oh my . . ." she whispered.

It was a windless, sunny day, and the sun was baking the wood of my rear deck. I got the plastic covers off two Adirondack chairs and we both settled down. The wood was fairly clear of sand and it was nice to sit down without worrying about a broom.

The waves were gently rolling in, the sky was clear, sharp blue, and there were little bits of color on the water where lobster pot buoys bobbed up and down. A few miles out, the scraggly white forms of the Isles of Shoals looked close enough to swim out to, if one were crazy enough to do so. Gwen settled down and stretched her legs out to one of the deck's railings.

"My God, what a view," she said. "If I lived here, young man, I'd spend most of my time out here."

I don't know why I spoke like I did, but I said, "No doubt sunbathing and teasing the neighbors."

Gwen laughed and laughed and then looked up the coast, at Weymouth's Point. "Hey, you can see Alice Crenshaw's old house from here," she said.

Those few words froze me. Gwen could not have surprised me more if she had said that she was originally from Indiana and was my long-lost aunt.

"Say again?" I managed to ask.

"Oh, Alice Crenshaw. That was her place up there, am I right?"

"Yes, you're absolutely right," I said, lots of unexpected memories flashing through me from years ago. "That was Alice's place."

"Did you know her?"

"We were friends for a while . . . until she moved out."

"That's right," Gwen said. "There was a scandal back then. Something to do with a body in the marsh from the 1940s, a fisherman getting blown up. Even the head of the chamber of commerce died in the mess. Am I right?"

God, was she ever right. "Yes, you're pretty much spot on. I had moved in just a while before all that happened."

"Alice was mixed up in it all, wasn't she?"

"She was." *And so was I,* I thought.

"We weren't the best of friends," Gwen said. "But we knew each other from my newspaper work, her being on some town boards and commissions. A real piece of work Alice was."

I stayed quiet and so did she, and we watched the ocean move its weight and water around, seagulls flapping overhead, other birds floating in the cove in front of us. Gwen stretched out her legs and closed her eyes, and it looked like she had dozed off. "Funny how history just flows along," she said. "You're living in a house that saw tremendous excitement and heroism back when it was a lifeboat station, and then a place for officers who shot off those big guns at Samson Point, and then that short time when it was basically a drunken party house."

She shifted her long legs. "Then life moves on. It's a quiet, beautiful day, you've got a lovely and quiet house, and what happened back there, it's all in the past. Seeing all this"—and she waved an arm—"hard to believe what happened here. Like sunbathing at the beaches on Normandy. But still . . ."

Gwen turned to me, face a bit more serious. "What did that Southern writer say, about the past?"

"It was Faulkner," I said. "He said, 'The past is never dead. It's not even past.'"

"Smart fellow."

"He sure was."

Gwen smiled. "I was talking about you, sport." A pause to look at her chunky watch, and she said, "Dear me, time to roll. Look, I'll get ahold of my old beau, Bobby Turcotte, see if I can pry him out of his rest home to get him to visit you."

She got up and so did I. "Do you think it'll be a problem?"

"Nah," she said. "I'll promise him a BJ like the good-old days and that should get him running."

I think she saw me blush, and that got another laugh. "Don't worry, Lewis, by the time we're done visiting, he'll have forgotten everything. Gosh, like I said before, you kids think you invented everything from sex and drugs to rock 'n' roll." She checked her watch. "Guess I'll go walk up to the Lafayette House and see if my niece needs some help beating up her boss."

At the sliding door leading into my house she turned to me, and like an old vision from years past, she touched my face like Alice Crenshaw did back in the day. "Oh, if only I were some years younger," she said.

I found it hard to talk. After a moment passed, I said, "That's sweet of you to say, Gwen."

"Never been accused of being the quiet one."

"My turn for a favor?"

"Sure."

"Where's Alice now?" I asked.

She took one step into my house, turned back to me. "Oh, you didn't know?"

"No," I said.

"Alice moved in with a niece over in Worcester—nowhere near the beach, poor girl—and got Alzheimer's, that nasty bitch of a disease. Suffered with that for years, and died two years back. By then, it was a mercy."

My throat was still thick. "I'm sure it was."

CHAPTER FOURTEEN

F elix gave me a ring later and asked me if I wanted dinner, and I said of
course; he said he was bringing company, and before I could ask him
what the hell was going on, he hung up.

I next checked in with Paula Quinn. "Poor Rollie, he's still sick," she
said.

"Poor guy indeed," I said. "Meaning you're still the editor?"

"For the foreseeable future, which means I'm off tonight and tomorrow
night."

"Off like in vacation?"

"Like hell," Paula said. "In a spirit of generosity, a couple of months ago
our corporate owners paid for Rollie to attend a two-day conference in
Boston, something called the New New Journalism or some idiocy. Poor
Rollie, I think it would have been wasted on him, but at least he would
have a chance to eat and sleep somewhere nice on the *Chronicle*'s dime.
But with him sick, the owners will be damned if this investment goes to
waste. So off I go."

"Pick me up a nice T-shirt, will you? Extra-large?"

"Sure, I'll get matching ones, and later this summer we can have a wet
T-shirt contest on your deck. How does that sound?"

"Best invite all day—hell, all week."

She laughed and her voice lowered a bit. "How are you doing?"

"As well as could be expected, and then some."

"Any report back yet?"

"If I get the energy and verve up, I might make a call today. If not, I'll take a nap."

"You all right emptying out your drains?"

"I've got a technique down pretty well, although if I run into a jam, Felix is coming over with dinner tonight."

Paula sighed. "Yeah, if there's one guy who knows his way around blood, it's him. You be careful, all right?"

"I promise I won't leave the house, and I'll make sure all the dishes are washed," I said. "Hey, quick question. You ever hear of a newspaper called the *Wentworth County Dispatch*?"

"Wow, you're really going back in time now," she said. "Sure. It was a small daily, covered Wentworth County, way back when there were rotary-dial phones and all us lady journalists wore poodle skirts and wrote for the Women's Pages. Probably sputtered out in the late sixties, early seventies. What are you looking for?"

"Oh, I'm not sure," I said. "Earlier today I spent a fascinating hour or so talking to a former reporter for the paper. Gwen Aubrey. Ever hear of her?"

"Nope."

"Any idea where there might be some back issues to look at?"

Paula said, "Best bet would be here, I guess, in our bound back-issues section, since the *Chronicle* bought it out about a month before it closed. Or the Tyler library, or the one up in Porter. Curious about something?"

"Always," I said, and after a bit more chit and chat, we parted ways.

I powered my way through the afternoon and managed to avoid a nap, and then I made a series of phone calls to my health-care system and listened to a lot of bad on-hold music. Eventually I talked to a very nice woman who expressed her sympathy with me, promised to do what she could to help me out this very day, and while putting me on hold to track something down, promptly disconnected me.

So that was that.

I decided to putter around on my MacBook Pro until Felix came; that gave me a thought, and then I buried myself in the odd world of rare silver from Sicily until there was a knock at the door.

It must be Felix, I thought, and as I got up and lumbered over to the door like a bear that's just escaped a bear trap, I wondered what kind of company he was bringing. Knowing Felix, I guessed it wasn't a single person, because he would have said "guest." He said "company," which meant more than one, and I was sure that the company would be young, pretty, and female.

I opened the door and saw Felix, flanked by two men in their early thirties with dark hair and brown eyes wearing blue khaki slacks and work shirts. I was embarrassed to see that I was wrong, wrong, and wrong.

"Hey," he said, walking in, carrying two paper bags with handles and a small drink cooler.

"Hello right back at you," I said. "Uh . . ."

The two men strolled in as well; they started talking to Felix in what seemed to be Greek. Felix replied, pointing to my living room, and then to the stairs, and both men nodded and trotted upstairs.

"Those two are my distant cousins, Dimitris and Michael, from the home country," Felix said.

"The other one?"

"Yeah," he said, going to the kitchen. "They tried to migrate up to France, got caught up and arrested, and they contacted the Red Cross—and then contacted me."

From upstairs came the noises of things being dragged around and opened up, and then water running. Felix started taking paper-wrapped packages from out of the bags, and then opened my cabinet doors.

"Well . . . what the hell are they doing here?" I asked.

Felix stared up at the cabinet. "Somebody moved your sea salt and pepper mills . . . oh, here we go. Huh? Oh. Michael and Dimitris wanted to thank me for getting them here, and until they get settled into something more productive and long term, they belong to me. I told them where I was going today, we talked about this and that, and now they're here."

"I can see that. What are they doing?"

"What I told them to do." He bent down, rummaged around some more, and said, "Hey, your cast-iron frying pan . . . hold on, here it is." He stood up and put it on my stove.

"Which is what?"

"Oh, don't be dense, my friend. The place needs a good cleaning, a good straightening out, and I know that having your books piled up in cardboard boxes is gnawing at you . . . like a fox chewing on some passed-out drunk's toes."

"Nice thought."

"Thanks, I thought you'd like it."

Despite the bandage on his wrist, Felix moved quickly and fluidly through the kitchen; he popped two potatoes in my microwave, heated them up and tossed them into the oven, made a salad, and then heated up the cast-iron pan.

"What do you have?"

"Nice, thick steaks."

I gestured out to my deck. "Isn't that what a grill's for?"

"That's what one usually does, but I want to try something else. Bear with me."

He heated up a mix of olive oil and coarse salt in my skillet, while upstairs there was a chattering of Greek voices and the sound of my washer and dryer being used. Then the sound of something being scraped on the floor, followed by the two men yelling at each other in Greek and the hum of a vacuum cleaner.

Felix unwrapped some yellow wax paper, tossed two beautiful thick, marbled steaks onto the very hot skillet. A burst of smoke and steam rose up; Felix kept a close look on the time while he charred one side, then the other, and then the edges as well. When he was satisfied, he put the skillet in the oven, washed his hands, and said, "Now we wait. What's going on with you? Any word yet on your tumors?"

"My tissue samples are still out there on the West Coast, probably having more fun than I am. I've talked to my health-care provider a couple of times, with no good answer."

"You making a list?"

"A list of what?"

"A list of those people screwing you over and making your life miserable. Then at some point, down the road, you can get back at them."

I rubbed at a spot on my kitchen counter. "Not the way I roll. Most times, that is."

"Yes," Felix said, "but think of the satisfaction you'll get, knowing someone who did you harm has been harmed in return."

"Sounds Sicilian," I said.

"Sounds human," he replied.

A little while later there was a shout from upstairs, and Felix walked over to the foot of the stairs, yelled something up in Greek. He walked back to the kitchen. "Silly brothers wanted permission to move your bed."

"Why?"

"Because they could," he said. "They were making progress in cleaning your bedroom and thought your bed would be better next to the window overlooking the ocean.

"Great idea," I said. "Except the wind and sand can cut through there when the weather is right, not to mention how bright the sun can be, coming up in the morning."

"You've thought it through."

"I did, during my first week here. Did you tell them not to move it?"

"You bet," Felix said. "I told them you'd be embarrassed by all the skin mags they'd find between the mattresses."

I changed the subject. "How goes your labors, tracking down the . . . local youths you encountered down in Lawrence?"

"Slow," he said. "They've either scattered or have gone to ground."

"Plus the cops are looking for them, both from here and from Massachusetts."

"Yeah, there is that. But I'm not going to let the little bastards think they've gotten away with it."

It was time, I thought. "This antique silver that belonged to your family. You said it was an old serving set, something like that."

"Correct, sir."

"Was it a plate? Or a platter? Or something on four little legs? With upturned sides?"

Felix had been making a salad over my sink and then turned. "It had four little legs. How the hell did you know that?"

I limped over, retrieved my laptop, brought it over, and put it on the counter, swung it around so the sun wasn't washing out the screen. "Check it out," I said.

Felix did that, leaning over, squinting his eyes. "Damn, that could be its twin."

"If so, you're one lucky guy."

"Why's that?"

"Because that one sold at auction two years ago," I said. "For just over a half-million dollars."

I had to give Felix credit because his thick eyebrows just lifted a bit, and he went back to preparing the meal. Using a thick pot holder, he took the skillet out, and the heavy aroma of the cooked steak filled the air. He removed the steaks with tongs, put them onto a dish, and covered the dish with foil.

"Five or so minutes in there, and it'll be perfect," he said. "People tend to forget it keeps on cooking if it just sits there, and this gives the juices a chance to stay inside."

He worked in a flurry for a few minutes more, making a sauce with water, flour, a bit of wine, and some juices.

The steak was charred, crispy, and tasty on the outside, and tender and juicy on the inside. The sauce he drizzled over the filets was practically a meal unto itself. It was one of the finest dinners I'd eaten in a long time.

"What about your two men overhead?" I asked.

Felix was working on his salad. "What about them?"

"I'd think they'd be hungry."

"Oh, they'll be fine," he said. "They ate before we got here. Filled up at a Greek restaurant in Newburyport."

"You didn't join them?"

Felix grimaced. "My father's Greek. My mom was Sicilian. I can speak Italian fluently, and Greek passably. The Greeks gave us a lot of wonderful things, from great plays and epics to the concepts of philosophy and democracy. Just don't ask me to eat their food."

"All right, I won't," I said, and we continued eating until both of us were stuffed. Felix did some initial cleaning, and then one of the brothers—I couldn't tell which one was Michael and which was Dimitris—came into the kitchen and started talking with Felix. It was more like talking at Felix, though, with plenty of raised voices and swinging arms. Felix gave back some of the same, and to add some emphasis, he picked up a carving knife and waved it around under Michael or Dimitris's throat.

I was wondering what in hell was going on until, after a heavy pause, Felix laughed and the cousin laughed back and slapped Felix's back cheerfully as he came around the counter.

"Michael's going to clean the kitchen," Felix told me, as he poured us two fresh glasses of Chile's finest. "And then his brother is coming down to start in your living room. Let's head out on the deck."

I got off the stool, gasped when a bit of pain rippled along one of my drainage tube outlets. "All that discussion over who gets to clean the kitchen?"

"Sure," Felix said, bending over to pull up the piece of wood blocking the runners, and then unlocking the door and sliding it free. "It's a macho kind of thing. I told him I didn't hire him to do dishes, and he told me that I had hired him and his brother to clean the house, and he said, expletive deleted, isn't the kitchen part of the house? A few hundred words later, we settled things without blood being shed."

"Enough blood's already been shed in this house, thank you very much."

It was a nice, sunny afternoon and we each took an Adirondack chair in the sun. Felix noted the slight breeze immediately and went back into the house to retrieve a wool blanket, which he draped over my legs.

"There you go, gramps," he said.

"You keep that up and you're out of the will."

"Good," Felix said. "I wouldn't know what to do with all those damn books anyway."

We each took a sip and I took note of the swells of the waves, the bright little dots marking lobster traps. I said, "That silver piece from your grandfather."

"My great-great grandfather."

"Any idea where he got it?"

"Stole it, I'm sure," Felix said. "That's my family's M.O., going back centuries."

"Gee, you sure sound shook up about it."

"Instead of looking at Roman history or World War II, you should take a look back at the feudalism that was in Sicily back then, and which hasn't changed much. So I won't begrudge his spirit that."

"What did you use it for?"

Felix chuckled. "Believe it or not, it was near the front door. A handy place to dump the mail that needed to be checked out later, or to drop my car keys."

"Nice handy place you got there, Felix, worth about a half-million dollars."

"What can I say?" he said, taking another sip. "Fortune sometimes favors the brave, the lucky, and those too dumb to know what they have."

"Why didn't you check it out on the Internet?"

"Didn't you tell me once that nobody knows you're a dog on the Internet? Same idea. Unlike you, I didn't have the time nor patience to scroll through lots of pages, trying to figure out what's what. Which is why I went to Maggie."

"She say anything to you at first?"

"Maggie was busy looking for a cat hiding somewhere in that barn, told me she'd get back to me, and just drop it on her desk. Which is what I did."

Out on the ocean a sailboat was doing an expert job, beating against the wind, nearly tipping over in the process but always moving on.

"Do you think that gang might have it?" I asked.

"They just might at that," he said. "And I'm not going to stop until I retrieve it."

"Especially since you found out its real value."

He shook his head. "No."

"No?"

He paused, held the wineglass in his two strong hands. "It doesn't matter if it's worth a half-million dollars or fifty cents. It's mine. It belongs to me. And I won't allow anyone to steal it and think they got away with stealing anything from me."

"Where do you go from here?"

The sound of vacuuming and more yelling came through the sliding glass doors. I turned and the two Greek brothers were at work in my living room, one working the vacuum, the other with a bunch of books under his arms, both yelling at each other.

Felix said, "Once the Spic 'n' Span lads wrap up, it's a visit to my own personal doc to see how my arm is doing, and then it's back to work. These guys, they tend to be bold and brave when they scamper off or go to ground, and for a couple of days, it's hard to track them. But at some point they loosen up. They go back to their hangouts, their girlfriends, their social clubs. And once you find one, that's all it takes."

"You got friends down there in Lawrence and Lowell?"

"No," Felix said, finishing off his wine. "But I have people I pay money to. In the long run, that's more important."

The sun felt good, and with the wine and big meal, I dozed off in the comfortable wooden chair, not minding the gentle scrape of the sliding glass door opening and closing, and some other sounds back there; I just slept some outside—for the first time in months, I was sure, and that's how the rest of my afternoon went.

A screeching seagull nearby woke me up; I yawned and stretched, careful not to disturb my drains. I got up and spent an extra few minutes folding the blanket, which gave me a nice small sense of accomplishment. Last week I would have dumped it on the chair and left it there for Paula or Diane to fold up, or for any renegade seagulls to use as a bathroom.

I opened the door and went inside. In the kitchen, everything had been washed and put away, and the counter and stovetop had been wiped down. I washed my face and hands, thinking this was the best I had felt in some time. I limped out into the living room with cane in hand, and I saw the two brothers had done a great job. I have bachelor sensibilities and can go a long way without cleaning, but even I could tell how things were clean, how furniture and shelves had been dusted.

All in all, things looked pretty good, though I would probably shift some things around and put those two bookshelves over there and—

Something was odd about my books.

I gimped forward and couldn't help myself.

I burst out laughing, for the two young men had carefully shelved every book—and it looked like each volume had been dusted beforehand—placing them not according to subject, title, or author. Nope, the hundreds of books I owned and displayed down here had been shelved according to the color of the book cover. Yellow, sliding into blue, sliding into gray.

"Well done, fellas," I said. "Well done."

Even though it looked like I was standing in the middle of a paper-made kaleidoscope, I had to give them credit for taking the time and puzzling it out.

A knock at the door.

I recalled what Mia, the nice waitress from across the street, had said. Maybe one of these days I'd install a doorbell. Lord knows I was getting tired of people knocking here.

But then again, I was here 24/7, so that meant when I could be mobile, I could stay away from my lovely home and the lovely beach for hours at a time, disappointing my visitors but cheering myself up.

Back to the front of the house, as the door knock was repeated.

I spared a glance through one of the windows. Young, dark-haired woman, standing by herself, holding what looked like a map or brochure in her hand.

Lost tourist or sightseer?

I've had my share of them before, but usually in the three months we laughingly called summer in this chilly state.

I opened the door and the woman, who looked Hispanic and about sixteen or seventeen, smiled at me, holding up a brochure from the Tyler Beach Chamber of Commerce.

"Excuse me, sir," she said shyly, her voice having just a trace of a Spanish accent. "Do you think you could help me?"

"Sure," I said. "What can I do for you?"

Then two large Hispanic men quickly walked around from the corner of my house; the larger of the two came up to me and punched me solidly in the face.

CHAPTER FIFTEEN

I was on the floor, chin aching, two dull spears digging into my back, staring up at the wood beams and dull white plaster of my ceiling. The two men came in and spoke Spanish, and then the young girl departed, and the door was closed. The bigger of the two men, the one who had punched me, looked down at me. He had on a short leather jacket, white T-shirt, jeans, and a Boston Red Sox cap worn sideways. I had been generally aware for the past few years that the latest fashion trend was wearing caps backward, but when did this sideways trend start?

His thick neck was seemingly secured by a number of gold chains, and he had a thin, almost two-inch-wide beard that ran to his chin and from ear to ear. He rubbed at his hand and said some words in Spanish.

The other man came over to look down at me. He was dressed nearly the same—his T-shirt was blue and his baseball cap was for the long-maligned Chicago Cubs. His face was clean-shaven and it seemed each ear was fitted with a diamond stud.

"Yo," he said, speaking with a faint trace of a Spanish accent. "What are you doing down there, man?"

"Looking up at my ceiling," I said. "It was replastered a few months ago, and I'm seeing where a few spots were missed."

He said something to his larger friend, and they both laughed, but I failed to see the humor in the situation. I was trying to recall where my weapons were, and I ran down the list in my mind: 9mm Beretta upstairs on my nightstand, 12-gauge Remington pump-action shotgun on a foam pad underneath my bed, and .32 Smith & Wesson semiautomatic pistol in a drawer in the kitchen.

Oh, and there was the stainless-steel Ruger .357 magnum revolver that had been seized some time ago by the Secret Service, and which they still hadn't returned.

If I got out of this current predicament, perhaps I would write a stern letter to the Boston office of the Secret Service.

Perhaps.

The smaller man—smaller only in comparison to his massive friend—squatted down next to me and said, "Hey, for real. What are you doing down there?"

"Your friend put me here."

"Not my friend, my cousin."

"Sorry," I said. "Missed the family resemblance."

"You comfortable down there?"

"Not really."

"Ramon!" he shouted, followed by a quick Spanish phrase—once upon a time I could read Russian and understand it spoken, if spoken by a five-year-old child and who was droopy and about to fall asleep, but that was the limit of my language skills—and Ramon came over and picked me up. I mean, he didn't help me up, or drag me up off the floor by grabbing my arms.

No, he picked me up and put me down on the couch.

I let out a breath.

My back was still aching and my jaw was right there with me. Not-Ramon pulled up a chair and stared at me, and stared. "What's that, running from your back?" he asked.

I twisted and saw both tubes were visible. "Drainage tubes," I explained. "I had surgery and the tubes are draining out blood and fluid, going into those little plastic pouches."

He nodded seriously. "Shit, yeah, I should have known that. A friend of mine, not a cousin, his name was Julius, he got shot in his junk, you know?

Had this tube running out of his Johnson, draining blood, piss, and every other liquid imaginable." He leaned forward, peered some more. "You get shot, bro?"

"No," I said, now having an idea of who these two gents were. "Surgery. Cut out two tumors."

He whistled. "That sucks. You gonna get that radiation, that chemo shit, make your hair fall out?"

"Don't know yet."

"Uh-huh." He rubbed his hands together. "Sorry, I was rude back there. The name's Pepe."

Neither of us offered each other a hand. "Oh, I thought the rude part was when Ramon slugged me."

Pepe shrugged. "Wanted to get your attention, bro. Heard some old guy say that years back. When you get a stubborn mule and you wanna communicate with it, you start off by whacking it in the head with a baseball bat or something. I wanted your attention."

"You certainly got it," I said. "So what can I do for you?"

"I'm sure you can think of something . . . am I right?"

"Sorry, I'm not in the market for your little bluebird heroin."

He grinned at that. "Our business plan sure is working, if an old guy like you knows our brand."

"Why a bluebird? I thought a hawk or an eagle would be more appropriate. Bird of prey, something like that. Show how tough and rough you guys are."

"No, no, no," he said. "You got that shit all wrong. We're not selling violence, man, we're selling stuff to help you through the day, help you through the night. Bluebird of happiness, you know what I mean?"

"I guess I do now," I said. "Tell me, Pepe, I'm enjoying this cross-cultural exchange we've got going on here, but what are you looking for?"

He smiled. "I think you know."

"Felix Tinios."

"Yeah, that's right," Pepe said.

At the sound of Felix's name, Ramon rumbled over to the couch and spoke loudly at me, face coloring. He looked like one of those trained Russian bears who never went beyond his first lesson on the tricycle because he tore off the head of his trainer.

Pepe spoke sharply and Ramon shut up. "Sorry 'bout that," he said. "Ramon . . . he got something personal going on with that Felix guy."

"I can see," I said. "Well, if you were here about an hour or so ago, you would have met him, face-to-face."

Pepe shook his head. "Not yet," he said. "Not yet. You see, I don't know much about the man. Can you help me with that?"

"For real?" I asked. "I thought you knew him pretty well, back the last time you and your . . . associates met up with him."

"Nah, I wasn't there for that particular meet and greet. I was down in the D.R., doing some business."

"D.R.?"

"Dominican Republic."

"Scouting for the Sox?"

His eyes flashed at me. "No, man, not scouting for the Sox. Can we get on with this shit?"

"Sure, Pepe. Whatever you say."

By now the pain in my jaw and back was easing, and so was my tension. Having these two men in the house was one hell of a disturbance, and I didn't like it. They were young, big, muscular, and utterly confident they could force their way in and do and say whatever they wanted. And based on my own condition and the location of my weapons, there was nothing I could do about it.

He nodded. "All right then. Who is this Felix guy?"

"Why are you asking me? I'm sure other people in your . . . field of interest would have the same kind of information."

"We asked around, that's why. Wanted to know who this clown's friends or acquaintances are. Got a bunch of names but lots of them were women, which I don't want to deal with, 'cause they get all emotional and shit, and the guys . . . well, they were too much like him. Or us. And then there's you. Even found out that you got him freed a while back on a murder charge."

"He did that pretty much all by his lonesome."

"Not what I heard."

"Should I feel honored, then?"

"Dunno. Learned you were a writer, that true?"

"Yes."

"What do you write? Newspaper? Video games? TV?"

"Magazine columnist."

He laughed. "Good luck with that, bro. Last time I held a magazine was ten years ago, and it was a whack-off mag, you know? Now, who needs it."

"Thanks," I said. "That's encouraging to know."

"Look," he said. "Me and Ramon, we're thirsty. You got any beer?"

"Maybe in the back of the fridge."

He spoke to Ramon, who came back with two bottles of Sam Adams Ale. I wasn't offended that he didn't offer me one, because I was pretty sure there had only been two in there before. They drank for a couple of minutes and Ramon belched when they had emptied the bottles.

Pepe sighed and said, "This Felix guy, why is he gunning after us?"

"He's gunning after you because he thinks you have something that belongs to him."

"Really? Like what?"

"Like an antique piece of silver."

"A . . . what?"

"Old silver."

Pepe looked confused. "Silver, like little bars? Coins?"

"No, like a serving platter. The sides curved up. With four little feet made to look like tigers."

A pause, then. Ramon still there, Pepe staring at me. "He thinks we got his platter, is that the case?"

"Yep."

"What? We supposed to have gotten this from some wedding reception he was at, his daughter or something, and we jacked it?"

"No," I said. "It was at an antiques dealer here in Tyler. Maggie Branch, on the Exonia Road. He had left it there for an appraisal, and it appears to be missing."

"So why does he think we nabbed it?"

"Because it was there before she was killed, and it was gone after she was killed. And some of your guys were there. A car with a license plate traced back to you, plus a packet of yours was left behind."

Pepe scratched behind his right ear. Ramon stood so still I wondered if his boots had accidentally stepped into some form of superglue and he couldn't move.

"That's bullshit, man," he said.

"What? That you weren't there? That your heroin was left behind? Oh, and the fact the cops from New Hampshire and Massachusetts are after you?"

Pepe shook his head. "Didn't kill the old lady. She was alive when we got there, alive when we left."

"Witnesses said they saw you leaving in a hurry."

"'Cause the old bitch was threatening to call the cops on us, that's why. We don't need that heat in this part of the world."

"Did she catch you, then?" I asked.

"Huh? Catch us, what?"

"I mean, did she come across you guys breaking in, trying to steal jewelry or cash."

"Wasn't like that, bro," he said, shaking his head.

"I'm not your bro," I said. "Then what was it like?"

He shrugged. "Pure business deal, that's all. And we couldn't reach an agreement, she got pissed, and that's that."

"A business deal? You guys were set to sell her stolen antiques? Or jewelry?"

Pepe grinned. "Shit, no. We were going to sell her smack."

I stared at him. He went on. "You know. Horse. White."

A pause. "Heroin."

That took me aback, and I couldn't say anything for a moment or three. Ramon was still standing like a carved piece of wood, and Pepe had a wide grin on his face. "What, you think our customers aren't all ages, all places?"

"Uh, let's just say I'm surprised."

"Shit, you shouldn't be, being a magazine writer, somebody who's supposed to know stuff. All this heroin epidemic people keep on talking about, it didn't mean shit when it was just brown and black people turning up dead in restrooms or parks, am I right?"

"Pretty much," I said.

He reached over, gently slapped me on the knee. "Man, an old white man who knows when I'm talking sense. You're one rare bird. So yeah, nobody gave a crap when it was those people keeling over and dying. Then some years back, the doctors, the big-pharma companies, they started pushing stronger and stronger painkillers, right? And the docs wanted to take care of their patients complaining their knees hurt, their hips hurt, so they wrote script after script. And what happened, then, huh?"

"A new class of addicts were created, and when they couldn't get the straight stuff, they went to the street stuff."

"That's right."

"And you don't mind doing it?"

"Doing what?"

"Poisoning people. Killing them. Ruining their lives."

Pepe held out a hand, ticked off finger by finger. "Let's see. Like cigarettes, like booze, like politicians who cut deals so kids drink water filled with lead. Yeah, I'm real broke up about my business."

"You say Maggie had pain problems, she wanted to score from you?"

"*Score*," he said, repeating my word. "Funny word. You watch a lot of gangster movies when you were younger?"

"Some."

"Nah," he said. "She didn't want to score for herself. She wanted it for some friends who were hurting, hurting in their joints or back, hurting because they had a little monkey on their backs and they needed help. Their family couldn't help, their docs couldn't help, so they went to Maggie, and she came to me."

I nodded. "All right. You guys went to see her for . . . what, negotiations?"

"Right. Negotiations. Yeah, we went there, wanted to talk, and we started dealing . . . and it didn't end well." He laughed. "Man, that old broad, she might have known the prices and shit for old pots and pans, but she didn't know anything about our business. That's for sure. Silly old lady wanted a senior discount. Hey, Ramon, remember that?"

He quickly spoke Spanish to Ramon, who grinned and nodded, and spoke back. "Yeah," Pepe said. "Gotta give her a lot of credit for that. Senior discount. Tough one."

"She was born tough."

"Huh?"

"Her family, they've been here since 1638, when the first settlers came here. A long line of tough men and women. So, you sure you didn't kill her?"

Pepe shook his head. "Christ, why the hell would we do that? She got pissed at us, told us that if we didn't get out in thirty seconds, she'd call the cops. At first we thought she was joking, but she picked up her phone, so we got the hell out. Quick."

"But no hard feelings?"

"No hard feelings, shit, no. I mean, that was the negotiations, you know? Opening salvo, everybody talks shit, and then you go back. Why would we want to hurt her? A nice piece of change, us doing business with an old lady like that. Who would ever suspect she'd be part of our business?"

"I see, but—"

He held up both hands. "Okay. Shut up, okay? Christ, I'm the one who came here, I'm the one wanting to ask questions, and I've been answering yours the past few minutes. Asshole."

I kept quiet. He stared at me. I still kept quiet.

"Well?" he said.

"Excuse me?"

"You're not talking."

"You haven't asked me anything."

There was a bit of noise from Ramon, as though he heard what I said and understood I was giving some grief to his boss. "Okay," Pepe said. "Back to the beginning. This Felix guy, he's after us 'cause he thinks we stole his silver, that's it?"

"That's it."

"But . . . none of my guys took it."

"Felix thinks otherwise," I said. "Are you sure one of your guys didn't slip it under a coat while you were running out?"

He didn't like that. "We wasn't running away from nothing. We were just moving quick. And no, I don't think my guys took it. Why does he have such a hard-on about it?"

"It belonged to his great-grandfather. From Sicily."

"So? If it was so important, why was he trying to sell it to that antiques lady?"

"It was cluttering up his house."

"Okay," Pepe said. "Was it worth a lot of money? Is that it?"

I shook my head. "I'm no antiques dealer. It could be worth money, it could be worth nothing. I don't know."

He grinned. "Nah, it's gotta be worth lots of money, with Felix wanting it back so much. Lots of money."

"No."

"Huh? You said earlier you didn't know how much it was worth."

"I don't," I said. "But don't assume that Felix is after you because that silver is worth money. It could be a cardboard plate and he'd still be after you. Because it's his, and because he thinks you stole it."

That seemed to get his attention. "Too bad."

"No, too bad for you," I said.

"From what I heard, he's old-fashioned. Boston North End, all that crap. Those tough guys, those made guys, they're either dead or in jail. Why should we be scared of him?"

"Because he's not dead, and he's not in jail."

"Can you tell him to back off?"

"I can suggest it, but don't think it'll mean anything."

"You're his friend."

"I'm his friend as much as one can be, but that doesn't mean I can tell him to do something he doesn't want to. You want a suggestion? You visit all your companions, and make sure nobody took that platter. If somebody has, you can contact me and I'll work with Felix to set up a nice, peaceful exchange. And if nobody has it, well, come up with a way to convince him otherwise."

He nodded and rubbed at his chin. "I got another idea. Maybe Ramon beats the shit out of you, sends a message to Felix not to fuck with us. Or maybe Ramon goes the distance, you know? Settle things once and for all. Really get Felix's attention, so this damn thing is over."

The air was cold and crisp in the living room, with an electric edge to it. I had no illusions of what was happening, or might happen.

"Beyond purely personal reasons, I wouldn't recommend it."

Pepe grinned. "Why's that, bro?"

"You keep on calling me bro," I said, "but we're not related."

"Like I care."

"Then care about this," I said. "If you're going to come at me, you better finish it. Otherwise the cops will be coming after you even harder."

"That sounds like an invite."

"Then tell me how this sounds. You finish it, the cops are going to check out the surveillance cameras over at the Lafayette House, keeping an eye on their parking lot and whoever comes down my driveway. Then they'll go through my house—maybe politely stepping over my body—and they're going to get your prints off the beer bottles, the kitchen, the furniture, the front door, and a host of other places. Now, I may be going out on a limb here, but I'm pretty sure you boys have records somewhere in the law enforcement community."

"Cops don't bother me."

"But I'm not done."

"Really?"

"Really," I said. "Earlier you said Felix is my friend. Pretty close to the truth. After he oversees my funeral and gets my affairs in order, he's coming after you."

"He's already coming after us."

"No, he's merely trying to get something back that he thinks you clowns took. That's not coming after you. If I'm dead or severely injured, he's going after every one of you, your friends, your family, your first-grade teacher. That's coming after you. Got that?"

Pepe stared at me and I stared right back at him.

The staring went on.

He got up and said, "You tell that Felix guy, you tell him to lighten up, okay? We'll be in touch."

"I'm sure he'll look forward to it."

Pepe spoke to Ramon, he spoke back, and the two of them left my house.

But not before Pepe stopped at a bookcase, slipped out a book, and held it up.

"This looks cool," he said. "And see? No misunderstandings. I'm taking it."

It was a copy of John Keegan's *The Face of Battle*, autographed to me personally by the now-deceased author.

The two left and shut the door behind them.

CHAPTER SIXTEEN

stared at the closed door, feeling like a sixth-grader who just got beat up for his lunch money by a couple of playground bullies.

Those two galoots had taken one of my prized possessions, and I had sat here and watched them do it. Damn.

I got up from the couch, went over to the kitchen, opened up a drawer, and took out my .32 Smith & Wesson semiautomatic pistol. I checked the magazine and action, put it on safe, and then tucked it into my left pajama pocket. My pajamas sagged but I didn't care.

I called Felix and there was no answer, but I left a message. I wandered around until Diane called. "Gotta make this quick," she said. "You up for dinner tomorrow?"

"That would be great, thanks."

"How are you doing?"

"Never better," I said.

"I think you're lying, but I don't have the time to figure it out. Later."

"You got it."

Then the night was all mine.

I spent a few minutes rearranging some of my books so it didn't look like I was living in the middle of a paint sample emporium, and then I made some toast and scrambled eggs for a late-night snack. All the adrenaline burning through my system after meeting Pepe and his big friend had made me hungry. I even placed the eggs on a plate, instead of eating from the frying pan, which seemed like another sign of progress.

After cleaning up, I went upstairs and measured my blood and fluid output, which was holding stable. Good to know that it wasn't increasing, but it wasn't declining either, meaning the drains weren't coming out soon. Damn. I was tired of feeling half-man, half-machine.

I stretched out on the bed and watched some more *Band of Brothers*, and as I was dozing off, the phone rang. It was Paula.

"How are you doing?" she asked.

"Doing all right," I said. "You got a good room over there in the Hub of the Universe?"

"Pretty good," she said, "since the paper's owners are paying for it. I'm considering doing some room service later."

"You wild woman, you," I said, and her laughter warmed me right through.

"Actually, some of us survivors of the newspaper age are gathering in the bar later to reminisce and plan our survival techniques."

"Boy, it makes changing out my little sacks of blood twice a day look like fun in comparison, right?"

Paula said something about waiting to be with my healthy body again, which warmed me even more. "You know, it looks like there might be a future in newspapers after all," she said. "If we can just get our bearings back . . . and not worry so much about making owners halfway across the country rich."

"You'll figure it out, young lady. If anybody can do it, you can."

"Thanks. I'll call you in the morning, okay?"

"Please do."

I was awake now and decided to make one more round of the house, in case Pepe and his man-mountain decided to pay me a late-night visit. I got out of bed, tickled that I could actually move without hurting anything, and then went downstairs with cane in hand. I found enough energy to reshelf one more bookcase and then, exhausted, I switched off the lights.

Just in time to see someone peeking in one of my living room windows.

I moved over to the entryway, flipped on the outside lights, opened the door, and leaned out.

A shadow, flickering its way up my driveway, and soon out of sight.

"Hey!" I called out.

No answer, not that I expected one.

It was nice to know that my trespasser was aware that I was awake. But who was it?

I flipped off the lights, moved back in, and shut and locked the door. In the darkness I said, "For an old house way off the road, we're sure as hell getting a lot of visitors."

Suddenly quite tired, I put my .32 Smith & Wesson back in the kitchen drawer and went to bed, making sure my Beretta was within easy reach. I stretched out, switched off the nightstand light, and stared up at the darkness. Nothing was happening, which should have comforted me, but it did the opposite.

I called Felix in the morning and didn't get him at home, but I did get him on his cell phone. He said he was busy, but when I told him who visited me the night before he said he'd be right over and hung up the phone.

Less than an hour later we were having crepes and bacon in my kitchen. When I started to say something to Felix, he had shook his head and kept on eating.

"Later," he said. "The older I've gotten, the more I want to enjoy my meals without any negative energy."

I nearly spat out a bite of crepe. "Negative energy? For real? What's next, healing crystals? Pyramid models? Feng shui for your gun collection?"

He just smiled and we continued eating.

When he had washed and I had dried, we sat on opposite sides of the kitchen counter, coffee mugs in hand. "All right," Felix said. "Go ahead. Tell me about your misadventures with the bluebirds of happiness."

I talked and talked. Felix just sat there, listening, and only asked a couple of questions. One was right at the beginning—"He nailed you in the chin?"—and the second question was at the end.

"Which book did he take?"

"*The Face of Battle* by John Keegan."

"Valuable?"

"To me," I said. "It's a signed first edition, made out to me. And he's been dead for a couple of years."

"Damn," Felix said. "All right, I'll make sure I get that back."

"Felix . . ."

"What, did I say something wrong?"

I smiled. "Come on, Felix. With all that's going on, you're going to get my book back?"

"What, you don't think I can multitask?"

"I have no doubt of any of your talents."

"All right, then," he said, and then he stared out my sliding glass doors to my first-floor deck. "Funny story Pepe told you."

"Didn't seem funny at the time."

"Yeah, well, I didn't mean funny in the hah-hah sense, but funny in the peculiar sense. He and his gang of drug dealers show up at Maggie's home . . . ready to be her dealer. Things go badly, and away they go. But at some point, Maggie is visited again by a killer who tears the place apart, and blows her head off."

"That's about what they said. You believe them?"

With a sharpness in his voice, Felix said, "Many, many years ago, probably about the time you were trying to save America from the godless communists, I learned something important. Never, ever, trust drug dealers or drug users. Never. No matter how sincere they sound, no matter how proper and smooth and good-looking or educated, never trust anybody involved with drugs."

"You want to tell me more?"

"No," he said.

A moment passed, and I caught a glimpse of something in Felix's past that he didn't want to share. A rare experience, but not one to be savored.

"So you can see why I doubt Pepe's sincerity."

"Yeah," I said. "Still, he made a strong case that they didn't have anything to do with your silver."

"Maybe," he said, and Felix rotated his wrist so I could see the bandage there. "Now he wants to talk. His folks didn't want to talk earlier."

"Everybody makes mistakes now and then."

"Sure," Felix said. "Still . . . then who killed Maggie?"

"Maybe it was another visitor, right after Pepe left. Maybe one of Pepe's crew came back and things got out of hand. Or . . ."

I hesitated, but Felix wouldn't let me hesitate for long.

"Go on."

"You know there was one other person in the vicinity, somebody with a criminal record."

"I do?"

"Felix. The man you had conducting a surveillance in the neighborhood. What, was he a Boy Scout leader? A church deacon? He was working for you."

"But—"

His eyes narrowed. I could tell Felix wasn't happy, and I sensed it was for two reasons: one, I had pointed out something he had missed, and two, the idea that someone under his hire might have been the one who had killed Maggie Branch.

When I thought it was safe, I said, "Who is he?"

"Rudy Gennaro."

"What's his background?"

"From my old haunts, until he went south to Providence. A dumb move. The North End gets all the news while Providence keeps its head down and focuses on business. Rudy thought that because he had the North End heritage, that gave him some weight and muscle when he went to Rhode Island. It didn't."

"You rescue him?"

"As a favor."

"For whom?"

Felix's face relaxed a bit, like he was recalling a fond memory. "An old girlfriend," he said. "Evie. She begged me. So I said yes. And now the knucklehead stays on the North Shore, does some errands and jobs for me."

"What's his criminal background?"

"This and that. Burglary. Loansharking. Passing on TVs and computer equipment that fell off someone's truck."

"But anything violent?"

That caused another pause from Felix, and I could sense he was working behind those cold brown eyes.

"Once," he admitted. "He was set to go on an armored car heist, set up by a crew from Charlestown. In Charlestown, that's pretty much a local business, like a town that has a coal mine or paper mill. That and robbing banks. Their proud community heritage. Thing was, Rudy wasn't part of the crew. He was an add-on, because one of the other crew members got his skull beaten in at some tavern."

"Occupational hazard," I observed.

"Always," he said. "Anyway, they did this job in Connecticut. Went well for all concerned. Guards were tied up, weren't even shoved around much. Nice little chunk of change. But when it came time to divvy up the loot, Rudy ended up with the short end of the stick. There were three others in the crew. Ten percent was sliced off the top to pay tribute to whoever was in charge that month, before the Feds snagged him. Rudy was expecting the rest of the haul to be split four ways. But in the end, he only got ten grand."

"And ten thousand dollars wasn't a quarter of what was left?"

"Not even close. Rudy tried to sweet talk his way into getting a bigger cut, and the head of the crew basically told him that he should be happy with the ten grand. That Rudy was hired as a one-off, that he wasn't part of the regular crew, and that he should be grateful he was getting money instead of two in the back of the head."

"What do you think?"

"I think Rudy should have negotiated the payoff before the show commenced, but anyway, things escalated real quick. There was some fighting, some gunshots in the air, and it was only by the slimmest of all margins that Rudy and the other three walked away with most of their blood supply intact. And he told me something later."

"Like what? To ask you to help with the negotiating next time?"

"No," Felix said. "Rudy told me, 'Felix, the next time I'm next to a major score and I'm in a position to take it, I'm gonna take it. Period.'"

Outside, the sky was slowly becoming overcast, and a fog bank was slowly obscuring the Isles of Shoals.

"How long did he do that surveillance for you?"

"A week."

"Long enough to case out the rest of the neighborhood."

"Yeah."

"Long enough to see an old farmhouse there filled up with antiques, including gold coins, jewelry, some antique silver."

Felix didn't say anything, but he didn't have to. I knew what was going on in that mind of his. He was thinking through past information, scenarios, probabilities, possibilities, and courses of action.

"Your Rudy said he was there when he saw the car with Massachusetts license plates roar out of the house, nearly get into an accident because they were moving too fast. Maybe he recognized someone in the car. Maybe he thinks they just did a job at Maggie's, maybe she's in there, already bound up and helpless, maybe he could go in and get some leftovers."

Felix slowly nodded. "But Maggie's dead."

"You know Maggie. She certainly had a mouth on her, wasn't one to take crap from anybody. Rudy comes in right after Pepe and his crew depart, she screams at him to get the hell out, but he's committed. He's already been seen. And he has a chance to make a score . . . and doesn't let that chance slip away again."

The sky was really graying. The Isles of Shoals were gone, and I thought of people on those scraggly islands looking my way, thinking, *Boy, the mainland is gone.*

All a matter of perspective.

Felix looked at me. "You think like that when you were back at the Pentagon?"

"Tried to. Sometimes the higher-ups thought better, or ignored what I said, or pretended my section and I didn't exist."

"Too bad," he said. "Bet if they had listened to you, the Cold War would have been over sooner."

"But to what end? To have it start up again sooner, too?"

He grinned, got up, and checked his watch. "And that's you. Always looking at the dark side of things, instead of just accepting little victories where you can."

"And what are you looking for, then?"

"Who else? My junior partner in crime, Rudy Gennaro. I want to talk him, face-to-face, see what he might know."

"Will my name be brought up?"

"Why, do you want it to?"

"No, it's just that I've got enough people rattling around my house. I don't need anybody else angry at me."

Felix reached over, gently touched my chin, rotated it back and forth. "How does it feel?"

"Like a very big and mean man punched me."

"Well, I don't feel anything clicking around in there. Just bruises coming your way."

"Lucky me."

He made a sighing motion, like he had a big day ahead of him. "Lucky me, too. Besides looking for my silver, I'm going to be looking for your book as well."

"I didn't ask you to do that."

He gave me a gentle slap on the shoulder.

"You didn't have to."

CHAPTER SEVENTEEN

The rest of the day just dribbled on in a gray and stormy kind of way, matching my mood. The phone rang once and it turned out to be my new best friend from Albany, Dave Hudson, trying to talk to me about how little time it would take for him to come into my house and measure things and take photos. I just hung up on him. When the phone rang again I ignored it.

After a nap, I tried once again to find out the status of my tumor samples, to see if they had been discovered in their westward trek, and if so, had they been checked out. I went round and round on the phone with my doctor's office, and had three attempts with my insurance carrier. I managed to navigate the prompt system and actually end up with a human being, which seemed promising, but the human being didn't seem to have a basic grasp of the English language, and the phone connection between here and Wherever was full of static and cut in and out. The next time I called, the prompts took me somewhere else, and then there was a silence. No music. Not even static. Then a recorded voice came on: "This session has expired," and the call was disconnected. Sure.

The last call was more successful, but not by very much. After some more prompts and voice commands that didn't work, I ended up talking to a woman named Mindy with a Midwestern accent that at least I could understand, and after some give and take, she said, "I'm afraid our records here don't indicate that your tissue sample has arrived in San Diego."

"Look further," I said. "The sample was supposed to go to Boston. Not San Diego."

Tap-tap of computer keys. "Oh . . . I see. Yes. Well, it seems that your physician is the one who—"

"No," I said. "My doctor's office says that it was sent under some sort of program conducted by you, to supposedly save money. They insist that any answer has to come from your company."

Tap-tap-tap.

"Oh, here we go," she said cheerfully, and I felt a bare flicker of optimism.

"Yes, what do you have?"

"A tracer has been put on the package with your tissue sample. We should hear back within three to five business days."

Boy, what a fight to keep my voice level. "It's been more than a week."

"Perhaps," she said, "but you have to take into account the weekend, the past holiday, and—"

"I have taken that all into account," I said. "Perhaps you should take this into account. Where are you located?"

"Excuse me?"

"Where are you physically located? Not Manila, I'm sure, or Mumbai. You sound too American for that."

"Topeka."

"Topeka!" I said. "Well, that's just great. I'm here in the seacoast of New Hampshire, my tissue sample has been sent to San Diego when it should have gone to Boston, and I've got someone from Topeka allegedly trying to help me. We've got a real Continental Congress here, trying to find my sample."

"Mr. Cole, if I can explain—"

"I'm sorry," I said. "I'm not sure if any explanation out there is going to make a difference. Let's look at the facts. I still don't know whether or not my two tumors are benign or malignant. The samples that will answer this question should have gone to a testing lab in Boston. They did not. They were mistakenly sent to San Diego. But they haven't arrived there either. So I'm in limbo, waiting day after day, because your company can't do its job right."

"Mr. Cole—"

I was really on a tear now. "How does it feel, sitting in your comfortable cubicle, answering phones from across the country, knowing that the only thing you have to fear is tripping on a comfortable rug on the way to a coffee break, knowing you and your company are hurting people, every second, minute, and hour of the day?"

I took a breath and she dove right in. "Excuse me, Mr. Cole, excuse me," she said. "I'll tell you how it feels, sitting in this cubicle, day after day. It sucks. It really, really sucks. I shouldn't be here. I have a master's degree in education and I should be teaching, but our school district's budget got cut and I got fired. I should be working with my husband on our wheat farm, but that's about to go under for a variety of reasons you Easterners wouldn't even know or care about, so our family needs a steady paycheck and health insurance. You all think your food pops up magically in supermarkets, and you don't realize the hard work and sacrifice from a farmer class that doesn't—"

By now she was sobbing, and I whispered, "Sorry," and hung up the phone.

The rest of the day didn't improve much after that. I had a lunch of Campbell's finest and a defrosted frozen roll I had to drench with butter to make edible. The rain came in, a steady downpour that matched my mood, and I watched the water pelt my outside deck until I felt dopey and dozy and fell asleep on the couch.

My dinner date was Diane Woods, who brought over a meal she cooked at home, some sort of haddock dish baked over rice with a side of salad. She was very proud of it as she served it up. I took one bite and nearly choked, for it was as dry as dust, and tasted like lemon gone bad.

Her face was eager. "What do you think? C'mon, you can tell me."

"I can't believe you went to the trouble of making me dinner. That's very thoughtful of you."

She dug in and ate across from me at the kitchen counter. "Maybe it's the maternal side of me coming out."

"Really?"

Diane made a face. "Just because I don't want to play with what you boys have to offer doesn't mean I can't be maternal."

"Point noted," I said. "And I thank you for it."

She ate while I struggled for a few minutes. "I guess that's why I'm applying for the deputy chief's job," she said.

"Your maternal side?"

"Yep."

I chewed and chewed, hoping enough saliva would kick in so I could swallow. "Begging your forgiveness, mom, but I'm not seeing the correlation."

"I knew you wouldn't," she said, but her voice was light. "What happens in two months?"

Now I had an idea. "Kara Miles makes an honest woman of you."

"Attempts to make an honest woman," she said. "But when we're married I'm going to take it very seriously, including being her partner. For example, putting her under my health insurance."

"Considering what I've been going through," I said, "I hope the two of you have a better experience than I do. All right, Kara is under your insurance. And . . . hold on. You two are going to need extra income, right?"

She nodded. "Yep again. For a long time Kara held her own with her little software and web-development business. Hell, in one year, she actually took home more than I did. But, my friend, those days are gone."

"Hard to compete against free website designs and cheap software engineers on the other side of the globe."

She energetically took another bite and I wondered if her taste buds had gone dull. "That's right. And I intend to support her, and if that means becoming deputy chief, well, that's what I'm going to do."

"How about Captain Nickerson? Isn't she next in line for the deputy job?"

"She is, but I have a touch more experience and background. Not much, but maybe enough to tilt the scales in my favor."

I tried another bite, and chewed and chewed again. "The other day you told me that the deputy's job is to be the chief's bitch. You sure didn't pump it up when we last talked. In fact, if anything, you said you might apply just because you didn't want to be seen as weak."

"That's right."

"But now your maternal side is pushing you to go for the job, so you can take care of Kara."

"Right again."

"And if you get the job?"

She shrugged. "I'll make it work. What else can I do? At least our chief here in Tyler is secure, and I get along with him. Plus, for the most part, it's a Monday–Friday, eight A.M. to five P.M. kind of job. That sounds appealing. At least I'm not up in Porter. There's a deranged mob after their chief, and it ain't a pretty sight."

"What does Kara think?"

"Not good. She feels, well, put upon and guilty. Like she's failing me, failing the relationship. I told her that things could have easily been the reverse. Like when I got tuned up at the nuclear power plant demonstration last fall, I could have been permanently disabled. Then she'd have to take care of me. Fair is fair."

I struggled with another piece of the dry fish. When I thought Diane wasn't looking, I placed a paper napkin up to my mouth, slipped it out, and clenched the napkin in my fist, then lowered it and dropped it to the floor.

It didn't look like she noticed.

"What's going on with Maggie's homicide?"

"Well, she's still dead, so I guess that still might be news." She took another bite. "All right, that was snarky, sorry. The state police and Assistant Attorney General Martin are still running the case, keeping us poor locals out of it. But from what I hear, they've got nothing. They had evidence that a gang connected with drugs had been in her place of business at about the same time she got shot, but the opioid task force can't find the guys. They've scattered, gone underground."

"Like they know the police are after them?"

"Nope, like something even more terrible is after them, something scary and deadly."

Knowing the scary and deadly thing going after them, I tried to keep a bland expression on my face, which was difficult considering the circumstances and what I was attempting to eat.

"I see."

"And what's up with you, my friend?" She motioned to my living room and said, "Love the fact you've gotten your books put away, but there's something odd about it."

I glanced back and knew what she meant, with the covers all being color-coded and lumped together. But if I told her how that had happened, I'd have to mention the Greek brothers who came here and did the work, and explain how the Greek brothers came to arrive at my doorstep, and that would lead to Felix Tinios, and I didn't want to bring up his name.

"Yeah, you're right," I said. "But I just can't put my finger on it."

"Uh-huh. Okay, besides your impressive book collection, how's your health?"

"If Maggie's still dead, I'm still alive."

"Just because I was a snarky bitch doesn't mean you have to follow my lead."

"Apologies." I went into a detailed description of how I had been going around in circles, squares, and parallelograms, trying to get the location of my tumor samples and test results. I ended with my last call to Topeka, and how I felt guilty about it.

Diane's chin scar was practically glowing white, meaning she was seriously upset at something, and I was pretty sure it wasn't me.

"Why should you feel guilty about anything?"

"Because the woman from Topeka was having a rough time of it," I said. "And I think I made her cry."

"Screw Topeka and the woman sitting there," Diane snapped. "She's not sitting there in her smelly pajamas, drains coming out of her, waiting to hear whether she has the Big C or not. This world of ours would get along much better if everybody just did their goddamn jobs."

She stared at me like she was daring me to contradict her. I managed to swallow another dry piece of fish and asked, "You think my pajamas are smelly?"

Diane laughed so hard I thought wine was going to come out of her nose. "All right," I said. "Next time we eat here, I'll open the slider and get a bit of a cross-breeze. I'll even let you sit upwind because you're such a special gal."

Diane laughed again and said, "Hey, have things been quiet around here?"

With the visit of Pepe and Ramon, plus Felix, I don't think *quiet* was the best word to use, but I said, "Relatively so, I guess."

"No more sneaky visitors?"

Now I knew where she was going. "No, not for a few days. It's been quiet. No late-night visitors."

"Uh-huh."

"Diane, some guy was coming into my house at night. I'm sure of it."

"I'm sure you are."

"And I'm not some ditsy uncle that you say sympathizing words to when he claims the Nazis built a secret underground UFO base in Antarctica."

Her eyes got wide. "You mean there is?"

At the meal's conclusion, Diane had cleared off her plate and so had I, although I had a pile of crumpled-up napkins on the floor near me. She did the dishes and apologized for not bringing dessert—which I said wasn't a problem, especially considering what she had given me earlier (though I didn't say that part aloud). "How's Paula?" she asked, as she sat down next to me.

"Paula's at a journalism conference in Boston, trying to see if the Fourth Estate is dead, or really, really dead."

"I'll deny ever saying this, but I miss the time when we had a bunch of newspapers, all competing with each other. That meant nobody set the narrative, and if one newspaper got lazy or cocky, another paper could whack them upside the head, keep them on the straight and narrow."

"Me, too," I said.

"Besides the journalist Paula, how's the girlfriend Paula?"

"She's . . . she's pretty special."

"Good. Years ago, you had a chance with her, and you blew it, didn't you."

"Why are you blaming me?"

"What, you think I'm going to blame the woman in any relationship?"

"All right," I said. "It was my fault. I'm making amends. And what about you? How goes the wedding planning?"

That got me a big smile. "Going well, which is a nice break from things. Not sure of the location but I don't care, and Kara has some distant uncle who's a Unitarian minister who'll gladly marry us."

"You going to be wearing your cop uniform when you walk down the aisle?"

"Are you out of your bloody mind? I will not. No, the both of us are going to go girly-frilly and wear nice gowns—gowns we can reuse down the road. No use in dropping big bucks on a gown that you wear once and looks like it was designed by a deranged Paris designer drunk on absinthe. And you?"

"What about me?"

"You have a tuxedo?"

"I'll have one in plenty of time. I'm thinking a retro-1970s look, you know, powder blue for the pants and jacket, big ruffled shirt, bowtie the size of a drone's propeller."

Without a smile or a trace of laughter, Diane said, "You show up like that, and there'll be an accidental shooting in the parking lot, guaranteed."

"Okay, I get the message."

"You better."

Before she left, Diane made one more sweep of the kitchen, and I flushed with embarrassment when she picked up my three crumpled paper napkins with fish in them.

Diane tossed them into the air, caught them. "Lewis, if you don't like fish, tell me."

I stood still. "How did you know?"

"I'm a detective," she said. "It's my job to know."

Then she gave me a kiss on the cheek and asked, "Time to empty your drains?"

"I can do it myself."

"Not tonight, you can't."

Twenty minutes later, we were through and she eyed the notes. "Your output hasn't changed much."

"I know."

"But that's not good news, is it."

"Hardly," I said. "The fluid output should be below eight ounces, and then I get the tubes out and I stop looking like a costume contestant at a science-fiction convention."

She gently slapped me on the butt. "Especially one with smell-o-gram pajamas."

Later I was on the couch, trying to stretch out my dining with some home-made peanut butter and crackers—my never-fail recipe of Jif peanut butter and saltine crackers—when Paula called from Boston. "Last full night of the conference, and I'm ready to come home after tomorrow's sessions."

"I'm ready, too," I said.

"Because you miss me or because you miss my nursing talents?"

"All of the above," I said. "How's the state of journalism today?"

"More like a disease-ridden province than a state," Paula said. "But you know what? Being here is a lot of fun, hanging out with your peers and guys and gals who've been through the same shit you have. Being a reporter or editor, you see the same damn faces all the time, the same town officials, the same 'concerned citizens' who come up to you every week with their particular tales of woe. Which reminds me, never trust a man who wears sandals and socks."

"Where did you get that little bit of info?"

Paula giggled. "At lunch earlier. A bunch of us were talking about the 'concerned citizen' approach to life, and how they all had their particular cranks to turn, from alleged corruption to fluoride in the water. But there was one thing in common. The male part of the species always wore leather sandals with socks. So always watch out for them, and never trust them."

"Duly noted."

"Okay, time to head out and—oh, forgot to tell you. Mystery solved."

"You mean Pluto really is a planet?"

"No, silly boy, the mystery of the missing silver sludge at the *Tyler Chronicle*."

I had been pretty close to drifting off to sleep with Paula's pleasant voice in my ear, but now I was wide awake. "Go on," I said. "Who's been arrested?"

"Nobody," she said. "But the mystery is no longer a mystery."

"What happened, then?"

"What happened is that Rollie Grandmaison, our increasingly forgetful editor at the *Chronicle*, suddenly remembered what happened to the sludge. It hadn't disappeared a few days back, when I heard the break-in the night I was working late. It went out the door a couple of years back, when our sole photographer departed the scene."

"Did he leave on his own?"

"Yeah, if you call a layoff notice stuck in your pay envelope leaving on one's own," she said. "Anyway, he was the last of the old-fashioned characters, the guys who could go into a darkroom with a piece of crap film, work some magic, and come out with a stunning page-one shot. That was when our corporate masters decided that with the arrival of digital cameras, anyone could be a photographer." A little snort. "Like anyone with a portable PC could be a journalist."

"So he stole the sludge?"

"Not really," Paula said. "When he was leaving, he asked Rollie if he could take some of the old supplies, chemicals, papers, stuff the newspaper wouldn't be needing anymore. Poor Rollie—probably half in the tank from a Rotary Club lunch—he said sure, not realizing later that the silver sludge was included in the deal."

"Did Rollie try to get it back?"

"Hell no. That would have been too embarrassing. He didn't want to let corporate know what happened, so he left it at that. Whatever the sludge was worth made up for a lack of severance pay. The end."

"So what were the people doing in the basement of the *Chronicle* if there wasn't anything valuable down there?"

"Not my job, dear one. Talk to my rival, Diane Woods."

"She's not your rival."

"Glad to know that. Gotta go."

She hung up and I disconnected the phone. I ate one more peanut butter cracker, trying to make sense of what I had just heard.

And instead, I dozed off.

I woke up gradually, wondering why I had spent the night on the couch when a perfectly good bedroom was just upstairs. I checked the time and saw it wasn't even midnight yet, so I got up, washed my hands, and switched off the lights in the kitchen and the living room. In the semidarkness I stood there, tired but refreshed, thinking of the two very different women in my life, one my lover and the other a long-term friend, reporter and cop, practically opposites in so many ways. Some women.

Then the gunfire broke out.

CHAPTER EIGHTEEN

At first I thought the television was still on. But I saw the flashes of gunfire through my windows and dropped to the floor as best as I could. The shooting went on and on. I crawled across the room, keeping low, until I made it to the counter. I reached up and grabbed the phone. On my back, in the darkness, it was easy enough to see the glow-in-the-dark numerals, and I dialed nine-one-one.

It was picked up instantly. "Tyler police, what's your emergency?"

"There's gunfire in the parking lot of the Lafayette House, Atlantic Avenue."

"Do you know who's doing the shooting?"

"No."

"When did it start?"

"About ninety seconds ago."

"Is anybody injured?"

"I don't know."

"Who is this, please?"

"Lewis Cole."

The dispatcher must have recognized my name from my constant visits to the police station to see Diane Woods. "You all right?"

"I'm on the floor."

"Good," he said. "Stay there."

I clicked the phone off and rolled over. The gunfire had slowed down but was still going on. Party A and Party B, it seemed like. There had been a sudden outburst—somebody made a move, somebody made an insult or stepped on a shiny pair of shoes?—but now it was only a couple of rounds here and there. It seemed like Party A and Party B had retreated to their respective corners.

I started crawling to the door, reached up and gave the doorknob a twist, and then propped the door open with my right hand.

Sirens were sounding off in the distance. A couple more shots.

It seemed to be slowing down.

The sound of a *thunk* came just as the door vibrated against my hand. A bullet had come my way.

I lowered my hand and decided to follow the kind dispatcher's advice.

The sirens grew louder and louder, and it seemed that was that for the gunshots. I didn't hear any more snap, crackle, or pop. I stared up at the dark ceiling, which was quickly illuminated by the flashing blue lights of the police cruisers.

Stronger lights were eventually set up, and the sound of the sirens drifted away. It seemed safe enough to finally get up and see what was going on in my neighborhood.

I opened the door again and peered out. Lots of lights up there, lots of movement, lots of shapes carrying flashlights.

There was a lump of something on my driveway, about thirty feet away. I went deeper into the house, got my flashlight and my borrowed cane, and made my way out into the darkness.

Flashlights were bobbing up and down as cops started coming down my driveway. I went closer to the lump and switched on the flashlight.

A dead man was sprawled out on his back.

I moved the light around. He was in loose black pants, white T-shirt shredded and bloody, and open black leather jacket.

Unmoving, not breathing, and very dead.

Ramon.

The bigger half of the Pepe and Ramon Traveling Enforcement Show, and the man who had punched me in the jaw yesterday.

I'd like to say I felt sorry for the big guy, but I didn't. But I was still curious as to how he ended up here.

Up on the driveway a cop yelled, "Freeze, right there! Show your hands!"

I switched off the flashlight, dropped the cane, and then the evening got more interesting.

One and then two Tyler cops approached me, flashlights and pistols in hand. "Who are you? What are you doing here?"

"I'm Lewis Cole," I said. "I live in that house. I heard gunfire, came out to see what's going on."

One cop kept his flashlight on me, and the other flashed it on the ground. "Holy shit," the second cop said. "What's going on is a crap show. Do you have ID?"

"Back in the house."

The first cop said, "Hey, I know him. He's a friend of the detective sergeant. He's okay."

With that, I could feel the tension go away. I could have been standing there with a bloody axe in my hand and one cop saying to a brother cop "He's okay" meant I was okay.

Another question came my way. "Do you know this guy?" The first cop knelt down and checked the neck for a pulse. "Christ, this one is gone."

I sort of knew Ramon, but not enough to name him or give anything else up for the cops. "No, I don't."

"Mind going back into the house?"

"No—but would it be all right if I just stand on the steps?"

"Why?"

"I'm a magazine writer. I just like to see what's going on."

"All right," the first cop said. I couldn't tell anything much about them, except they were young, lean, and had close-cropped hair. "Just stay out of the way."

"I'll do that."

With some difficulty, I picked up the flashlight, switched it on. I was going for the cane when the near officer picked it up for me. "What happened to you?"

"Had a run-in with a couple of surgeons," I said.

"Who won?" he asked. "You or the surgeons?"

"Still don't know."

I ducked back into the house to get a jacket, then stood on the granite steps watching more and more lights show up, flashing so much up at the parking lot of the Lafayette House that it looked like a thunderstorm was coming through. Soon the blue lights were joined by some red lights from the fire department ambulances. More cops traipsed down my driveway and set up high-powered lights on tripods to illuminate Ramon's body. There were flashes as photographs were taken, and measurements were made, and I could make out voices from the parking lot. The harsh glare of lights from the television crew lit up.

Television. That meant something big had just happened, right here in Tyler Beach, and right here on my doorstep.

Cops started moving up and down my rugged driveway, and then one form separated itself from the line and came over.

"Detective Sergeant Woods," I said.

"Mr. Cole."

She joined me on the concrete steps. "What a mess," she said.

"You mean the dead guy over there?"

"No, there's more up at the parking lot."

"What happened?" I asked.

"Why don't you tell me what you saw or heard, and I'll try to fill in the blanks."

"Okay," I said. "About thirty-five minutes ago I was getting ready to go to bed—"

"Pretty late for you," she said.

"Certainly is," I said, "but I dozed some on the couch earlier."

"Very well," she said. "What happened thirty-five minutes ago?"

"Sounded like the O.K. Corral up there. Shooting broke out, pretty fast and plentiful, and then tapered off."

"How many shooters?"

"Four, maybe five."

"Then what?"

"I went to the door, opened it up, wanted to see what was going on."

"Pretty dumb," she said.

"Pretty me," I said.

More television lights were lit up, harshly illuminating my side of the parking lot.

"What did you see?"

"Muzzle flashes from up the way."

"Did you see that guy get dropped?"

"No."

"Anything else?"

I moved and aimed the flashlight to the lower half of my wooden door, noted the fresh scarring of wood.

"When your folks get around to it," I said. "There's a bullet in there. Random shot I guess."

"I'll be damned." She looked down as well and squatted, put a finger in the hole. "Feels like the slug's still there."

"A couple of feet lower, you'd be digging it out of my skull."

She twisted her finger into the door some more, then stood up. "All right, fair's fair. This is what we got up there, best we figure. Two sets of folks rolled in separate vehicles. One's a Mercedes, not sure about the other. Some sort of SUV. People got out, started chatting in the middle of the parking lot. The chatting grew louder. Then things got serious."

"Anybody else get hit besides my new friend over there?"

"Two other young gentlemen, struck in the legs and abdomen. As far as I know, they've both forgotten how to speak English."

Even more lights appeared. It looked like the parking lot up there had been turned into day. "Diane."

"Yeah."

"Not that I'm being critical or anything, but why are you here and not . . . you know, working?"

"I am working," she said. "I'm being support. See the really bright television lights up there? That's because Assistant Attorney General Martin has arrived with his state police unit, taking over this awful gang-land-type shooting as part of the ongoing opioid crisis. Blah-blah-blah, yadda-yadda-yadda."

Two bulky men in ill-cut suits were gingerly walking around the dead man, and I knew they were detectives from the state police.

"So besides chatting with me . . ."

"I'm not chatting with you," Diane said. "You're a witness, and I'm conducting a witness interview."

"Oh," I said. "My bad. Sorry."

"You heard the gunshots. You saw the muzzle flashes. You poked your head out and nearly got it blown off. Pretty fair description so far?"

"Very fair."

"Did you see that bulky guy over there come down your driveway?"

"No, I didn't."

"Hear any shouts, any voices? Anything else?"

"Nope."

"All right," she said. Over by the deceased Ramon, the state cops were taking photos and making measurements. "Lewis . . ."

I was hoping she wasn't going to press me, because I didn't want to be pressed, and I was relieved at what she said next.

"That hunk of man meat over there, any chance he was your mysterious visitor who's been coming in at night when you've been upstairs in bed?"

Good question, one I was very happy to answer.

"No, not a chance."

"Why are you so sure?"

"Hard to explain. When I heard the guy come into my place, he moved softly. Like he was barely disturbing anything. That big boy over there"—I pointed for emphasis—"would have sounded like a small tank going across the floorboards. I would have easily heard that."

Diane nodded. "Yeah. Wonder why, though, he ended up in your driveway. It was almost like he was coming down here for a reason."

I had been asking myself the same thing. "I don't know. Maybe he got scared, decided to run away, find a place to hide. Maybe he saw the lights on. Maybe he had already been shot and was looking for help."

"Maybe," she said. "But one thing's for certain. Somewhere out there a woman is sleeping, maybe that guy's wife, girlfriend, or mother. She's sleeping deeply, with no idea that the man she loves, the one she's either coupled with or raised as a little boy, is dead."

I could hear Diane take a breath. "And I'm not the one who's going to make the call tonight, to wake her up, to shatter her life. Not me. It's going to be somebody else, and at my age, and at this hour of the night, that's all right by me. I have no problem with that."

"I can see," I said.

Diane gently nudged me with her shoulder. "Hey, recovering patient, don't you think it's time to get back to bed?"

"Going to be hard, with all that noise and lights."

"Yeah, well, it's cold out here. Better to be inside and warm. Don't want you to catch cold. Or worse."

She gave me a quick embrace and I said, "This one should be relatively quick to get leads on, don't you think?"

"Maybe," I said. "The Lafayette House still has surveillance cameras on their front lawn and the parking lot, right? With the streetlights up there, the footage you might get from tollbooth cameras, it might be easy to get a trace."

"Dear me," Diane said. "I'll make sure to pass that along to the big bad state police detectives. Maybe you can get a shiny badge from them when this is over."

"Only if you put in a good word for me."

"As if."

Diane left and I stood for a while on my steps, feeling the coldness of the granite seep into my shoes. The glare from the television cameras had switched off, meaning that Assistant Attorney General Martin had finished his statements and left for the night.

Two men with a wheeled gurney came down the driveway, holding onto its sides as it rattled and shook over the rough ground. They were firefighter/EMTs from the Tyler Fire Department, and with the state police detectives looking on, they went to work. They undid the belts on the gurney, took off a flat object that they unfolded into a very familiar shape: a body bag. They unzipped it and got to work, clumsily maneuvering Ramon into the bag, securing his limbs, and zipping the bag shut.

The detectives took a step back, either out of respect or because they didn't want the body to fall on their feet when the EMTs picked it up. With a "one-two-heave," Ramon was picked up, strapped onto the gurney, and wheeled back up my lumpy driveway. I suppose this was the time to think grand philosophical thoughts about Life and Death and The Meaning of it All, but I wasn't in the mood.

I went for the door. "Sir! Sir! Can you hold on for a moment?" one of the detectives called out.

The two detectives came over and identified themselves, and I promptly forgot their names. "Can we ask you a few questions?"

"I talked to Detective Sergeant Woods just a few minutes ago," I said. "Doesn't that count?"

The larger of the detectives crisply said, "No. Now, your name, sir, and how long have you been living here?"

So I stood out there in the cold and gathering darkness—one by one, sets of red and blue lights from the parking lot started to wink out—answering their questions. At one point, one of them knelt down and gently pried the bullet from my door, slipping it into a little clear glassine bag. The questions went on until they didn't, and when the smaller of the detectives said, "I think we're through, Walter," I was pleased indeed.

Still, I had one question of my own to ask. "Detectives," I said. "With no disrespect, don't you think this should be a Tyler case?"

"Yeah, in a perfect world, it should," the larger detective said. "But the governor's gone ape over the opioid epidemic, and what she wants, the AG and the state police try to deliver. There was heroin found on this character that just went up the driveway, and in one of the cars that got shot up."

The smaller detective added, "It's a statewide crisis, and the state's gotta respond. Can't have a dozen jurisdictions squabbling over who did what and who gets what evidence. Besides, the OT is damn sweet."

His companion passed over a business card. "Just in case you think of anything else."

"Sure," I said, pocketing the card.

"Nice place you got here," the detective said. "Remote. Out of the way. Bet you got one hell of a view when the sun comes up. And you know what? That nasty white powder can reach anywhere, touch anyone. You have a good rest of the night."

The detectives turned and went back up the driveway, their flashlights bobbing along as they went up to the Lafayette House parking lot.

⌘

Back inside, I put the flashlight on the counter, shook off my jacket, and went into the kitchen to wash my hands and get a long swallow of orange juice. My poor house had a bullet wound on the front door. It still hadn't been put back together properly since the arson, and a couple of months ago, another bullet had gone through two of my bedroom windows.

I slapped an exposed beam as I made my way out of the kitchen.

"Jesus, sweetie, you've been one roughed-up gal over the years."

Out in the living room I switched off more lights, and I stopped.

Wood was creaking.

In an old house like mine, over the years you get used to the creaking of wood. It's like one's old bones and tendons, you know when they stretch and strain. So you know that this certain creak is from the stairs, that little moan is from the roof, and the little *tap-tap-taps* are the hot water pipes expanding when the oil furnace kicks on.

I didn't recognize what I was hearing.

I waited.

The creaking noise returned.

I slowly rotated as I stood in one spot, like one of those old-fashioned radar dishes, trying to pick up a ghost out there.

A ghost. How cheerful. A thought I never really wanted to consider much over the years, but considering this was once a lifeboat station, I'm sure a number of drowned or nearly-drowned seamen had spent their last moments under this roof.

More creaking.

I stopped moving my head. The noise was coming from outside. The rear deck.

I moved a hand forward in the near darkness, slid open a drawer by the telephone, took out my .32 Smith & Wesson semiautomatic pistol, clicked back the hammer.

No children in the house—I kept all of my weapons loaded.

I lowered my hand and limped back to the kitchen, taking my time.

Another creak, louder.

By the counter and cabinets was a set of light switches that I rarely use. One was a floodlight that lit up the entire narrow strip of rocks that was laughingly called my rear yard, and the other were two smaller lamps that illuminated my rear deck.

What the heck, I thought. *Let's go for it.*

I slapped them both on, stepped back, and nearly stumbled as a man came into view, standing right up against the sliding door, blood streaming down the side of his face, holding something in his right hand, aiming right at me.

CHAPTER NINETEEN

I dropped my cane and nearly dropped my pistol too, but I managed to bring it up in a two-handed stance, aiming right at my trespasser. "Freeze! Hold it right there!" I yelled.

The guy looked shocked and dropped what he had, lifted up his hands. We stared at each other through the glass. "Keep your hands up and stand still," I said.

He was in his late twenties or early thirties, wide-eyed and disheveled, his brown hair wet with blood. I stepped closer to the glass so he could hear me better.

"Who the hell are you?" I demanded.

He shook his head, mouthed the words "I can't hear you." I cursed the new energy-efficient glass doors and stepped closer. Even though I had told him to stand still, he did the same, and this time, he beat me to it.

"Are you Lewis Cole?" he asked.

Usually in the movies or books, this is when the hero says, "I'm the one asking the questions here!" But the guy looked so scared and dopey, and all I said was, "Yeah, I am."

"You're friends with Felix Tinios?"

"Yeah."

He nodded, attempted a smile. "I'm Rudy Gennaro. I work for Felix."

Well. He glanced around. "Hey, can I come in?" he asked. "There's a lot of cops running around out there, they're making me nervous."

"Step back a few steps," I said, and the bleeding young man did just that. I unlocked the door, took out the wooden stick, and slid the door open. A blast of salt air and cold came in, and he came in, hands still up, like this was a routine he was very familiar with. I traded outdoor illumination for indoor illumination by slapping some more light switches, and stepped back, keeping a good distance between us.

"You armed?" I asked.

"Shit, no, not with the record I got. That's a first-class ticket right back to the joint. Hey, can I lower my arms? They're getting tired."

On the deck he had looked deranged and dangerous, looking to break in and cause me harm, but inside, under the warm glow of my interior lights, he looked sad and a bit pathetic. It was like going to your high school reunion ten years later and seeing that the once-admired high school quarterback had gained twenty pounds and was now working as a greeter for Walmart.

I went around the kitchen counter, lowered the pistol, but made sure he saw me slip it into a pocket. "Okay, lower your hands, but I'm jumpy tonight, with all the shooting going on up at the parking lot. You stay over there and I'll stay over here. Okay?"

Rudy lowered his arms with relief. "Yeah, thanks."

I got some paper towels. I wet a bunch and kept another bunch dry, then passed them over to him. "Your head's bleeding pretty bad," I said. "You get caught up in that shooting up there?"

He wiped the blood away with the wet towel, winced. "Shit, no."

"You mean you weren't part of it?"

He wiped and wiped and most of the blood came away, and I saw an ugly gash on the left side of his forehead, just under his hairline. "Didn't you hear me earlier? No guns, don't even want to be near 'em. Nope, I was trying to sneak around that whole shit-show up there when I fell in your rocks. Damn nasty things, sharp and slippery."

"You think you're okay?"

"Yeah, yeah," he said. "I got dinged up in my scalp, and believe you me, those cuts bleed like a bastard. Won't kill you or nothin', but boy, it just won't stop bleeding." He dabbed and dabbed at the wound, and the helpful homeowner part of me wanted to grab my first aid kit—but later.

"All right," I said. "Then why are you here, at this time of the night?"

"I didn't plan it that way."

"What did you plan, Rudy?"

"Well, I wasn't sure at first, but you see, I heard Felix was looking for me, and I got scared. There's looking, and then there's . . . *looking*. One means kicking back and having some beers at a strip club in Salisbury, and the other means digging a hole in the ground and being told to step inside. You got it?"

"I got it."

"And I heard you were his friend, a magazine writer who lived in this remote cottage on the beach. That's you, right?"

"Right."

"And you being his friend and all, well, I hoped you could, what's that word? Inter . . . inter . . ."

"Intercede."

He nodded his head with pleasure. He might be bleeding out in a stranger's dining area, but at least the conversation was making progress.

"Not sure if I can do that, Rudy, when he gets into one of his moods. You know why he's looking for you?"

Rudy nodded. "He thinks I have something that belongs to him."

"Okay, and—hold on a moment."

I remembered what I saw, not more than two minutes ago, when he had first shown up at my place. I said, "Is it on the deck?"

Another nod.

"You sure?"

"Hell, yes, I'm sure. I brought it all the way down here, and then tried to walk across all those slippery fucking rocks, so yeah, I'm sure."

"Why did you drop it?"

His eyes glared at me. "Hey, you told me! You said, 'hands up,' and I saw you were pointing a piece at me, so I put my hands up. What else was I going to do?"

Sure, I thought. *What else could he have done?*

"Okay, Rudy, not that I don't trust you, but we've just met. I want you to slowly go out on my deck, retrieve what you were carrying, and bring it back inside. Hold it with one hand, no sudden moves. You got it?"

His eyes still glared at me. "Okay, but you better know this, Mr. Lewis Cole."

"What's that?"

"If it's broken, it's your fault."

It took less than a minute and he came in, carrying something a couple of feet long, covered in what looked to be bubble wrap and a black piece of cloth. He put it down on my kitchen counter and took two steps back without waiting for me to ask. I passed over a fresh collection of paper towels and he squeezed them against his forehead.

"Like I said, if it's broken, it's your fault."

I took my time removing the black cloth, which was just a torn T-shirt, and the bubble wrap. Sure enough, Felix's silver serving set came into view. I put it down on the counter on its four little legs and rubbed the tarnished silver, trying to make out the archaic Sicilian lettering on the surface.

"It doesn't look like much, does it," he said. "I was gonna get some silver polish and really give it a good scrub."

I winced. "Good thing you didn't. Silver this old and tarnished, if it's going to be cleaned, needs to be done by an expert. Using store-bought polish would ruin the value."

For a few seconds I was entranced with the feel and the look of the old ornate piece. Hard to believe that something made for some long dead and forgotten King of Sicily had now ended up at my home. The currents of history sure run wide, and often drop off the most unexpected pieces.

"How did you get it?"

Rudy got defensive. "Well, I think that's what you call, you know, trade secrets and—"

"You stole it from Maggie Branch's antiques shop, just up the road from where you were conducting surveillance on a house. Do tell me, Rudy, how did you end up stealing it?"

He looked confused and angry, and it was late and I was tired. I took out my .32 Smith & Wesson and said, "Rudy, do you really want to go sit on the couch over there and have a seat as I call Felix and have him come over? He'll be in a real rotten mood, no matter what. Or do you want to answer me and then get the hell out of here, while I turn this over to Felix?"

Rudy still wasn't saying anything, so I nudged him. "Was it before or after you saw that car race out with the Massachusetts license plates?"

His shoulders sagged. "After."

"How much longer?"

"I don't know. Maybe ten, fifteen minutes. Then I heard something."

"What was the something?"

"A woman screaming, and then a gunshot. Sounded like a shotgun."

"How can you tell?"

"Shit, you can tell. The sound, it echoes right in your chest."

"But you said you were in your car, watching. How did you hear a scream and the sound of a shotgun?"

He took the paper towel off, looked at the blood, put it back up against his forehead. "I was outside, taking a leak. Okay? That's the damn thing about watching a house you never see on the TV or the movies. At some point you gotta piss."

"All right," I said. "Did you see another car go up the driveway?"

"Nope."

"Just the scream and the shotgun."

"Yeah."

"No car anywhere?"

"Well . . ."

"Rudy."

"Well, when I was in the woods with my pecker out, there was this car that went by the driveway, slowed down, and kept on going. It might have pulled over a ways up. The woods there are thin. Easy to walk through if you need to."

By now things seemed calm enough that I put the .32 back into my pajama bottoms. "Okay. You're doing a surveillance, you just saw a car zip out, you're outside urinating, and you hear a scream and the shot."

"That's right."

"And then you decided to go over and check things out?"

"Yeah."

"Why?"

"Huh?" Rudy asked.

"You heard me. There you are, outside draining your bladder, you hear a woman scream and then a shotgun being fire. Most people would leave the area. Why didn't you do that?"

"Opportunity, man," Rudy said. "I mean, things like this, a shotgun going off, a woman screaming, it means something somewhere's gotten in trouble, there's a screwup, things are a mess."

"And you were going to swoop in and take advantage."

"Yeah, whatever. I could see the lights of the place from where I was pissing. So I went through the woods, went up to the barn next to the house, the lights on and bright and shit, and I poked my head in." He paused. "Now, with me giving up this silver without getting a dime, I wish I hadn't. It was a real bloody mess. I mean, I've seen shit over the years, I've done shit over the years, and blood don't bother me none. But I got there right after the old broad must have gotten shot. I could still smell the gunshot."

"What did you see?"

"What the hell do you think I saw?" Rudy said, grimacing either from the memory or the blood still trickling down his wrist. "The poor broad was dead. Practically falling out of her chair. Everything up from the chest . . . I gave it a quick look and that was that. Then I saw that piece of silver, resting right out on the open on her desk, and I grabbed that and got the hell out."

"Anything else?"

"Shit, besides her wet blood and brains still on the wall behind her?"

"Yeah, besides that."

Rudy wiped at the blood on his wrist. "Papers. There were papers all over the floor and a couple of cabinet drawers were open. Shit, I don't know what they were. I had the silver, ran out, happy I hadn't touched a goddamn thing besides that."

I picked up the silver plate, slowly moved it around, and put it back on the counter. "All right. Tell you what, I'll give Felix a call in the morning. Tell him that you were remorseful—"

"What's remorseful?"

"I'll tell him you were sorry for everything. I'll say that you couldn't find him or call him, and you did the next best thing, you left the silver with me."

"But I know where he lives. He might think that's a bullshit story."

"All right, I'll tell him that you—well, it was late. And you didn't want to disturb him. But you knew he and I were friends, so you thought of dropping it off with me, someone you could trust, and that you're still sorry about the whole thing."

"Fresh paper towel?"

"Sure." I moved back into the kitchen—still facing him, for even though we were doing all right, I didn't want to turn my back to him—and I tore off another few sheets of towel.

He bunched up the dry sheets against the sodden ones. "Sounds okay. I'm just worried he's still going to come after me and tune me up."

"I'll take care of that."

"How?"

"I'll ask him not to hurt you."

"C'mon, for real, how can you take care of me?"

"I just told you," I said. "I'll ask him not to hurt you, and he won't."

"The hell you say."

"I just said it twice, so let's leave it at that, all right?"

"Okay but . . . what do you have on him? Some photos? An affidavit hidden somewhere? You got a brother who's a cop or FBI agent or something? What's the deal?"

"The deal is friendship, Rudy."

He snorted at that. "You don't say. Then I'm glad I got what I got with him, which is pretty much lined out straight. Boss and worker. You say you're friends? Okay, but you're like one of those survivors on a zombie show, you decide to keep some decaying zombie as a friend and pet. That zombie will leave you alone at first, but one of these days, when you least expect it, that bastard will turn around and rip out your guts and eat 'em in front of you."

"That's some analogy."

"Some what?"

"Forget it," I said. I picked up the silver plate on its four tiny legs, slid open a nearly empty drawer, and put it in, closed the drawer. "I think we're through here. You all set?"

"Yep."

"All right."

I started out of my kitchen and Rudy stood still. "Where are you going?" he asked.

"To the front door," I said. "You can walk up my driveway and you'll be all set."

Rudy shook his head. "Christ, no. There's a lot of cops still up there." He went to the sliding glass door and opened it up. "That's how I came in, and that's how I'm going out. Later, bud."

He closed the door, and that was that. I spent a few minutes cleaning up, locking the door, putting the wooden stick back in, and then went upstairs. I had to pause halfway up.

I was so terribly tired, and my back and shoulders ached.

"Just a few more steps," I whispered, leaning into the cane. "Just a few steps more."

I pushed myself off and got into my bedroom. Rudy was right. There were still lights up there, and two cruisers still had their blue strobes flashing. I dropped the cane to the floor and dropped myself onto the bed.

Even with the blue strobes reflecting off the flat white of my ceiling, I fell asleep right away.

It seemed like just five minutes had passed before my phone rang. I rolled over like a beached dolphin and grabbed the phone. It was 8:05 A.M.

"Yeah."

"This definitely isn't the charming and happy Lewis Cole I'm used to," she said.

I yawned. "Dear me, Detective Sergeant Woods, do you know what time it is?"

"I do," she said. "And I bet I woke you up."

"You did."

"Tough," she said. "I haven't gone to bed yet, but it's about twenty minutes in my future, and I wanted to let you know about the little O.K. Corral reenactment that took place on your doorstep last night."

"Please do."

"The large gentleman found in your front yard was a Ramon Martinez, from Lawrence, Massachusetts. We also have two seriously wounded at Exonia Hospital, one Raul Gortez and Santiago Garcia, from Lowell. Plus we have one stolen Mercedes-Benz sedan with enough bullet holes to give passengers a nice shower if it were to rain. Other than that, lots of questions."

"Any idea what triggered the gun fight?"

"Hah-hah-hah," she said in a monotone. "You made a funny with a pun. Well, our friends in the Massachusetts State Police have told us that the guys from Lowell and the guys from Lawrence belonged to rival social organizations. It seems like they had a meet over at the Lafayette House parking lot last night when a disagreement broke out—along with the gunfire."

"Over the chess club results, I'm sure," I said. "Anything from the surveillance cameras from the Lafayette House?"

"If there is, the New Hampshire staties aren't saying," she said. "Usually we get along just fine with the boys and girls from Manchester, but now—just a lot going on. By the by . . ."

"Yes?"

"I'm still puzzling over young Ramon going to your house. Doesn't quite make sense. Lots of nice places to hide in among all those rocks and boulders."

"Maybe he panicked with all the shooting going on."

"Or maybe he was coming for you. Or for something you have. You ever think of that?"

"I'm trying not to."

"You have anything to tell me?"

What could I tell her? That Ramon and his boss Pepe were here earlier, about Felix's missing silver, which was no longer missing, but was in one of my kitchen drawers?

"Not a word."

She laughed. "Good. Time for this old broad to get some sleep."

"Time for this old man to do the same."

Just as I was falling back asleep and the whispers of dreams started to make themselves known, the phone rang once more. I fumbled some and a young woman's voice said, "Mr. Cole?"

"That's me."

"This is Mia Harrison calling. The niece of Gwen Aubrey?"

Two unfamiliar names and I was rubbing my face when—"Oh, yes," I said. "I wasn't paying attention. Sorry about that."

"Me, too. Did I wake you?"

I yawned. "Not really. Please, go on."

"Oh, well, you remember the last time we visited? My Aunt Gwen said she knew a man who had served for a while at your house? When it was a training facility for the Navy and its corpsmen?"

My mind was clearing, like mist lifting off a sodden farmer's field. "That's right, that's right."

"Well, we can come by this afternoon. Would that be all right? Do you have the time?"

"Time is what I've got a lot of," I said. "What time?"

"How does three P.M. sound?"

"Perfect."

Then I said, "There was a shoot-out in the parking lot of the Lafayette House last night. Did you hear about it?"

"No, I didn't. What happened?"

"It seems like rival drug gangs from Massachusetts had a disagreement. Lots of shooting. One dead. Two wounded."

"Good," she said.

"Good?"

"Sure," she said, sounding cheerful. "That means investigators, reporters, nosy people stopping by . . . and more customers for the restaurant. See you later, Mr. Cole."

I hung up the phone, checked the clock. Still plenty of time to catch up on my sleep. My drains would need to be emptied, but I could gamble. I settled myself in, brought the blankets up, and stared out the window, imagining all the ghosts and people who had been in this little house of mine, and how many of them had seen this exact stretch of ocean.

My eyes closed, my breathing slowed, and the whispers of dreams out there on the horizon began, and the phone rang once more.

∞

I was getting the feeling that the gods of slumber had something against me, so I was a bit grumpy answering the phone for the third time, and I got a laughing voice in return that made me warm right from the start.

"Tsk, tsk," Paula Quinn said. "Here I am, on the last day of my conference, feeling all jazzed up and frisky, and wanting to know if you were up for a visit after I get to work and straighten things out."

"Always up for a visit," I said. "How are you?"

"Fine," she said. "Question is, what the hell happened in your neighborhood last night? One of my interns said there was a gun battle in the Lafayette House parking lot."

I gave her what info I could, secretly quite pleased that she didn't ask to quote me as a witness.

I didn't feel much like a witness. Only a guy who happened to be around.

When we got through that piece of journalism, I asked her about the conference.

"A newspaper conference like this, it's like a meeting of survivors from some sunken ship, making plans to go out on another cruise. Sounds silly but what else can you do?"

"Lots of possibilities," I said. "None of which I should probably mention."

"Probably," Paula said. "You hear anything from your doctor? About the tumor results?"

"Nary a word," I said. "It sounds like my tissue samples are touring the finest post offices in California."

"Damn."

"Double damn," I said.

She sighed. "Look, I know I said earlier I'd be coming by for a visit, but I'm torn."

"How?"

"Besides making sure the folks at the *Chronicle* get this story right and don't print a headline upside down, there's other stuff. Got a bunch of laundry to do, mail to check when I get back to Tyler, need to talk to the condo manager about a rattling pipe . . . I was thinking of visiting you tomorrow. Is that all right?"

Maybe it was because I was still short on sleep, or feeling strained because of the events of last night, but I paused.

Paula caught on my pause. "All right, sunshine, I'll be around later tonight. As a surprise. How does that sound?"

"Sounds great," I said. "Thanks."

And with that, I hung up the phone, rolled over, and actually managed to get to sleep, realizing only some hours later that what I had just done—having Paula come over—was going to prove to be a horrible mistake.

CHAPTER TWENTY

I slept until midmorning, when it was my turn to make a phone call. I dialed Felix twice, at his home number and his cell phone. Each time he wasn't there, and each time I said the same thing: "Felix, I have a present for you, from the home country. Call me when you can. It'll be a hell of a story. And don't pick on Rudy Gennaro anymore."

Then I checked the output from my tubes—about the same, damn it once more—did some laundry, had a late breakfast or early lunch, dozed some more. Realizing I was expecting company in the afternoon, I did my best to straighten up the place before a much-needed early-afternoon nap.

At exactly three P.M., there was a knock on the door, and my little house suddenly seemed to be filled with people.

First in was Mia Harrison, followed by her loud and brash Aunt Gwen Aubrey, and then a very slim older man with light tan pants belted up just below his breastbone. He was introduced to me as Bobby Turcotte, and when we shook hands I immediately noticed the old, faded tattoos on his wrinkled forearms, one of a mermaid and the other with faded U.S.N. and an anchor. It made me wonder if he ever thought those bright and powerful tattoos would fade away, along with his strength and perhaps his memory. Even at his age his white hair was thick, combed back in a pompadour, and behind his wire-rimmed eyeglasses, his eyes were twinkling.

"My God, my word, I never, ever, thought I'd be back in here again. Wow! Who would have thought."

My visitors situated themselves on the couch and a chair, and I moved a chair around so we could hear each other easily. I gave them all glasses of lemonade, with a shot of gin in Aunt Gwen's glass. Mr. Turcotte (I couldn't call a man of his age and experience Bobby) took a healthy sip and started talking. "So? Gwennie tells me you're looking for info about this joint when it was a barracks back when we was doing medic training?"

"That's right," I said. "What was it like?"

He laughed, took another sip. "Don't ask me what year it was . . . must have been the last year of the Korean War, 'cause I remember getting discharged soon after. For the second time, you know."

"What do you mean?" I asked.

Turcotte's voice laughed and quaked at the same time. "Oh, I was in the Pacific for the first go-around, you know? Was at Leyte Gulf, invasion of Okinawa. Medical orderly aboard one of the support ships. Jesus Freakin' Christ, you wouldn't believe what those poor Marines looked like, coming aboard, bandages and wraps, most of them dopey 'cause of the morphine they got, sweet Jesus. The burns, the shrapnel wounds, the missing arms and legs . . . Christ. I remember one corporal, we started undoing a big bloody bandage around his belly, and shit, his intestines just oozed out on the deck."

Gwen patted him on his thin leg. "Now, now, Bobby, we appreciate your service and all, but how about telling us what it was like, being in this cottage back in the day, back when Elvis was just about ready to get famous?"

Mia looked like she was going to get sick, but Turcotte giggled and leaned into Gwen. "Hell, Gwen, I still appreciate all the good times you and I shared back in the day. Christ, you still look good. Me, I'm a thin and old wreck, but God, you sure kept yourself together."

"Well, it sure as hell wasn't from clean living," Gwen said, and the two of them laughed.

Turcotte looked around my home. "Jesus, this place, it looks a lot different, but a bit familiar, you know? I mean, that deck wasn't there, but the view, that's the same. And back then, this room seemed much bigger. We had a hi-fi system over there, lots of chairs and couches. No books, though. Upstairs were the bunks. And the cellar—oh yeah, the cellar . . ." Turcotte started laughing again.

"What about the cellar?" I asked.

He stopped and looked to Gwen, Mia, and me. "Oh, hell, enough time's passed. It's not like the Navy's gonna worry about it, right, Gwen? And the girls, hell, they're grown up, have kids. I hope they have fond memories. Lord knows, I still do."

Gwen patted his leg again. "Bobby, come along now, get to the point. Mr. Cole lives here now, and he's curious about what it was like back in the day."

Turcotte smiled but he wasn't laughing, and it was like a bit of coolness was running through his veins. He gave off a rattling sigh and settled back in the couch. "You folks, you still don't know the whole story, you know? Nobody knows. The movies, the books, the documentaries, it's like all you've got is a bunch of puzzle pieces on the floor, and you pick up a bunch and try to get the whole picture. You know? You might get the general view of what's what, but there's a lot of pieces, a lot of stories still missing."

"Like what?" I asked.

Turcotte smiled, wiped at his lips. "Those of us who made it during the Pacific, we cheered when the A-bombs got dropped, you know? There was no debate, no shit talk about morality, about hitting those two cities. War and morality? Please. Shit, we had already turned Tokyo and its residents into cinders. All we knew was that we were going to live. We weren't going to get wounded, shot, burnt, or have our balls blown off trying to invade the Home Islands. The war ended and I came back here to Tyler. I started lobstering again, dumped my uniform in a trunk, and the nightmares faded away. Then those shit-ass North Koreans started a war in '50." A pause. "Assholes. You know why? Because just when we were settling back into civilian life, lots of us were being called up again. To go back to our old duty. And most of us . . . shit, earlier, we didn't mind going out to the

Pacific. It was our job. Our duty. Goddamn Japs had started it. But Korea? Shit, who cares about Korea? But some of us lucked out. The ones that came here. Hah."

Mia and Gwen were quiet, so I stepped in. "How did you luck out?"

He grinned. "Me and the other fellas, we had been around. We knew the Navy, knew how their minds worked. And we played the system. And why not? All of us were vets, and we weren't so eager to go back to sea, or to that frozen Korea place, fight the freakin' Chinese. Nope. So our job was to delay, delay, delay. And that's what we did. Ask for training, take leave time, get sick here and there, do this, do that . . . and before you know it, we was here, getting trained on stuff we already knew. Oh, damn, it was sweet duty."

"How sweet?" I asked.

He laughed again. "Real damn sweet. In fact, by the time we got here, the fighting had died down, the armistice talks were going on. Most of us stopped going to class over at the old artillery station. Stayed here, got drunk, got suntanned, had lots and lots of parties. And the cellar . . ."

The second time he had mentioned the cellar. "And what was in the cellar?"

"You don't know?"

"Only thing down there is dirt and an oil furnace."

"Well, there was no oil furnace back then," he said, grinning. "But the dirt was there, a good place to sop up the drinks and piss and vomit when things got out of hand. A bar in the corner that served all the time, day and night. And once the little girls in the area knew what was going on here, man, it was pure pleasure."

Mia's face flushed, and I remembered what her aunt had said earlier: Each generation thinks they invented sex, drugs, and drink, and each generation is wrong.

"What did you give them, then?" I asked.

"Mmm," he said. "You know."

I smiled at him, trying to put him at some sort of ease. "I think I know, but why don't you tell me?"

"Uh, the usual," Turcotte said, glancing a bit nervously at Mia and her aunt. "Most of those girls had never tasted beer before. Rum. The trick with the rum and Coke was to put just enough rum in the Coke to give the sweetie a nice little buzz, but not enough so she could taste it."

"Other things, too?" I asked. "Marijuana, maybe? Other stuff?"

He grinned shyly, nodded his head. "It was party central back then. I mean, most of us, we skipped classes—with the war over, what were they going to do, send us to Korea? Even the instructors let up on us. We had rock and roll on the hi-fi, a barbecue pit out back, dancing, drinking, smoking, lots of fun stuff."

Mia still looked one part horrified, one part amused. I'm sure her generation was like my generation, thinking they had invented it all, had sampled it all, and for the very first time in human history.

"But didn't—I mean, didn't you have inspections every now and then?" I asked.

"Sure, but I mean, c'mon. Most of the officers were in the reserves, just like us. And they weren't going to go out of their way to give us shit. I mean, there were a couple of hard cases, but we always got tipped off that they were coming. Hell, we never got caught."

Turcotte swiveled on the couch. "Hey, Gwen, how come I never saw you stop by? You were a fine piece back in the day."

She gave him a not-so-gentle slap to the leg. "I'll have you know that many men still consider me fine, no matter what day it is."

Turcotte grinned but wouldn't let it go. "Still, you would have learned a lot back then, right here. Gotten a real fine education."

Gwen smiled sweetly, put her hand on his upper leg, and leaned in. "Bobby Turcotte, if you don't turn around and answer Mr. Cole's questions, straight and true, then Mia and I are going to trot up that driveway and leave you behind, and then you'll be late going back to your room and tapioca pudding. So what's it going to be?"

His red face turned even redder. "Ah, just joshing around, Gwen, that's all. You don't need to take offense. Okay. What else do you want to know, Mr. Cole?"

"When did all this happy time end?"

"Well, it happened around August of that year, when things were really hopping. Seems like this cop—can't remember what town he was from—"

"North Tyler," I said.

"Yeah, that's right, North Tyler. Well, he heard his niece was sampling the fun times down here. Betty, Bambi, something like that. Jesus. She had this flaming red hair, light freckles. She had hooked up with this big sailor, a guy named Mahoney—"

Gwen interrupted. "Focus, Bobby, focus."

"Oh, yeah. Well, this North Tyler cop tries to come down and pick up his niece, and all hell broke loose. Okay, she told us she was eighteen, how were we to know otherwise? Am I right? So this cop was on a one-way suicide mission, trying to get his niece out, and a bunch of us tuned him up and tossed him into the Atlantic Ocean."

Mia spoke for the first time. "Were you one of those who tuned him up?"

The smile was still on his face. "Long time ago, lady."

"You must have known it wouldn't stop there."

"Shit, what did we know? We were all young, strong, drunk, high, or strung out. We didn't care. But I did luck out when the shit came down."

"And how was that?" I asked.

"I was out on a beer run. I was the only one who had a car. Not like today, when every kid gets a car on their sixteenth birthday, the spoiled brats. I drove down to Bubba's in Falconer, stocked up on a few cases, and when I came back here . . . Christ, what a show was going on."

"What kind of show?" I asked.

"State cops, cops from Tyler and North Tyler, even the goddamn shore patrol. I drove into the parking lot up there, it was dirt at the time, and when I saw all those cars and some of my buds being led away in chains and handcuffs, well, shit, I turned around, dumped that beer, and went to the hospital in Exonia, all spiffed up and ready for afternoon class. Hah!"

"You didn't get into trouble?" Gwen asked.

"Oh, a bit, but nothing they could prove. Besides, the whole mess was an embarrassment to the Navy and the town, and it was in everybody's interest to keep things quiet. So that's what happened. I hung out at a boarding house in Exonia for a few weeks, went to class a few times, and then diddled around until I was discharged. Maybe a week or so later I came by to see what was what, and the place was clean. I mean, clean. Everything had been pulled out, stripped. All the furniture was gone, even the hi-fi, which was a pretty piece of equipment. You know, I looked around, to see if any of my gear was there, but nope. But one place I didn't look was the cellar. You sure the bar down there is gone?"

"It sure is," I said.

"Mmm," he murmured. "Lots of fun memories about that cellar. You sure I can't go down there for a peek?"

"There's nothing down there except dirt and a furnace."

He grinned. "That's how we got the girls down there. 'Come see our special party room.' Hah. Hey, can I ask you a question?"

"Sure."

"How did you end up living here? I mean, it's always been government owned."

"The government gave it to me a few years back."

"Shit, for real?"

"Shit, for real."

Gwen nudged him with an elbow. "You got anything else to say to Mr. Cole?"

"No, but—"

"But what?"

"Damn it, Gwen, why in hell didn't you stop by back then? We would have had a good time, you and I. Honest to God."

Gwen got up, and she and Mia assisted Turcotte to his feet. "I may have been wild, but I was smart. Come along, Bobby, you don't want to miss tapioca pudding night."

We got outside, Turcotte leaning onto Mia's grasp, and Gwen asked me, "How are you feeling?"

"Tired," I said. "Always tired."

She touched my cheek. "Hell of a thing, isn't it. You grow older, and older, and friends and family start dropping off, and there you are. Death is just God's sniper, one of my ex-husbands told me. Just don't ask me which one."

Gwen gestured at Turcotte, slowly going up my rugged driveway. "I know this wasn't your plan, but it was good to get Bobby out, let him come back here, let him be a hell-raising young corpsman again for just a while. That was a good thing."

"It was an accident on my part," I said.

"It was still a good thing."

She kissed my cheek. "Ah, if only you were a couple decades older . . ."

"Stick around," I said. "I plan to get there eventually."

Gwen laughed. "But that's a goddamn race I'll never win."

Back inside the place seemed empty without my visitors. I imagined the ghosts of the past enjoyed the little visit from Bobby Turcotte. I sat down on the couch, slowly oozed over, and slept and slept until knocking on the door woke me up.

I rolled off, yawning, the cane with the ugly wolf's head falling to the floor. "Hold on, hold on!" I yelled out, stumbling up, grabbing my cane, and lumbering over to the door.

On the other side, looking big, well-dressed, and very professional, were the two state police detectives from last night.

I squinted from the sunlight. "Have you guys gotten any sleep yet?"

One said to the other, "Steve, you get any sleep?"

"Frank, if I did, I'm not telling," he said. "Sorry to disturb you, Mr. Cole, but we're just wondering if you've thought of anything else since last night's events."

"Not a thing," I said.

"Are you sure?"

"Very sure."

A photograph of a dead Ramon was produced. "Do you know this man?"

I made a point of giving it a good look. "I do not."

"Are you sure?" the other detective asked. "Are you sure you don't know him, that he wasn't coming to see you for a reason?"

"I still don't know him, and if there was a reason, I would bet that he was trying to get away from all of the shooting in the parking lot and didn't make it."

Frank looked to Steve, who looked back, and the photo went away.

I asked, "How goes the investigation?"

"It's going," Steve said. "Trouble is, nobody wants to talk."

Frank corrected him. "Not true. Some people want to talk. It's just the wrong people."

I yawned again. "But it seemed like there were two groups of guys up there, two gangs, shooting it out."

"Maybe," Steve said. "Or maybe it was one gang, splitting apart under the pressure, deciding to settle things on neutral territory, and then bam, the shooting starts and the Germans take Slovakia."

"Huh?" Frank was confused.

"Nice analogy," I said.

Steve said, "See, Frank? See? There are some smart people out there in the world. I just happen to not be working with one. Mr. Cole, you still have our business cards, correct?"

"Correct."

"Then we'll leave you be," Steve said. "But if you think of anything, or see anything, do give us a call."

"I will."

"And us, well, we'll keep on digging."

"And digging," his partner said.

And back to sleep I went, though I didn't have enough energy to get back to bed. The couch again.

When I woke up it was dark outside. I felt troubled. I dozed some, woke up, wondered about things.

If it was already dark, Paula should be here. I moved around on the couch. She'll get here, I thought. She'll get here.

Digging, I thought. Those poor detectives, digging. Looking. Searching. Like . . .

Like the killers of Maggie Tyler Branch. They apparently didn't take anything from her antiques shop. Certainly hadn't taken Felix's antique silver service.

Like the crew who had broken into the *Tyler Chronicle* and had torn apart the cellar. They hadn't stolen the silver sludge that everyone assumed had gone missing due to theft. Nope.

In each case it had been—papers. Old files. Back issues of newspapers. Information.

The crew had been looking for information?

And Maggie's voice came back to me, pointing to her old wooden filing cabinets:

In there are old documents, papers, invoices, receipts, and such concerning the history of the Tyler family, the history of the town and its famous buildings . . .

"Famous buildings," I whispered into the darkness. "Like the one I'm living in."

It was there. Almost there.

And I remembered my incessant visitors from Albany, who kept on wanting to come into my house, again and again.

For photographs? For history? For something else?

Dave Hudson's voice came to me as well:

The basics of your house, the foundation of your house, it's remained the same . . .

It certainly has, I thought. Even with the fire, the extensive repairs, the earlier reconstruction. The basics had stayed the same.

I got off the couch with my cane, switched on some lights, grabbed a flashlight, and then went to the cellar.

CHAPTER TWENTY-ONE

switched on the light and slowly descended, one step at a time. At the bottom I had to sit on a step to catch my breath. I switched on the flashlight and examined the place.

Not much to look at, to be honest.

The floor was hard-packed dirt. In one corner was a small oil furnace and small oil tank that warmed the water for the radiator system that kept both floors heated. The foundation was old stone, carefully assembled and cemented in the old style from the mid-1800s. One old historian told me years ago that these types of foundations are rare. The masons back then took pride in their work, making sure every piece fit right and was level. Definitely not like today, when the goal isn't doing it right, but doing it by next Thursday. I let the light move across the cellar, checking the stonework and the dirt. A couple of years ago, in a fit of energy and idealism, I had used a spoon and an old colander to dig some in the dirt down here, looking for archaeological artifacts from my predecessors. But I had come up with exactly nothing. Just dirt.

I closed my eyes, thought about Bobby Turcotte and his merry band of naval corpsmen, setting up a bar down here. Why in the cellar? Why not upstairs in the light and openness? Because it was easy to hide. It was easy to be out of sight, out of the way. To bring down giggling young girls, some of them just teenagers, to show them the world of the adults.

Booze, of course. Marijuana, definitely. And—other things, as well. Turcotte had said that. Other things as well.

I opened my eyes, heaved my way off the step, and with cane in one hand and flashlight in the other, I went up to the stone foundation. Started looking, examining, feeling foolish that this was the first time I had given this cellar—it was just a cellar, after all!—such a close examination.

The stone foundation went up to about head high, and then thick beams of wood called sills were on top, which supported the rest of the house. I moved along, moved along, and—

Came to a place where there was more than just a sill.

There was a length of dark wood, almost like a plank, that was nailed to the sill. The color of the wood neatly matched the sill. No wonder I had never noticed it before.

I leaned on my cane, breathing hard, feeling that pressure on my back that told me I really, really should empty my drains before I made a mess.

But it could wait.

It would have to wait.

I ran my fingers across the plank.

It was definitely out of place, definitely didn't belong. So what was it doing here?

I set the flashlight on top of the oil furnace so it was illuminating the part of the sill were the plank was located, and limped back.

I put my fingers under the plank, gave it a good tug.

Nothing moved.

Of course.

I tried again, grunting and groaning.

Nope.

Upstairs in one of the closets was a toolbox, with screwdrivers, hammers, wrenches, and a pry bar. All I had to do was to go back upstairs, grab the necessary tools, and come back down.

Right.

But I was a dumb and impatient man. I grabbed the cane from Felix's uncle and managed to shove the tip of the cane underneath a small gap in the wood. I pressed, pressed, and there was squeaking as some nails started to let loose.

"Almost there," I whispered.

I pushed in again and used the cane as a pry bar, hoping the spirit of Felix's uncle would forgive me.

The wood came apart a couple of inches. I moved the cane down, and repeated the process two more times.

Now I had a good grip. I reached in, tugged up, tugged up hard, and with one ungodly screech, the plank came free. I felt cold air on my face, and wondered how much of an opening I had just discovered. I limped back to the furnace, grabbed the flashlight, and then went back and peered inside.

Lots of stuff was piled back there.

For some reason I recalled the discovery of King Tut's tomb. When Howard Carter opened the tomb and thrust a candle inside, he was asked, "Can you see anything?" "Yes," Carter responded. "Wonderful things."

Me?

I saw things. None particularly wonderful.

I carefully reached in and pulled out one, two, and three bottles of Four Roses bourbon. Then some rusted cans of Pabst Blue Ribbon and Narragansett Ale. Soggy cartons of Lucky Strike cigarettes. A plastic-wrapped package of what the police would have probably called "green leafy matter" at the time.

I carefully placed everything on the dirt floor. Turned back to the opening.

There were three other soggy cardboard boxes back there, almost falling apart in my hand as I slowly pulled them out.

There was official lettering on the covers. I opened one soggy cover and saw little yellow cardboard boxes, nestled in rows, scores of them, each about the size of a small travel toothpaste box.

I flipped one open with my thumb, holding the flashlight in my other hand. A little glass ampule with a needle came out.

A morphine syrette. Made to be used on a battlefield by a corpsman or a medic, or even a wounded soldier or marine. Break the tip by tugging on a little wire, insert the needle under the skin at a certain angle, and squeeze, and the person in question in terrible pain will get some relief.

Morphine.

Opioid.

Lots and lots of it.

All piled up in my house, undisturbed from one century to the next, until now.

From upstairs I heard my front door open, and the familiar voice of Paula Quinn calling out.

"Lewis? You here?"

"Be right up," I said. "You won't believe what I've found."

I stuffed one of the cardboard packages in my pocket, and then gimped upstairs, feeling full of energy and vigor. Now it all made sense.

Finally.

The search hadn't been for silver.

It had been for this old stockpile of opioids.

At the top of the stairs I bore right, and Paula was standing in my open doorway, not looking very happy to see me.

"Hey, it's okay," I said. "I don't mind you being late."

Her face . . .

Then she was shoved into my house, nearly stumbling.

Dave Hudson came in, face set, eyes hard. "Then I hope you don't mind we're late, as well," he said.

He was followed by his wife, Marjorie.

Who was holding a shotgun aimed at Paula's head.

CHAPTER TWENTY-TWO

I said very carefully and plainly, "Let her go. It's just us. Not her."

With bitterness in his voice, Dave said, "Oh, now you're friendly, now you're open for reason. Too late now, fool. We could have done this easy, we could have done this in a friendly manner. You could have stayed up here with Marjorie while I went in the cellar and quickly did what had to be done, but no, you had to be a stubborn, arrogant prick. Well, now you're going to pay the price, and pay it in full."

The three of them were now in my house and Dave closed the front door, locked it. "There. We won't be disturbed now, will we."

Thoughts were trampling fast through my head like horses on the last stretch of the Preakness. "Dave, I told you before, I've been sick. I've got two tubes draining blood and fluid out of my back and—"

"Shut up!" Dave shouted. A revolver was now in his right hand. "Just shut up. So you're sick. So what? Lots and lots of people are sick out there, and what do you care?"

I tried to catch Paula's eye but she wasn't looking at anyone, just at the floor. My heart felt like a lump of cold lead. Marjorie prodded Paula with the shotgun and I remembered.

The first time I had seen Marjorie.

Picking up dropped papers in my yard, how she winced, like her arm and shoulder were hurting—

Hurting from the kick of a shotgun blast the night before.

"Why did you kill Maggie? For God's sake, why?"

Marjorie spoke up, eyes flashing. "Yap, yap, yap. That's all the old bitch did. Yap, yap, yap. I told her if she didn't stop talking, I'd blow her goddamn head off. She laughed, said I didn't have brass to do that. So she yapped some more—and I showed her."

Words and thoughts failed me.

Marjorie looked to her husband. "David, I need it."

"Not now, hon."

"David, I really . . . I need something."

"Wait until I go in the cellar."

"I can't wait that long!" The shotgun was wavering in her hands. "Please . . . please . . ."

"I can't help you, Marjorie. Not now."

The shotgun was now pointed at him. Paula sat down on the couch, head slumped forward. Marjorie took a long, hacking breath. "David, you always carry something for me. Something for an emergency. This . . . this is it."

Dave looked at me with despair and I matched his look. "Okay, honey," he said. "Relax. Just relax, all right? The shotgun, go put it up against the fireplace, okay?"

As she walked over, Dave said to me, "You don't move, all right? I mean it. You move and your girlfriend gets shot. I'll aim for her leg or shoulder, but I'm not that good of a shot, and I might miss and hit something more vital. Got it?"

Paula had both hands up to her face.

"I'm not moving," I said.

"Good."

As Dave moved around the coffee table he reached into his pocket and pulled out a couple of folded dollar bills. He opened one of the bills to reveal a pill of some sort inside; Marjorie smiled and her eyes lit up like Christmas had come eight months early.

With trembling hands, she took the dollar bill and folded it back up again. I watched, horrified and fascinated at the same time. She took the folded bill and put it in her mouth, and crunched down with her teeth. Chewing and chewing the bill, crushing the pill and crushing the pill.

She ignored all of us—slumped-over Paula, Dave, and me watching. The trembling in her hands halted as she removed the bill, carefully placing it on the table. She knelt down and rolled the second bill into a thin tube. She placed one end of the paper tube onto the crushed pill and the other in her left nostril, then she took a deep snort. She moved the tube to the other line, and snorted in one more time.

Then she licked the dollar bill, rubbed her nostrils, and sat down on her haunches. Her eyes were watery and red-rimmed, and she looked up at her husband with devotion and appreciation.

"Oh, honey, I love you so much," she said.

"Me, too," Dave said. Marjorie closed her eyes and rocked back on her heels, as the chemical pleasure rippled through her brain.

Dave looked at me. "A few months ago she fell off the steps. Compound ankle fracture. Her doctor put her on a heavy-duty painkiller, and when the prescription ran out and nothing else would work . . ."

"Did you try—"

"I swear to God, if you're going to tell me if I tried rehab for my wife, I'll shoot you right here and now."

I kept my mouth shut.

"Of course I did, you idiot," he said. "Rehab. There are no available beds, and when one miraculously pops up, you ever try dealing with an insurance company?"

"All the time," I said. "All the time."

"Yeah, well, you know how it is."

"David," Marjorie said. "I'm doing okay. Honest. I'm doing okay." She went over to the fireplace, retrieved the shotgun, went back to Paula. "I'm doing much better."

"Good girl," he said. He turned to me and said, "Go ahead, Lewis. Show us what you've found."

"I—I don't know what you're talking about."

Dave smiled. "Good try. You know how this whole goddamn adventure started? Really? I did a report back in high school, one of those greatest generation pieces, interviewed my idiot uncle. He had a diary of what he did back during the Korean War, when he got called up. Most of it was about him boozing and partying and the horses. Loved showing the girls the horses. Talked about Susan and Joyce and Delilah, how he showed them the fun of horses."

"Horse being heroin."

"Aren't you the smart son of a bitch. And he wrote about having to hide everything when the petty officer came by. He got busted a couple of days later. Thus endeth the naval history of my idiot uncle."

He paused. "But not the history of what he did. Now. You. Move."

I moved.

I opened the cellar door, started descending, Dave behind me, occasionally poking me in the back with his revolver, making me wince from the tugging of my drain tubes. "What the hell do you plan to do after you leave?" I asked.

"You ever live with an addict? You get through the next ten minutes without a crisis, without a fight, without blood spilling, then that's a good time. All you can do is hope and pray for the best. Take it one hour, one day at time."

On the dirt floor now, I took my time, moving slowly, but Dave was having none of it. "Move it, Lewis. What, you think the cavalry is coming to save you? Not anytime soon."

Over to the opening in the sill. Dave said, "Flashlight?"

"Hold on."

The flashlight was on the ground, where I had left it; I grunted, leaned over, and picked it up, the cane still heavy in my grasp. "Nice cane you got there."

"It's from a friend."

"Bulky piece of shit."

"It does its job," I said. I handed the flashlight over to him. He flicked it on, glanced in, and gave a low whistle. "Uncle Bert, you were a drunk and a bastard, but at least you got this right."

He worked for a few minutes, pulling out one and then two and ultimately six bright yellow boxes containing scores and scores of morphine syrettes.

"Those are decades old," I pointed out. "How do you know if they're even potent anymore?"

"Doesn't matter if I know or you know or if a chemist knows. All that counts is that certain folks think that what's here is good stuff, enough to trade for the real deal. Enough to keep Marjorie maintained for months to come. This way we don't have to go out on the street and deal with the sketchiest bastards you've ever come across, don't have to worry about getting arrested or knifed or shot."

"That shoot-out up on my parking lot?"

"Yeah, I had a quick business meeting with those Lowell jerks that didn't go well. I told them what was going on, what I had planned. Half of 'em wanted to stick with the plan, but the other half wanted to come down here, guns blazing, and splatter you all over these nice old wooden walls."

Dave stood up on his toes, flashed the light once again into the tiny cavern. "There. Clear."

"Dave."

"Still looking to apologize, ask for forgiveness? Way, way too late."

"Then just grab the stuff, get out."

Dave released a big sigh, knelt down, put the flashlight on the dirt, the revolver next to it, and took a large white plastic bag out of a coat pocket. He started stuffing the soggy cardboard boxes into the bag.

"What, and just go on like nothing happened? Well, shit happened. My wife got so hopped up that she blew off the head of that old lady, and now we're breaking and entering, and threating you and your girlfriend."

He looked up at me, hand in the bag. "We've been in this so-called drug war for decades, Lewis. Lots of casualties, lots of innocents dead. That's the way it is."

His hands were busy with stuffing the bag with the syrettes. The flashlight was on the ground, near me. The revolver was at his side.

Now.

Dave looked on, stunned, as I took the cane Felix leant me in both hands, grabbed the ornate, heavy top and the lower section, and tugged hard.

Revealing the cane's secret, that it was a sword cane, concealing at least two feet of fine Italian steel, with a needle point that could go through a person like a barbecue spit going through a hunk of beef. It was good for close-quarter combat, to terrorize or impress an opponent—for who would expect such a weapon to appear?—and I was eager to use it.

About a foot of the shiny steel came out, and—

Stopped.

Stuck.

I tugged again.

Still stuck.

Dave laughed.

I swung the cane by its lower shaft, catching him in the chin, and he yelped and fell back. I scooped up the flashlight, switched it off, and with another swing of the cane, I smashed the overhead dangling light bulb.

The cellar flashed into darkness.

I stumbled and ran as best as I could up the stairs, hearing Dave groan behind me, and at the top of the stairs, where the main fuse box was located, and I slapped the door open and tossed the main circuit breaker, at the same time yelling, "Paula! Get down!"

CHAPTER TWENTY-THREE

T he house was plunged into darkness. From the other side of the first floor, Marjorie yelled, "Hey! Hey! What's going on?"

I moved forward in the blackness of the kitchen, hand out, and found one of the backed stools I use to sit at the counter. I dragged the stool back to the cellar door and shoved it hard up against the doorknob, blocking Dave's escape.

Good job.

But the scraping noise of me putting the stool into place identified where I was, and that was a bad job indeed.

A hollow sounding *boom!* tore through the living room as I fell back against the floor. Glassware shattered and broke, and I think Paula screamed. I yelled out, "Paula! Quiet as you can, get safe!"

I crawled on the floor, my fairly useless sword cane behind me, hoping to scurry across to the left, to the living room and the shelves and where the phone was. I moved as quickly as I could, my ears ringing from the shotgun blast, the room smelling strongly of gunpowder.

"Cole!" Marjorie yelled. "Stop it, stop it right now."

Closer.

Okay. Close enough to reach the phone now. An old-fashioned landline but I was an old-fashioned landline kind of guy. My fingers found the power cord and the phone line that snaked up the side of the counter.

But what?

Another shot, another flare of light, and I spotted Marjorie standing in front of the closed and locked door.

Another scream from Paula.

"Cole!" Marjorie shouted out. "I was co-captain of my high school skeet team, I know how to use this. Lights or no lights, I'll just start shooting from one side of the room to the other, spraying everything out there with double-oh buckshot. Got that?"

I ran my fingers up the phone line and power cord, tried to keep my voice even and clear.

"I got that," I said. "What do we have to do to calm everything down?"

Wood creaking out there in the night. Was Paula crawling away, or was Marjorie stepping closer to where she thought I was?"

"Where's David?"

"In the cellar."

"David!" she yelled. "You okay?"

There was no answer, and she yelled louder, "David!"

Again, relative quiet. More wood creaking.

"You—what did you do to my David?"

"Sorry," I said. My fingers were on the base of the phone. I managed to pick up the receiver and hold it tight in my shaking hand. "I bopped him in the head with my cane."

"Did you hurt my David?"

"I guess I did," I said. "But he started it."

More wood creaking and something metallic being clicked. Marjorie putting more shells into her shotgun magazine?

"You . . . you hurt my David? That sweet man, he's kept me alive, he's kept me going. To hell with you. I'm going to kill all of you."

I lowered myself down to the ground, got the phone—

Dropped it on the floor.

Well, damn.

I fumbled around, my hand moving frantically, and there was that bone-marrow chilling sound of *snick-snack*, of a fresh shotgun shell being chambered. I found the phone, I found the phone, and God bless whoever came up with numerals that glow in the dark; I punched in 9–1–1 and tossed the phone in the direction of Marjorie, just as she fired off another blast.

Somewhere on the other side of the room, Paula screamed.

I scuttled like a bug across the floor, trying to get to where I thought Paula was.

Another *snick-snack*, and Marjorie's taunting voice. "Sometimes high-priced shotguns are known as street sweepers. This ain't a street sweeper, but it's close enough."

A metallic sound again, and—

I bumped into Paula, trembling and shaking.

I wanted to whisper to her, tell her to hold on, but I didn't want to make a sound.

Instead I crawled around so I was over her, holding her, shielding her, as I waited for what was coming next—which was *not* what I was expecting.

Light came in from somewhere, a woman's voice said, "Hey!" A heavy thump, followed by a heavier thump, and the lights came on.

My eyes hurt. I blinked. Blood was on my hand. I stayed where I was, protecting Paula.

I looked to the door.

Mia Harrison, the waitress from across the way, was standing there, eyes wide, face pale.

"I think I hurt her," she said. In her right hand she held a chunk of my boulder-strewn front yard, with blood on it. Marjorie Hudson was on the floor.

"I think that's just fine," I said.

"Okay," she said, voice light. "I'm going to drop this on the floor. Okay?"

"Absolutely."

She dropped the boulder, denting my wooden floor—like I cared—and then came the sound of the sirens.

Chaos arrived, and then sorted itself out into something nearing controlled chaos. I stayed with Paula, who was bleeding from her forehead—I couldn't tell if it was from a stray shotgun pellet or from falling on the floor—and I held her and kissed her on the cheek and told her she would be all right, and she didn't say anything, even when the Tyler Fire Department EMTs bandaged and bundled her up and took her out.

I said what I could to the arriving officers, pointing out first that Marjorie Hudson, on the floor, moaning and holding the back of her head, was the probable killer of Maggie Tyler Branch, and that her husband was in my cellar. I warned them that Dave was armed and dangerous, and two brave officers tugged my stool away and opened the door partway. They shouted with Dave, negotiating from the kitchen to the cellar, until an arriving Tyler police sergeant threatened to toss a tear gas canister down there.

The thought of my house being shrouded in tear gas almost made me volunteer to go down and get him myself, but the threat got Dave's attention, and at the direction of the Tyler police, he crawled up the stairs on his hands and knees. He emerged slowly into my very crowded kitchen, whereupon he was thrown on his face and handcuffed.

By now, the two Tyler Fire Department ambulances were engaged, one transporting Paula, the other transporting Marjorie Hudson, so the officers had to wait for a North Tyler Fire Department crew to take away Dave Hudson.

Still bleeding from his cheek and nose, Dave turned to me before leaving. "Fool," he said. "If you had that sword cane working, what would you have done?"

"I would have stabbed you in the heart."

"Why?"

"Because the throat's a harder target."

More cops arrived after he was bundled off, including Detective Sergeant Diane Woods. I was about to give her a statement when the two state police detectives arrived and took over the scene. I talked to them for several minutes, with a promise to talk more later. My house was now under assault—measuring tapes, the flashes from cameras, and then the real heavy stuff: television news crews from Boston and Manchester setting up shop on my front lawn.

My front door was still open, with forensics technicians at work dusting for prints, and then the whole place lit up like a UFO mothership had landed out there, but it was just Assistant Attorney General Camden Martin, giving a press conference. He was slim, with thick blond hair and round wire-rimmed glasses, and Diane stood next to me as he started talking quickly, hands gesticulating.

I asked Diane, "Is he taking credit for . . . for whatever this mess is?"

"Nope," she said. "He's just saying what happened here was a testimonial to police cooperation including Tyler, the New Hampshire State Police, and the Massachusetts State Police. He's also saying that he hopes this . . . matter will lead to the arrest and conviction of a heroin-dealing gang that was operating here in the state."

"A testimonial," I said, now oh so tired. "I hope that doesn't mean they'll be issuing a plaque anytime soon."

"Only if Mr. Martin becomes governor one of these days."

"Sure," I said. "One of these days."

I sat on my couch and watched another state police detective come up from my cellar, holding aloft a clear plastic bag with the old morphine syrettes contained. Somebody asked, "What's that?" and I was going to say something about the stuff that dreams are made of, but I didn't have the energy.

But what I did have was the energy to wave at young Mia Harrison, who came over and sat down next to me.

"Hey," I said.

"Hey," she said back at me. Her face was pale and her hands were trembling.

"You saved us," I said. "Thanks."

"I . . . well, it was the right thing to do."

I squeezed her hand, then let it go.

"Ask you a question?"

"Of course."

I made sure she was looking right at me. "I'm curious, how long have you been coming in and spending the night here?"

She didn't hesitate. "Just over a month."

"When you saw no one was home," I said. "When I was in the hospital, and afterwards. How did you get in?"

"My dad . . ."

"Construction. Was part of the crew that worked on revamping my house after the arson. Probably had a key to the place to let himself in when he had to."

"That's right," she said. "And I never stole anything. Not ever."

"I know that," I said. "But you were coming here . . . why?"

"I was tired, that's all. Working all these shifts, trying to stay awake going back to my place in Porter, where my moron roommates might be having a party. I asked the Lafayette House if they could help me out, and you'd think I was asking to set up a tent in the lobby."

Tears started rolling down her cheeks. "I heard you . . . calling out. And I knew I was taking advantage of you, and I'm sorry. But I started coming in here while you were away, and I knew you couldn't move fast, or move much, since you got home from the hospital."

"But there was one time," I recalled. "I was pretty sure I heard you. And the door was locked, and I looked. I even fell while I was in the cellar."

She nodded. "I was so scared."

"Where were you then?"

"In your downstairs coat closet, curled up in a ball. Scared out of my wits. Like . . . right now."

I squeezed her hand again. "No need to be scared. You did okay."

"That's the first time I hurt anyone."

"She deserved it."

"But—"

"You did something brave," I said. "You saw the flashes from the shotgun blasts, you knew there was a shooter in here, and you still came in and knocked her on the head."

"I missed," she said. "I just wanted to hit her shoulder."

"That'll be our secret," I said.

After some hours the place slowly emptied out, until I was alone with Diane Woods, who plopped herself down on my couch and said, "Wild evening."

"One for the books, that's for sure," I said.

"You okay?"

"At some point, I guess I will be," I said. "How about you?"

She leaned into me and yawned. "There's been a number of nights when you've let me sleep on your couch because of late work or other things. You might be able to convince me again."

"Want to spend the night on the couch?"

"No."

"All right, you want to spend the night in my bed upstairs?"

"No again, silly boy," she said, sighing. "I was just playing with you. Nope, this old broad has a sweet woman waiting for her when she gets home, and that's worth it all."

"I'm glad."

"How's your sweet woman?"

"One of the EMTs said she got a wound on her forehead, maybe a ricochet from a shotgun pellet."

"You take care of her."

"Always."

We sat there in silence for a few minutes; Diane's breathing slowed down, and then there was gentle snoring. She had fallen asleep. What to do?

Nothing.

I closed my eyes and joined her.

I woke up a while later to a voice saying, "You naughty man, you seduced me into staying here."

Eyes open, and there Diane was, standing in front of me, gathering her gear. "What can I say," I said. "We macho men, sometimes our pheromones do their own bidding."

"Hah." She leaned over, gave me a quick and sweet kiss on the lips. "You need help getting upstairs?"

I stood up, with Felix's uncle's sword cane still stuck. "Nope, I'll be fine."

My oldest and dearest friend smiled. "Tell you a secret?"

"You don't have natural brown hair?"

"I'm all natural," she said. "And intend to remain so. I'm not applying for the deputy chief's job."

"Good for you."

"Why good for me?" she asked. "I didn't even tell you why."

"Doesn't matter. You made the decision, it was the right one. That's all I need to know."

She smiled. "I decided it was more important for me and Kara for me to . . . remain who I am. What I do. And where I go. We're getting married in two months. We'll make it work."

"You sure will."

"Now," Diane said. "Upstairs you go, and you make it work, too."

Before any more time passed, I called the Exonia Hospital to check in on Paula Quinn's condition. Because I wasn't her relative, in any format currently fashionable, all they would tell me was that she was a patient and resting comfortably.

I hung up and clomped upstairs, wondering what I was going to tell Felix later about the not-so-deadly cane. I know what he would tell me, that in life and in sword canes, you have to practice, practice, practice. In my bathroom I slowly went about emptying the plastic bladders and measuring the output.

I paused, reading the numbers carefully. Even though I was late, even though it was practically the start of a new day, the output from both tubes had been cut in half.

It was finally time for the two drains to be removed.

"How about that," I said, and I went to bed.

I woke up to the sensation of someone in bed with me. I moved around, and in the dim light there she was.

Cissy Manning.

Smiling as before, her thick red hair over the pillow, lacy straps of something black on her shoulders, sweet white skin and rust-colored freckles.

I tried to speak but I couldn't.

All I could do was stare, and that I did, staring and trying to remember everything I was seeing and even smelling, for her old scent was there, tickling my nose and memories.

"Let it go," she whispered.

And it was dark.

CHAPTER TWENTY-FOUR

The next morning I did my best to push back the memories of the previous day and night—save for one special dream—and I checked the drain output and it was even less than before. After a quick breakfast in my disturbed kitchen, Felix called and I told him what was going on, including the good news about my drains.

"What's the name of your doctor again?" he asked.

I told him and he said, "Hold on," and there was that funny *click-click* as he made another call. I was thinking of telling him not to waste his time, that even now, scheduling something could take a few hours, but then he came back on and said, "Get dressed. I'll be picking you up in thirty minutes."

"But I've already eaten."

"So have I," he said, "but you've got a doctor's appointment in an hour."

"How the hell did you manage that?"

"Trade secrets," he said. "Always trade secrets—just like you."

"What?"

"Man, all of this excitement must be getting to your memory," Felix said. "You told me you had something for me from the home country, and that I should stop picking on Rudy Gennaro. Or was that your evil twin, Skippy?"

"Skippy's out raising hell," I said. "Come on over."

True to his word, an hour later we were on the outskirts of Exonia in an office park dedicated to medical professionals. Felix sat in the waiting room and read *Glamour* with his precious silver serving set next to him—"This thing isn't leaving my sight for a while"—while I was brought into a back office and weighed, poked, and prodded. I changed into hospital scrubs and a licensed nurse practitioner named Molly Samuels started her work.

Her hair was as dark as a raven and her voice had a delightful lilt to it. "Ireland?" I asked her.

"Northern Ireland," she said. "County Armagh."

"Same here," I said. "Long time ago. How do you like it here?"

She laughed. "Not as much rain, which is a delight. All right, Mr. Cole, if you please."

I was up on an examining table, the kind with the endless roll of white thin paper, I flopped around on my side, and I felt her gentle fingers poking and probing. "Ah," she said. "Here we go, then. You're gonna feel a slight pinch there, Mr. Cole."

I sighed. "Sure. Whatever you say."

She stopped. "Why's that?"

"Why's what?"

"Are you expecting something else?"

"Sorry, it's just I know from experience that when a medical professional says 'a slight pinch,' my toes usually curl from the pain."

"Ah, don't you worry none," she said, her hands again moving softly along my back and my shoulder. "We of the Irish blood, we need to stick together, for as my grannie told me once, we sometimes have the power of the fairies with us. Here we go."

By God, there was just a slight pinch, and then there was—it was hard to describe. A slippery sensation like a worm or thin snake was rapidly being tugged out. It was an odd feeling, but not entirely unpleasant.

"There we go, then," she said, cheerful. "And . . ."

This time it went quicker.

"Hold on just a moment before you go dancing," she said. I heard things rustling around and felt a cool sensation back there; two bandages were gently placed on, and she helped me off the table.

"You're done, then, Mr. Cole."

"No follow-up?"

She shook her head. "No, dearie. I put a couple of butterfly bandages back there. Give yourself a week, and you should heal up pretty well." Molly went over to the medical terminal and started typing. "You must be one happy man," she said.

"Some days, I guess. Why did you say that?"

"Oh," she said. "I see here that your biopsy results came back yesterday. Benign."

Felix helped me out of the doctor's office, and when we got back into his Mercedes convertible, I said, "Please indulge me."

"Sure."

"Take me over to the Exonia Hospital."

"What, you didn't get enough health care today?"

"No, I want to see Paula Quinn."

"You got it." He started up the car and said, "Oh, how could I forget this? Hold on for a second."

Felix reached back and grabbed a Shaw's plastic shopping bag, plopping it in my lap. I reached inside and took out my recently stolen John Keegan book.

I flipped it open, saw the inscription, "To Lewis Cole, with all best wishes. John Keegan."

I closed the book cover, rubbed it once.

"Good job," I said.

"That's what we do."

Then we left.

At the hospital the day was sunny and perfect, and just outside the main entrance we stopped in a little oval park with wide granite benches. I said to Felix, "Being that I'm still in recovery, I'm going to sit out here and catch some sun. Be a dear boy and go inside and find out what room Paula's in."

"You need to go to the bathroom first, in case your bum needs to be wiped?"

"Thanks for the offer," I said. "I'm going to try to hold it in."

He helped me over to the bench, his uncle's cane still in my hand, even with part of it exposed. I already felt lighter and walked better, without the harness back there and the tubes running out of my skin. I sat on the stone bench, stretched my legs, and let the sun warm my face and hands.

Felix came back about five minutes later. "She's been discharged," he said. "About a half hour ago."

"Then you're going to take me to her house," I said, getting up.

"That's not going to work."

"Why?"

"Because she's not home. And she's not at the *Chronicle*. Looks like she's . . . gone."

I sat and thought and sat some more, and Felix said, "How about a ride home?"

"How about," I said.

When we got to the parking lot of the Lafayette House, I asked him to stop for a moment, and he found a parking spot that overlooked the ocean. If you leaned forward some and turned your head, you could make out the very top of my old and battered house.

Old and battered. What a coincidence.

Felix said, "Over the years, I've been in a tight spot or two with a woman friend who had been there either by accident or on purpose. Sometimes they were injured along the way. And when it was over, my friend, I usually never saw them, ever again. Just to let you know."

I sat there, the old and now silly-looking cane in my hands. I kept quiet.

"Not that they necessarily blamed me, you understand. But they couldn't be with me anymore. No matter my charm, my skills, anything else, when they were with me, the first and only thought that came to their mind was remembering the time they were with me, hurt and terrified. And they never wanted to relive that experience, ever again. And that's how it would end, and you'd just have to accept it and move on."

"You thinking that about Paula?"

"Hell, no," he said. "I hardly know anything about her, except that she's not too fond of me. I was just speaking randomly, to fill up the empty space."

"All right," I said. "Bring me down, will you?"

He backed his Mercedes out and with some careful driving, maneuvering, and one muttered Italian oath, he got me down the driveway and to my house without once bottoming out. "I'll check in with you later," he said.

"Thanks for the ride," I said. "And for getting my book back."

"Thanks for the silver. I think I'm going to hold on to it for a while."

"Good idea."

I got out and he moved up and around, and when I went up to the steps, the door opened, and there was Paula Quinn, waiting for me.

I just stood there, looking up at her. Her face was pale but smiling, and there was a little square bandage on the side of her forehead. She looked comfortable, and wonderful, in tight jeans and a black pullover sweater with the sleeves rolled up.

"You okay?" I asked.

"Pretty good," she said, briefly touching the bandage. "It looks like when I took a tumble to the floor, I scraped it on a bookcase."

"I'm glad it wasn't worse."

"Me, too," she said. "And . . . I have a couple of bruised ribs, too. From some gallant man who covered me with his body to protect me."

"Gallant's my middle name."

"No, it isn't," she said. "Where have you been?"

"The doctor's office," I said. "Getting my tubes out. I'm no longer carrying plastic bladders back there, filled with blood and fluid."

"Good news," she said. "I hear chicks dig the non-bladder look for spring."

"I also hear they dig the non-malignant look as well."

It was like a flash of light flickered in her eyes, and she brought her hand to her face for a moment. Then she took something out of her jeans pocket. "Recognize this?"

"Sure," I said. "My cell phone."

She wiggled it in her hand. "In this interconnected world of ours, it's customary to carry it around so people can contact you."

"But I did try to call you," I said.

"No you didn't."

"But—oh. It was Felix making the calls."

Paula nodded. "And you think I'd want to talk to him for any particular reason when I saw his name come up on the screen?"

"You know, this is fun and all, but I'd really like to come in. After all, it is my house."

She took my hand and so several pleasant minutes passed.

We were on the rear deck, a light breeze blowing, and she said, "All right, sport. I promised to take some time off and take care of you here, and so the fun will start. You okay with that?"

I thought and said, "No."

"What?"

I squeezed her hand. "No. I want to spend time with you, it will be my greatest pleasure. But not here, not in my house."

"But you love this place!"

I squeezed her hand again. "I do. And I'll want to come back. But right now, there's too much history, too much past . . . And there's some repair work that'll need to be done from Marjorie Hudson's shotgun play. I don't want to be around for that. I want to go away with you. So pick the place, pick the duration."

She smiled, leaned over, and kissed me. "I'll give that some serious thought. How about we head out tomorrow?"

"Tomorrow's fine," I said.

"Good. Because my stuff is upstairs in the bedroom, and I really don't want to repack it. I even changed the sheets and made your bed—but don't think that's going to be a habit."

"I won't."

"I'm glad, because you still need to come up with an explanation for this," she said, carefully digging into a side pocket.

"This" turned out to be a folded piece of white tissue paper. She unfolded it, and unfolded it, and then picked up something in triumph. "Have you been cheating on me, Mr. Cole?"

I took it from her fingers.

It was a long strand of hair.

Red hair.

"No," I said. "I've not been cheating on you."

She laughed. "Care to explain it, then?"

I held the length of red hair up to the sunlight, let it twist and dangle.

Then I let my fingers go and the passing breeze took it away.

"Not today, Paula," I said. "Not today."

ACKNOWLEDGMENTS

Once again, the entire publishing team at Pegasus Books—Claiborne Hancock, Jessica Case, Iris Blasi, and Bowen Dunnan (the new and talented kid on the block)—were a joy to deal with.

I'd also like to thank my very patient first readers, my wife Mona Pinette and my brother Michael DuBois, who are always the first to learn of Lewis Cole's new outings, and who are dedicated to seeking out my errors.

Finally, my thanks to Elaine Rogers for keeping me legal, and my deep thanks and appreciation to the one and only James Patterson.